M.J. KEELEY

TURNING THE HOURGLASS

Black Rose Writing | Texas

ISBN: 978-1-68433-268-7
PUBLISHED BY BLACK ROSE WRITING
www.blackrosewriting.com

Printed in the United States of America
Suggested Retail Price (SRP) $19.95

Turning the Hourglass is printed in Calluna

For Cecil

TURNING THE HOURGLASS

1
AUGUST 2270

Dyrne's hands glistened blue under the electric light tubes. He rubbed his palms on his trousers as the elevator clunked downward and a drip trickled from his armpit to his bony hip.

Like always.

Juddering to a halt, the cage doors rattled open, and he stepped into the corridor that stretched ahead like elastic. His heels clipped the concrete floor as he passed under the white lights dotted along both edges of the ceiling. Silver doors lined the way, all labeled with numbers and complex names of equipment, half of which he still didn't understand. The air was much cooler down here and apart from his own echoing footsteps, the only other sound was the muffled buzz of machinery behind thick walls.

Reaching the end of the tunnel, Dyrne glanced right, wondering if he might catch sight of Phoebe leaving one of the chambers, but the heavy doors were all clamped shut. She must still be in the middle of a visit. Turning left instead, he marched toward the entrance of the one open room. Pod chamber 3.

"Hey, pal. Right on time as usual." Alex's rare American drawl couldn't be mistaken.

Dyrne faked a smile and shuffled inside the dim, stone room. The electronic hums and clicks emanating from the control panels around the walls were louder in here. On a dais against the back wall stood the pod itself: the waiting pink sphere barricaded behind metal railings. Alex sat in his chair on the raised platform, wheeling from screen to screen, tapping buttons and pressing lights with quick fingers.

Dyrne coughed before asking, "can I change now?" He wiped his palms on the small of his back now.

"Sure. Go ahead and suit up," Alex called over his shoulder. "Everything's pretty much ready."

Turning to the corner-bench by the door, Dyrne pulled the flapping, grey bodysuit from the shelf and unfolded it with care. He'd perfected each swift step of the process. He faced away from Alex, tugged off his shoes, unzipped his trousers, slid them off and flung them onto the shelf. Halfway. Next, he stepped into the elastic suit, pulled it up over his shins and thighs, unclipped the white shirt, tossed it to the floor, yanked the rest of the suit into place, and zipped it to his collarbone. His scars remained hidden. A small success.

"What'd you say?" Alex asked.

Dyrne realised he'd been mumbling to himself again.

"... Nothing." He turned. "Sorry."

"Well, when you're finished saying nothing to yourself..." Alex had twirled in his chair to face Dyrne, grinning. The physicist's madly-patterned shirt beamed from behind his unclipped labcoat. "You ready to see how all this shit started?"

"Mm."

Dyrne stepped toward the pod. A section of railing had unlocked itself, and the neat door slid open, inviting him in. He climbed the stone stairs to the platform and crossed the threshold, stepping inside the enveloping orb. It supported his weight without budging. He touched its pearly smoothness with both hands.

"Observation date 09.03.2141. First North American attack. Say hi to them for me."

"Yes..." Dyrne replied, too busy picturing what he might find to laugh.

The sheath door glided into place behind him. Click. The pod chamber sounds beyond the sphere became muted as if he'd been submerged underwater. Static shivered in his ears. Then the familiar shuddering overhead. The groan and whirr of gargantuan machinery shifting, compressing all its power into this little egg. He swallowed a throatful of sand. The rosiness of the surrounding shell began to swirl and melt, like ink dropped in water. The pink twirled into brown, black, navy, green, lime. Then the smoothness of the concave pod morphed and melded into angular shapes and lines and edges. Objects. Furniture. Walls. Shelves. A flat ceiling. Carpet. The light settled into mustard. Dyrne stepped forward and felt the now-invisible pod move under him. The surrounding images of the dull room shifted with him.

He was here. The desk in front of him. And behind it, the slumped President.

2
SEPTEMBER 2141

Worn books filled the mahogany shelves in Mason's office, and the window tints had been turned on so that the glass was black. The single, heavy door was locked from inside. One lamp glowed mustard in the corner.

Mason shivered in his chair behind a bulky bureau, too big for the small room. His fingers traced the Presidential seal imprinted on the leather inlay of the desktop. A transmitter whistled behind him, and he twisted to listen, a twinge pulling at his neck. But nothing. No words. No updates on the bunkers. No news of the attacks. Nothing since the confirmation that South America was gone. The radio's metal casing reflected his sallow eyes and wrinkles. He still wore a suit, but the commanding demeanor presented in news footage and holographs was long gone. In its place, an old man with shaking hands waited to find out if this room would be his sarcophagus. He glanced around at the histories and fictions filling the shelves and thought of them as treasures that might be carried with him to the afterlife. Only the 'necessities' would be cataloged and stored in the bunkers: books of medicine, technology, architecture, agriculture.

I mustn't be a necessity.

The transmitter whistled, snapping him to attention again. He leaned close to it, but just as quickly it returned to its crinkling fuzz, taunting him with nothing but static whispers.

The mustard light blinked. A dull thump in the corner. Books shifted on one shelf. Mason bolted up and scanned the tiny room. Reaching to his side, he pulled open a drawer and laid his hand on the gun. Another sound—not the transmitter. Distant footsteps? Knocking? Seconds passed before he realised it was the thud of his own heartbeat.

He waited again, commanding his breath and pulse to slow, as if they were soldiers who would obey. He rose from behind the desk and edged around it, moving toward the door, then pressed an ear against it and waited. Nothing but his thick pulse again. Easing back, he turned to the darkened window. He pressed the control in the frame, decreasing the tint by a few degrees and peering out. A hard rattling distracted him, and he glanced down at the gun tapping against the pane in his shaking hand. He sighed, lowering his arm, then looked outside again. The street beyond the metal gates at the end of the lawn was empty. And every other street, he knew. Looking back to the cold weapon, he wondered what the point would be in trying to fight an intruder now. Waiting for anything but fatal news from the transmitter was delusional.

He returned to the chair, curling over again, and dropped the gun back into the drawer on top of the red "Synthetic Repopulation Programme" disk. Another futile effort to make things better? Detailed versions of the programme were held in the bunkers, too. Since the server attacks and internet viruses, physical copies were all they could rely on now. He stared at the disk for a while, letting his hand fall to his leg.

After his breath stopped shaking him, he lay back and rubbed his face.

The radio squealed alive.

"ATTACK IMMIN-"

As he clamped his hands to his ears, light burst through the blackened windows. Rumbling thunder crashed into his eardrums. Then ringing. The room trembled. The blast barged him to the floor as the glass shattered, firing at him, cutting his hands and head.

The last thing Mason saw before the heat and the fire was the blurred shape of a man in the corner of the room. Watching him.

3
AUGUST 2270

Central New London—one minute, glowed the amber countdown from above. The platform of the Line station thrummed with footsteps, garbled announcements and hurried chatter. Dyrne alternated between looking down at his shoes and surveying the passing people. He gripped his frontpack with both hands, his left fingers double-checking that it was sealed shut, its contents hidden.

He had learned most of the faces who passed back and forth and milled around. He'd even come to imagine jobs and destinations for each of them. Thin, black-haired lady: political aide, according to her fascination with the giant news screen in the station and the election holographs on her frontpack. Short man with grey hat and limp: a literature translator, if such things existed anymore; Dyrne had peered over his shoulder on several mornings, glimpsing foreign language articles on his Net screen. Tall lady with short, brown hair and a mole: from what he had gleaned from the snippets of her Netcalls she worked in construction with the occasional day off to meet her lover while her wife stayed at home. He wondered what they might predict about *his* occupation from his appearance. Journalist? Teacher?

Highly classified government employee?

One of the women lifted her head, looking straight at him. He blinked several times, taking a step back. He hadn't really considered until now that they might be aware of being watched every morning. Occupational hazard he supposed: staring at people as if it was normal. Squirming beneath his stiff shirt, he felt the dampness of his armpits. Again.

Central New London—approaching, flashed green as the silver Line carriage zoomed toward them before stopping silently. Once aboard he found his usual seat in the plain, white interior. The other commuters around him were already poring over glowing, hand-held Nets and after surveying those around him, Dyrne removed his own outdated Mobile from his frontpack. A younger man in a suit smirked. Dyrne pretended not to notice, waiting another moment before peering back into the bag. He fingered the corners of the printouts and documents. Apart from Phoebe, he was probably the only other person still researching with physical paper. Storing it on his Mobile or Net was too risky just now. At least if anyone found this bag, he could always pretend he was a biographer. A very thorough biographer.

He shook the concerns from his head and sealed the frontpack closed, turning the Mobile on instead. After the usual wait of a few seconds for the scratched, shabby thing to come to life, an article written by one of his old colleagues back at the University illuminated the glass. It focused on 22nd Century pre-War propaganda—or what was left of it—from some of the lost countries: China, India, the Africas. But Dyrne couldn't absorb anything, caught in the familiar cycle of reading the same two or three sentences over and over. The image of President Mason burning alive still scorched his mind.

Then it appeared. As he rubbed fatigue from his face, the words flashed onto the screen: '*NEWS ALERT ON A SUBJECT YOU'VE BEEN TRACKING.*'

His stomach seized like a clenched fist. Acid slithered up his throat. He pushed himself back against the chair and pressed the screen. The news site headline page zoomed forward.

'Synth equality activist, Sarai Tailor, dies, aged 66.'

The bold black letters glared out at him.

Fuck.

He read the short headline again to make sure.

She's fucking dead.

Eyes dry and squinting, he skimmed down the news site.

'... Colleagues say she died peacefully at 5.30 a.m. this morning...'

Hurried fingers scrolled through, the surroundings of the Line compartment non-existent to him now.

'... had been in a coma for the past month following a severe stroke.'

He'd thought his reaction would be different. That, when she had died, he would be calmer, prepared. But all he wanted was to be sick. The familiar line beeping roused him from his daze—an alarm clock growing louder as the world re-formed. He slipped the Mobile away and stood to alight, his body weightless. Following the steady stream of people, Dyrne left the concrete Line station and emerged into the heat of the Central Gardens, clutching his frontpack a little tighter. He counted in his head.

One, two, three, four, five, six...

Straight, paved walkways shot from the station entrance through the too-perfect plant beds out into the gulch of towering scrapers ahead. He glided through his habitual route, watching his feet flit over the pavement.

One hundred and one, one hundred and two...

Occasionally he looked up to the bobbing heads in front of him: volts of electricity flowing along wires and branching off one by one pulled to different parts of a machine. And he was being drawn to a part hidden beneath everything else.

After two hundred and thirty seconds, he glanced up at one of the huge news screens mounted onto a corner building, scanning the various headlines flashing below the announcer's face. It was there again.

'Sarai Tailor dies aged 66.'

He hadn't hallucinated it.

Turning right, he floated across the road. The huge grey scraper in front of him was marked only with the street number—84. The silver-tinted glass doors reflected the same silver-tinted glass doors in the building opposite. Identical rectangular windows—all false—spread up evenly across the walls, revealing nothing, presenting an inconspicuous disguise to the city. The façade had fooled him on his first day two years ago. He had assumed, like anyone else, that there were offices on all those floors. 'Department of Historical Research' was nowhere to be seen, not even inside, although 'DOHR' was occasionally printed on a document or mentioned in an alert.

Dyrne stepped up to the entrance. Some days he still felt the irrational anxiety that the face scanners wouldn't recognise him; that he'd cause chaos and draw unwanted attention to the facility. Security officers would arrive to interrogate him and he'd be jostled from public view. It never happened, of course. He was just a historian like everyone else. And now he was too preoccupied for this simple worry.

He presented his pale face to the glass square. A light flashed, and he heard the familiar beep from the speaker. The glass door clicked and vanished downward.

Sarai Tailor was dead.

Five hundred.

Now he could begin.

4
MAY 2265

Breathing in the smell and heat of the city, Dyrne stopped and listened. Everything was awake. Steps away from the station entrance, he veered off and sauntered along another path.

Although the sun was beginning to bake the air, there was enough of a breeze every now and then to cool him. The occasional car rumbled distantly; the rare sunshine had encouraged most commuters to walk. Faint chatter and laughter ahead grew louder as Dyrne walked. Skipping out of a playground, pairs of children holding hands were led by two women away from the adjacent school building. Their little voices and excited squeals made Dyrne smile as he watched the miniature heads and matching bright frontpack straps toddling along. Two boys at the back whispered and giggled as they all crossed the road, meandering off in a different direction from Dyrne.

Sweat seeped through his shirt to the new suit already. But he was used to this in the warmer months and carried on, squinting up at the sky through the gaps in the patchwork of green leaves overhead. No one seemed to be looking at him anyway, and he could take off the jacket as soon as he arrived at his office.

While walking, others he recognized from his route began to appear in front of and around him, all migrating to the centre of New London for another day, suited, with frontpacks and smiles. He nodded to a familiar man who crossed his path and was even gifted a "good morning" from a woman who stopped beside him at a kerb as a quiet car drove by.

The journey reminded Dyrne of ancient pilgrimages and caravans traveling to havens. He'd studied them when he was a student himself.

He'd even read some interesting findings and theories from his own students on the subject of religion.

The car-lanes had vanished now. The roads here were for pedestrians, who swarmed in the same direction as Dyrne, their bee-humming rising higher and higher as they crowded toward the hive. Looking up, he watched the memorised, brown stone archway pass over his head, welcoming him and protecting him inside the railings. The freshly tended University grounds stretched out and around, and the grand, central building towered up ahead, gleaming from its multitude of windows, with other smaller extensions and faculty offices branching off. Friendly young faces passed around him, some older History students beaming at him.

"Good morning, Professor Samson."

"Good morning, Ember."

Following the wide, stone-slabbed pathway to the main hall, Dyrne examined the familiar exterior. Its faux pre-War aesthetic was still admirable. He'd always marveled at the work he knew had gone into creating this place just decades ago. They'd recreated and rendered the buildings from remaining holographs and even older photographs of some of the lost universities and other ancient architecture, trying to copy their facades. He didn't care that it wasn't authentic. He straightened his back and beamed proud smiles to more students passing by.

The surrounding laughter and chatter warmed him. Until a different sound sliced through. A sneer, piercing the film of everything else. Still cutting across the open green toward his office, Dyrne slowed as he glanced back in the direction of the cacklings.

In a clearing amongst the clumps of students, he saw three neat-haired boys in smart blazers—first years by the look of it—huddled together, smirking, one of them pointing. Another boy perched on the grass in the middle, down on one knee. His open frontpack hung from one shoulder, falling down his arm. A few books and a Net lay scattered on the ground. No one else had stopped what they were doing.

"Copil," Dyrne called, approaching.

The blazered boys scarpered like insects. Copil peered up through wet strands of flopping fringe.

"What were they doing?" Dyrne gripped his forearm, helping him up.

"Nothing," Copil sighed. "Just mucking about." He bent to gather his books, shoving them in the frontpack with red, jittery hands.

Dyrne tilted his head, raising his eyebrows. "Just mucking about? Who were they?"

"Honestly, I tripped over, and they were laughing about it. Who cares?" He rubbed at a grass stain on his knee, hiding his face from Dyrne.

"Do you know them?"

"Sir, it's fine. Please."

Dyrne chewed the inside of his lip, looking at Copil as if he was a magnifying mirror.

"Hmm. See you in class then?"

"Yeah, just need to finish something off at the library. Bye, sir."

As Copil scarpered, Dyrne opened his mouth to call after him, but stopped. He watched the boy shuffle off across the grass, head bowed.

It's fine. He won't be like me. Not with his mother.

5
AUGUST 2270

Dyrne didn't even notice his stomach dropping anymore. When he began working at DOHR it had felt so odd—that feeling of plummeting down in the elevator after expecting to travel up to a higher storey of the scraper. The young man at the reception desk in the pretend lobby—whose name he still didn't know—hadn't braced him for it. Dyrne never knew how far down the labs were. He'd stopped wondering long ago.

The elevator slowed to a stop, and the metal doors slid open. Dyrne emerged into the white, stretching lab. The difference between the muted world outside and the sanitised shininess of DOHR was still jarring. Today it took him longer to adjust to the brightness.

Passing by a couple of other historians who were buzzing around their hive of glass workstations with purpose, he studied the expressions on their faces and listened to their hushed words. Nothing about Sarai Tailor. Then again, why *would* there be? They wouldn't care like he did. Upon catching some eyes, he offered the subtlest of nods before shuffling ahead and manoeuvring toward his own desk. Unlike the others, which were covered in piles of papers open to anyone's prowling view, Dyrne's documents were locked in his drawers. Safe. Sliding onto his seat, he scanned into the Net. The white icon of a new alert blinked at him from the glass. He tapped it and held his breath. It could be the overdue announcement—the next submission date for historian bids; their chance to request visits.

He groaned. The alert was from Martin Daley, the historian for whom Dyrne had been conducting visits this month. A secure file waited to be opened—the recording of yesterday's observation: President Mason. 130 years ago. Reviewing the recordings used to be a novelty, and most other historians would have been thrilled to be part of this particular cycle. Dr.

Hould had called it 'monumental'.

Now the rigmarole of sightwriting beckoned him. At least it might distract him from the news of Tailor for half an hour. But he couldn't let the others see him struggling. He must look content. Normal.

Dyrne had been at school when the sightwriting software was created and had never picked it up like the other children back then. Or since. He often wondered if it was something in his DNA that caused the problem. His DNA caused most of his problems.

Opening an empty page on his second screen to the left, he pressed his shoulders back and pushed the chair a little farther from the desk, trying to get the distance just right; he was usually too close. He blinked several times before opening his eyes wider and staring at the bare, luminous glass:

31.08.2270
COMMISSIONED BY DR. C. HOULD ON 3.08.2270
HISTORIAN: D.5AMSON
VISITATION DAATE: 03.09.2141
LLOCATION: WWASHINGTON D.C., UE (FORMER USA))
SIGHTINGS: 1

A few errors already but good enough. He wriggled, blinking a few times again before breathing heavily through his nose. He pressed Play. Translucent images glowed on the screen. The footage showed a warped two-dimensional version of himself in the pink interior of the pod, swirling and shining. After a few moments, he returned to the blank report on the second screen and continued sightwriting. He flitted between both screens, desperately trying to keep up: watching the visit recording on one screen; sightwriting the report on the other as impartially as possible, according to procedure. He watched the pixelated image of himself gliding along the shelved edges of the room he had been in over a century ago, knocking some of the books.

Idiot.

(PARTIAL <u>SIGHTING</u> BY MASON—KINETIC TRANSFERENCE.) MASON REMOED GUN FROM DESK DRAWR AND NOVED NERVOUSLY TWARD DOOR.

He watched his own hollow outline shift around the room toward the desk while Mason peered out of the window pointlessly. That was when he'd seen it in the drawer.

The red disk.

'*Synthetic Repopulation Programme*'.

Not that he'd mention this to Martin. Or even include it in the report. Researching synths wasn't the focus of these visits.

As he turned to continue watching the recording, he felt something new. He knew what he was about to see; had watched it all in the pod. But looking at the helpless burning body of President Mason, he felt a cold, steel lump rolling around in his guts. Shivers spread over his skin.

'Sarai Tailor dead' flashed again in his mind.

•   •   •

The Hub emerged from the maze of glass walls, dark Net screens lining the large circular table. One screen glowed. Yusuf Sarin, one of the physicists, stood in front of it. This formality of coming here never served much purpose other than to initiate socialising. Dyrne only continued to do it out of a compulsion to follow routine.

"Good morning, Mr. Samson."

"Morning, Yusuf," Dyrne smiled for the first time that day. "So… busy day for you?"

"I'm supervising Miss Schue's final visit of this cycle. Late 19th Century. You should take a look at her reports when you have a moment."

Dyrne nodded. "Have you seen Phoebe yet?"

"Off making some revisions to her bid perhaps?"

"Mm," he mumbled, feigning a smile. "Wait, does that mean the ballot is open? Has Dr. Hould sent out the alert? Can we bid now?"

"Not quite." Yusuf smiled as if to calm Dyrne. "Well, Dr. Hould has sent out an alert. But the ballot hasn't been opened for bids..."

"Dyrne! I take it you've heard?" Piercing his focus, the bounding voice of Phoebe called to him as she strode around the Hub. "Well, have you?" Her eyes looked even brighter green than usual.

Shit. She's read about Tailor.

"Yes. Yes, I've heard. On the way here," Dyrne muttered.

"On the way here?" Phoebe tilted her head and screwed up her nose. "How did you manage that? I just got the alert a few minutes ago."

Realisation settled over Dyrne. She wasn't talking about Tailor. He waited, letting Phoebe fill the silence as he knew she would.

"You got the alert from Charlotte?"

"Oh. No, sorry. Getting mixed up. What does it say?" He swallowed loudly.

"She's postponed them, Dyrne. Visits are off."

6
MAY 2265

"Not long left now, guys." Dyrne grinned as he leaned back in the desk chair, clasping his hands behind his head. "Summer plans, Edward?" He realised his sweat stains would be showing and lowered his arms, hands to his lap again.

Edward sat perched sideways on Dyrne's desk while Herman lounged in the chair opposite Dyrne.

"Actually, yes." Edward grinned and drummed his fingers on the table dramatically. "Artemis and I are flying to the Europa mainland."

Herman gave a thumbs up, and Dyrne sprang forward. "Seriously? You got permission to travel?"

"Confirmation came in last night. We have approval to travel at least to France. Hopefully even farther east if we can manage. Not sure how tight restrictions will be once we get there."

"Good job, pal." Herman leaned over, slapping him on the knee.

"That'll be wonderful," Dyrne congratulated him, shaking his head in amazement.

"I'm hoping to do a little research there if possible... Yes, I know it's supposed to be a holiday!"

"And, um, does Artemis know about this research yet?" Herman raised an eyebrow.

"Well..."

The trio laughed.

"Anyway, what about you Dyrne? End of term plans?" Edward asked.

"Yeah, I heard you might be spending some time with Dr. Keller, eh?" Herman added. "Been up in that Physics department a lot recently." He gave Dyrne a nudge.

Edward winked. "You and her going on any trips of your own? Your apartment perhaps?"

Dyrne stood, laughing along. "Time to go, guys. Class about to start."

· · ·

An obscured, shadowy arm tapped three times on the frosted glass of the tutorial room door.

"Come on in, folks," Dyrne called after waiting a few seconds. He lowered his head back to the notes he'd been reading on his Mobile. The door creaked open, and a soft voice spoke.

"Hi, sir."

Recognising it, Dyrne looked up again to see Copil stepping toward his desk, holding out a white pile of paper. "My assignment. It's done."

"You know this wasn't due for another week."

Copil shrugged. Dyrne looked at the boy's cheek, wondering if the red mark he thought he saw was only painted by paranoia. "Copil are you...". The boy turned and rushed to a seat at the back of the room. "...OK?" Dyrne finished, pathetically.

He looked down at the assignment—handwritten, just like *he* had always preferred to do when he could. He'd always handed in his work at University weeks before deadlines too. Even now he obsessed over punctuality. He looked to Copil huddled over the desk in the corner of the room and wondered if their similarities could be explained biologically.

Dyrne had seen Copil's mother so often on news sites that he felt somehow closer to the kid, as if he was the son of a friend. He had even met Sarai once, during the introductory matriculation week, as she paraded beside her adopted synth son. He never stood a chance of hiding his birth status. Unlike Dyrne.

This 'fame' also explained why Copil had handed the essay in before any of the other students had arrived for class. There was a silent understanding between the two: he wouldn't have dared expose himself to any more easy ridicule in front of the others.

Taking the chance before any of the other students walked in, Dyrne felt his face heat up as he spoke across the room. "Copil, when I saw you outside the other morning... those boys... I know you said they weren't bothering you, but..."

The teenager recoiled, tucking back loose mouse-brown hair behind his ears and looking down to the desk. "No." He adjusted his frontpack needlessly, trying to occupy his nervous hands.

"No what?"

"No, they weren't bothering me. I'm fine, I told you." His eyebrows had hunched in gathered defence.

Before Dyrne could consider another way of probing him, the door was shoved open as the rest of the class members filed into the faux wood-paneled room, finishing noisy conversations with one another and taking over the space with their own loud words. After a few minutes they'd settled into the rows of desks, Nets prepped.

"So... Pre-War London," Dyrne announced. "Today we're going to be considering original location, developments through the ages and its most recent infrastructure and geography prior to the War. We have a lot to get through!"

He spent most of the session resting against his desk at the front, displaying large holographs of relics, city maps and salvaged photographs of the lost city whilst condensing the surviving literature and hypotheses he had meticulously studied on the subject. Some members of the class recorded his voice to their Nets while others sightwrote at impressive speed. Sometimes Dyrne found it off-putting. At the back, Copil scribbled notes by hand onto small pieces of paper.

Every now and then, Dyrne paused to ask questions, sometimes to gather the students' thoughts on a particular theory and sometimes to check they had been listening at all. An outspoken handful could usually be relied on to answer. However, when there were silences and mute starings of twenty vacant pairs of eyes, Dyrne would look to Copil. He knew the boy would always have an answer or idea in his head, bursting to escape. They had even discussed fields of study in great detail before or after classes at times—areas that even some of his colleagues would have very limited knowledge of. But Copil would never volunteer his thoughts in front of the others. All of those whirring ideas and speculations inside his mind would remain locked in there, undiscovered. Dyrne remembered the feeling.

One such silence had fallen now—he'd asked a question about Former British government. Stoic faces peered back at him over the shining edges of Nets, refusing to speak. The topic wasn't thrilling. Most of them had chosen to study History out of a naïve sense of adventure, expecting to uncover gory details of the past and truths behind War conspiracy theories, perhaps even garner fame through breaking discoveries. Some had been forced into it by parents and a sense of prestige or because other classes were full. Only a few seemed to understand the real value in looking back on what had been lost. Dyrne swung toward Copil, sitting in some imaginary shadow near the farthest wall of the room. He willed the boy to speak out. But Copil chewed his lip and looked away, ignoring the plea, no doubt churning through multiple answers to the proposition in his head.

Dyrne abandoned the unanswered question.

"We're going to get ready for a new group project running over the next month," he announced. Some students sighed. Others shifted chairs to face friends.

Rather than abandoning the quieter teenagers like Copil to the humiliation of finding their own teams, he assigned the students to groups. Eyes rolled and exaggerated sighs puffed here and there. Had he been like this at their age? This job must have been so much easier when University was somewhere people enrolled when they were eighteen, nineteen, even older. Dyrne placed Copil in a team of four with one other boy and two girls who were already sitting near his desk. He remained in his seat, scratching a pencil into his notepad in a circular pattern. Dyrne bent toward him.

"I know you prefer working on your own, but it's good to coordinate your research with others sometimes." Copil glanced up. "Besides," Dyrne whispered, "I think they'll need all the help they can get from you." An edge of Copil's lip curled in a half-smile, and he dragged his chair to the others' desks.

Dyrne issued instructions and circulated the room for the remaining minutes of the class, listening to initial ideas and suggestions, some more inventive than others. When arriving at the back-corner group, he heard no more than a few mutters and shrugged suggestions. Copil's hands were tucked underneath his thighs, face down with his eyes lifted, spying through the long strands of his hair.

"Bearing in mind, everyone," Dyrne interrupted, "that the aim is to use your investigative skills to pull together information that perhaps hasn't been collated so thoroughly thus far." He was sure he heard one of the girls snort, subtly mocking the advice. He felt himself wince then looked to the withdrawn boy. "Cop—" he began to utter, but before he could finish was cut off by the boy pushing his chair back and standing.

"Sir, can I leave early, please? Need to go to the toilet before next class on the other side of campus." Without waiting for an answer, he fastened his frontpack, thrust his hands into his pockets and squeezed past Dyrne, weaving his way through the other grouped students to the door. Dyrne hadn't noticed earlier, but Copil was limping.

Watching the boy go, he was sure he heard another smirk from the left-behind trio. Feeling the familiar scenario drag his own memories to the surface, he turned and stepped back toward his desk, just in time for the hourly alarm to buzz through every Net in the room.

"... See you all tomorrow," he murmured over his shoulder, listening to them already shoving chairs around and gathering frontpacks together. He grabbed the small hourglass on his desk and twirled it. Copil had given it to him as a gift at the end of his first year.

"Just a little thing. Stupid," he'd mumbled, blushing, on the last day of the semester. It was the first present Dyrne had been given by a student.

As the teenagers now piled out just as loudly as they'd arrived, the final group—Copil's—left together at the tail-end, still muttering and laughing insipidly between themselves, one of them mumbling "... stuck with him."

More jibes followed, striking Dyrne with an even sharper sting.

"... probably off to the Biology labs to meet some of his clone pals."

"Well, they do have a pretty good supply of cadavers up there."

So they knew. Of course. And they mocked him. Of course. More laughter prickled against Dyrne's skin as the students reached to close the door behind them and he said nothing.

7
AUGUST 2270

A dull electric hum filled the DOHR labs. Two historians chatted in a distant workstation and blurry shapes bobbed behind the mottled glass door of Dr. Hould's office every now and then.

Dyrne missed having a door to work behind. At the university, he'd had an office door, and after that he'd worked alone behind the door of his flat, scrawling notes and re-reading every research book he owned. But now he was here in this open-plan communal workspace, helpless. He hadn't heard another word about the postponement of bids for visits. Instead, the news had been left to fester on the office floor for the rest of the day like a rotting piece of fruit. The other historians picked at it for meaning, concocting all sorts of theories and rumours: Dr. Hould was being replaced; there would only be one single visit a month now; the whole department was being shut down. Dyrne hid himself away; a recluse in his transparent corner, scanning innumerable pages of information.

'Tailor was an early campaigner for the improvement in metaganic rights... her early work as an aide to Minister Dujohn...'

He skimmed one bland obituary after another. Most of them were now using the politically correct 'metaganic', rather than 'synth'. What difference would it make? Then one column stopped him.

'Tailor was also an adoptive mother to son, Copil."

One mention. In all of these articles. The next sentence blurred in front of his eyes. He skipped it, swallowing back the burning ice that had risen in his throat, and jumped to the next section.

'... Tailor largely faded from the public eye. Her campaigning came to an abrupt end.'

He lingered on the last sentence, the shimmering pixels hypnotising him.

'It was assumed by most that personal tragedy turned her into a recluse…"

My fault too?

"Apparently those screens work better from far away, y'know."

Dyrne jumped.

"Relax, I'm not that bad."

It took Dyrne a few moments to adjust from the Net's glow to the dimness of the office. He already recognised the voice before the blonde-grey hair and bright shirt came into focus.

"Alex, hi. What are you still doing here?"

"Just rounding up historians who need to see life above ground at some point. I've been calibrating the pods and tuning things up, seeing as we have the extra time now. Didn't you wanna take advantage and go home early?"

"Oh, I just wanted to get on with some research for my next bid," Dyrne swiveled his chair so that he was between Alex and the Net screen. "If I'm ever going to get a next bid…"

"Yeah. What do you think is going on? Think there's some kinda problem?"

"No idea. Hope not. Hould will tell us tomorrow hopefully."

"Hmm."

"You don't think she will?"

"Whatever it is, doesn't affect me much. I just punch in numbers, show you guys what you need to see." Alex shrugged, grinning. "We're just the techs after all."

"Hould always refers to you as 'physicists', doesn't she?" Dyrne always made sure to use the correct term for Alex and his colleagues.

"Yeah, but she always makes a point of saying it, trying to prove at every meeting that she values us as 'part of the team'." He rolled his eyes and laughed. "Aah, who cares anyway?" Alex reached around to grab a chair from the adjoining workstation.

Dyrne realised his colleague was enjoying the company—enough to make himself comfortable. As he rubbed his chin, conjuring something else to say, he noticed Alex, now in a new position, look beyond him to the Net screen. Dyrne shifted his body again to hide the glowing glass, but the move only drew attention.

"Sarai Tailor." Alex nodded to the screen, before nudging Dyrne's knee. "Thought your bids were supposed to be impartial."

Dyrne forced a pretend laugh, his hot brain pushing through his skull to escape to some other place.

"She was... interesting."

"Yes. She was," Dyrne mumbled, wiping his forehead. He desperately tried to conjure something to manoeuvre the conversation away from Tailor and after an unbearable freeze of three or four seconds, Alex leaned forward, as if ready to stand again.

"Don't stay too long."

Not wanting their meeting to end on such an uncomfortable note, Dyrne pressed his moist palms together, pushing Tailor from his mind.

"I won't, no, but now you've got me thinking about things... about why Hould might have postponed everything..."

Alex smiled. At Dyrne's theorising? Or out of sympathy for his blatant discomfort?

"Wasn't a historian let go at some point for trying to tamper with things? Do you think that's going on again?" he blurted. Had this even happened? Why did he let this thought slip out?

Stupid.

Alex leaned back in the chair again, nodding.

"We were about a year into the programme," he began. Dyrne's panic had struck gold. "One of the other physicists, Donson, and I were monitoring an observation cycle of a younger historian—we used to pair up and follow a whole series of observations right through a study. They obviously change us around now, you know, keep the techs on a rotation, no teaming up and scheming." He shook his head, grinning.

"Anyway, Donson was leading; I was just backing up. After a couple of observations we noticed an unusual amount of transference. Donson started reviewing the recordings—I only caught glimpses of one or two sections—and he became convinced this guy was deliberately transferring, trying to be seen by people in the past, hundreds of years back. A couple of observations later and we hear this guy thrashing around in the pod, yelling, kinetic transference, the whole lot. Donson had been right. This historian was trying to do something on purpose. I wouldn't have even realised it myself. Still wasn't convinced up until that last one."

"Trying to change something? Like what?" Dyrne croaked; his mask of pretence slipping.

"Who knows? We cut off the feed to the pod and hauled him outta there on that last one. After that he was 're-assigned to another government department' Never seen him since. Don't know anyone who has. Funny thing is, I can't even remember his name now..."

An electronic beep cracked their cocoon. Both men looked over to see Dr. Hould locking her office door behind her, old-fashioned leather briefcase in hand. She turned toward them, her blocky frame silhouetted in the dim lighting. Alex looked away, and Dyrne jumped, pushing his chair back.

She's been listening to us.

"Goodnight, gents."

Dyrne wondered if it was a nicety or a subtle command. He felt compelled to offer a polite wave. She faded in the direction of the elevator and Alex took his cue.

"More history for another time, maybe."

"Yes... night."

The physicist walked to the pod elevator at the opposite end of the labs, whistling. Dyrne watched him go, waiting until he disappeared through the doors.

Unlocking his drawer and pulling out his piles of research, Dyrne spread everything across the desk. Timelines and names and dates tangled themselves together in one enormous sprawl. How far back would he need to go? Five years? Ten? A holograph of Copil gazed out at him from a catalogued newssite article, watching him with deep, black eyes.

Ignoring Dr. Hould's suggestion, Dyrne spent three more hours at his desk.

The sky was dark now. The glass doors of the DOHR building slid open, and Dyrne emerged, crossing the road. The streets lay silent in the unnatural orange light of the scattered lightposts. He clenched his hands in the pockets of his overcoat and trod onward. The streams of people were gone, and the city was like a barren bed of a deep river run dry. There was no need for anyone to be here this late; they'd all be indoors in the residential zones. Dyrne was a solitary unit meandering alone. Anyone else might have felt frightened, but his mind swirled with other thoughts.

As he passed through each desolate block, he dissected his conversation with Alex and pictured over and over what Alex had seen on the Net screen. Sarai Tailor had revealed far too much.

'Thought your bids were supposed to be impartial.'

He heard Alex's words again and winced.

He knows about me. He must.

Of course, Dyrne had responded with such predictable awkwardness. He tried to rationalise: Alex wouldn't have thought about it any longer than their conversation had lasted; Dyrne was definitely over-thinking it; he had covered his embarrassment well. Easy to say now. And he didn't believe himself. It would still be several hours until he might accept that it was unchangeable and that moments like this would unavoidably arise again.

As if to cement his paranoia, when he reached the Central Gardens, a small, folded sheet of garish yellow paper scraped along the pavement, drawing itself to his foot. He glanced down, leant over and grabbed it, barely interrupting his pace. He unfolded the thing.

'Metaganic Support: Coming Together.'

'Metaganic'? Just say fucking 'synth'.

'Weekly anonymous meetings to help you cope with discrimination, meet others from your community, and combat prejudice together.'

'We are not synthetic. We are not conspiracy theories. We are human.'

Details of a meeting place were printed underneath.

To an onlooker, he would seem impassive. Inwardly, he felt he had invited it like a helpless magnet. Followers of omni, like Phoebe and her husband, would say it was some sort of karmic attraction.

He arrived at the station in time for the last Line train. Scrunching the leaflet, he concealed the unwanted message deep in his pocket and glanced around like a nervous animal. No predators had spotted his catch.

8
JUNE 2265

"The Tower of London was many things: a royal residence, a display of grandeur… a prison." As Dyrne spoke he darted several glances toward Copil who had arrived uncharacteristically later than most of the others, yet still managed to manoeuvre his way to a seat at the far edge of the room. He kept his grey coat on, buttoned up to his chin, and fumbled with the sleeves of a thick sweater.

"The fact that we know even this much is extraordinary, considering there are barely even ruins left as far as we can tell from the aerial holographs of the area. And obviously, everything online was obliterated. It will still be decades before the radiation's dissipated enough for closer human inspection. All that we know about it has been gathered from salvaged writings, paintings, even tourism literature found hundreds of miles away."

The students gazed back, seemingly attentive, listening, recording, sightwriting as always. Dyrne looked to the group at the back of the room who had been working with Copil. Had he imagined their disdain for him? Misinterpreted their comments? Maybe it was an in-joke, or something kids said nowadays that he wasn't familiar with.

Or maybe he was trying too hard to make excuses for them.

He showed a new holograph, asking the students to take notes, while he rehearsed what he might say to them. Some sort of speech about the language they use to refer to other students; that they would encounter all sorts of people in their lives who they'd have to interact with; that all of their knowledge and expertise would mean nothing without also learning tolerance. They'd be ashamed of themselves, maybe even apologise, and he would inspire them to act differently from then on. No more synthphobic comments.

But looking to Copil, the right words couldn't form in his mouth. Wouldn't he just embarrass the boy? Push him even further into the corner? Shine a spotlight in his face? Dyrne refocused on the holograph, rambling on with more facts, information, ancient history; words he couldn't screw up. Perhaps he could orchestrate a way to make Copil leave the room—deliver a message; collect something from an office—then talk to the others alone.

He realised he'd stopped speaking. The notetaking and sightwriting had halted.

"... I've chosen the Tower as an example today," he carried on after gulping, "because it seems none of you have opted for anything this far back for your group projects." He paused again. "In fact, raise your hand if you hadn't even heard of it." Some obnoxious arms shot up from students proud of their ignorance, while others lifted elbows from the desks slowly, looking around to see who else was admitting to it. Copil hadn't moved an inch. To another professor it might seem he wasn't even listening—gawking out of the window, slumped in the chair, coat still bunched up around him—but Dyrne knew he was absorbing every word.

"Well," he continued, "today will be important for the majority of you." He eased his stance, stepping back behind the desk, readying a new holograph to project to the waiting class. Maybe now the speech would come.

"Professor Samson," a hesitant voice piped up from somewhere in the room.

"Yes?" Dyrne raised his head, scanning the faces in front of him. Copil had sat upright with a half-raised hand wavering beside his head. "Copil?"

"What do you think we'll achieve?" he asked, his words wavering but his face stoic. The other students had turned in his direction, either out of surprise or anticipation—Dyrne couldn't tell.

"Achieve? In what sense?"

"From learning all of this. I don't mean in this class. I mean history, in general. Do you think there's really any point? It's not like engineering or medicine."

Some members of the class looked back to Dyrne to hear their professor's response, grins at the ready. Others continued staring at Copil, screwing their eyes, examining the specimen.

"I think learning about our past is important. Figuring out where we came from." Dyrne immediately regretted his choice of phrase. "I mean—understanding how our world came to be as it is."

"But will it ever get us anywhere?"

Dyrne stepped around to the front of his desk, resting back on it.

He's speaking. Don't put him off.

"I… thought you enjoyed learning about history, Copil."

"I do. I mean, it's obviously interesting," the boy continued. "I've read about the Tower of London already." Some eyes rolled. A whisper and a laugh. Copil didn't seem to notice. Or if he did, he was a better actor than Dyrne. "But what's been the *point* in learning about it? Just because it's interesting, doesn't mean it's useful." He shook his head a little, as if urging himself either to make more sense or stop talking altogether. More mutters spread around the room.

"It kind of seems like so much of what has happened just repeats itself—it moves in cycles," he carried on. "And back then, before the War, everything was recorded. All they wanted to know was there for them, and it didn't seem to make a difference. Why are we going to such extremes to rediscover it? Maybe we'd be better off forgetting the past."

Dyrne was the one squinting now. It was the most he'd heard Copil speak in front of the whole class. Or anywhere.

"That's ironic." The sneer came from a different direction. Another student: Daniel, sitting near the front. "Everyone knows they're cloning synths from DNA of the dead now. Not exactly forgetting the past is it?"

Copil returned to his curled, position, hiding behind the flimsy protection of his desk. Sweat glistened on his forehead.

Thick, viscous seconds passed while Dyrne concocted some way of moving on; of shifting attention away from Copil.

"Daniel, don't be a prick." One solitary response from a desk at the front. A redheaded girl. Ember. She raised angry eyebrows.

"I think, Copil, this is a more philosophical discussion—an interesting one that could take us a whole semester to explore. But not for now, unfortunately." Dyrne turned to move behind the barrier of his desk. 'And not one that most of your classmates would understand,' he wanted to add, but couldn't, compressing it in the back of his throat.

Shuffling movements and murmurs. Different voices merged, along with memories in Dyrne's head—voices from school, lodged deep in some cavity he thought he had sealed.

Turning to face the class again, readying himself to dissolve the dissent, a lightning realisation flashed. He had assumed the taunt was aimed at Copil—now invisible, shrinking into his chair, further and further away.

Is it me they're talking about? How do they know?

Perhaps they sensed the connection between the two synths, had noticed the extra time conversing before and after classes.

His mouth dry and sticky, Dyrne chewed all the wrong words, unable to say what he knew he should.

"Listen… we'll continue on your group projects tomorrow. Let's stop there today."

Ember laughed quietly in disbelief, shoving her Net away.

"Sir?" Another girl spoke from the back of the room—one of the students working in Copil's team. Dyrne swallowed hard, suspecting she too was about to highlight his inadequacy as an authority figure. "Do we have to stay with the groups you assigned?"

The others hushed to listen, awaiting his response.

"Well… Yes. Yes, I want you to work with the groups I placed you in."

The girl sighed and huffed, reaching over to one side to grab her frontpack. At the front of the room, Daniel stood, his athletic frame towering above everyone else. He reminded Dyrne of his brother.

"Don't blame you for asking," he grunted.

Ember, standing too, urged Dyrne to speak with her glare.

Dyrne's thoughts tangled together like an impossible, taut, knotted rope stuffed into his skull.

He knew what he ought to do. But he also knew that defending Copil would amplify the flare illuminating him. As a synth. A meta. A rat. A plug. A filler. A clone. All of the words Dyrne had been called himself and all of the words that still made him wince and cower. He struggled for the solution he knew he couldn't grasp until the hourly bell buzzed through the students' Nets. One by one they finished gathering their belongings, some still watching Dyrne the entire time. No dismissal. No parting message. His body remained pinned on the spot, a useless mannequin masquerading as a man.

As they disappeared through the classroom door, leaving the foul atmosphere behind, Dyrne knew he could speak to Copil alone, keep him behind, console him privately, fix this. But looking over to his empty seat by the window, he realised the boy was gone.

9
AUGUST 2270

Dyrne dressed for work making sure to leave the top clip undone underneath his tie. Too hot otherwise. He parted his dark hair as neatly as he could, judging with his fingers—there were no mirrors in the apartment. Lastly, he gathered his damp bedsheets and bundled them into the wall-dryer before stepping out through the frosted glass door at the edge of his living area and into the small entrance vestibule.

He turned to glance back at his semi-reflection in the shining inner door. A bleary outline of a man looked back like a broken holograph. He glanced up and down to make sure everything was in place but spotted a clump of hair sticking up at the back of his head. He tried to smooth it down with one hand, before forcing it with both. At the same time, his white shirt lifted, untucking itself from his belted trousers. He felt it instantly and looked down. He could see the marks even in this dull light. The mottled maroon and pink circular scars were reflected back at him through the gaps between shirt clips. Logic told him that they were minor, faded marks but insecurity magnified and distorted them into deformities. He shoved the shirt back in and hurried out of the flat door, almost forgetting to lock all three bolts, muttering.

"Fucking synth hair."

. . . . .

He wouldn't observe the travelers around him today. Instead, he let an endless parade of feet march across his stretched shadow on the paved platform.

Once aboard the Line, the city whizzed by in quiet streaks. Dyrne gazed out of the carriage window. His dark, puffy eyes craved rest.

He'd had another of his dreams.

Copil.

Exhaustion made focusing on the Mobile too difficult. He floated in numbness, for now, knowing it wouldn't last long. Most commuters were silent each morning, transfixed with work and reading Nets. But soon enough, Dyrne's radar ears hit a conversation. Two similar male voices muttered behind him.

"That candidate I saw yesterday wants to cut the Line back again. More walking, less power."

"Yeah, a few of the people in the running seem keen on that. Don't know why. We're not like the other cities further north—I thought the point of nuclear was that the energy's practically limitless."

"Must not be."

Dyrne hardly knew anything about any of the candidates running for election this year, a worrying realisation. Every other year at campaign time he'd have studied the specific agenda and policies of every one. Things were different now.

"Apparently Louis Apol is running again with that same artistic bullshit as before. Wants to open another theatre." Both men tutted.

Dyrne had at least heard of Apol—he had spoken at one of Sarai Tailor's synth equality events years ago. Dyrne turned his head, looking forward. The glossy sheen of the plastic chairback in front showed him an elongated reflection of the two suited men behind. Even this couldn't help him distinguish between the two; both with folded arms, the same hair colour, build and stern expression. They looked to be in their mid-thirties, not much younger than Dyrne. If not for their overlapping voices, he could've been spying a double reflection of one man.

Watching their reflections reminded him of what he'd seen on visits—those old television rectangles people would sit around staring at in unison. Now here he was, engrossed in his own version—the shiny image of two strangers talking mindlessly.

"Some of the operators in my office like the doctor," the black suit continued. "Scholtz, I think his name is. Seems pretty confident. And wants to put an end to this synth shit."

An electric jolt in Dyrne's core. He locked his eyes on the floor, studying the edges of his shoes.

"At least now that Tailor lunatic won't be around to keep interfering."

"Exactly. Although she sort of buggered off in the past few years."

"I mean, I'm not synthphobic, but why do they keep making more of them? Or whatever they do with that DNA. I mean, it's dead people. We're cloning dead people, that's what everyone seems to be forgetting. And the population's growing on its own now.'

The other man grunted. "I know. And that sweating is gross."

Both men chuckled, one of them snorting.

"My wife has synth friends at work, and that's fine, but I keep telling her—the War's over and done with. We don't need any more lab rats."

Rats. The reaction was innate. He felt the word breathe on the back of his neck and seep into his skin like a virus. He couldn't tell if the men had stopped talking at that point or if his brain had clamped into self-defence, locking them out.

He spent the remainder of the short journey willing Central New London into existence on the other side of the doors. Were others now looking at him too? Was that woman up a few rows away only pretending to read her Net? It was conveniently angled toward Dyrne. When the carriage slowed to a stop after a blistering age, he was the first to dive from his seat and leave. The waiting crowd at the busy station granted him quick anonymity.

Each step of the memorised path restored him piece by piece, like a morphine drip blanketing pain. By the time he'd traveled several blocks and had just about cooled to a bearable temperature, an imposing news site screen beamed down at him. Images of current election candidates glowed above, filling the glass. No coverage of Tailor's funeral.

Both of Dyrne's Net screens buzzed full of information. His eyes pulsed dully. Phone records, University enrolments, news site articles, discrimination legislation. Adoption documentation. Tailor's name was littered across each. Plenty to consider since his research was Post-War. Investigating anything before 2241 in detail was virtually impossible. But that's what Dyrne had spent his adult life devoted to. Researching recent 'history' was never something he bid for, even though Dr. Hould allowed it in certain circumstances. Now he felt more like a spy than a historian.

Not that he could do any spying yet. The hiatus on bids for visits still stood. And whenever— if ever—the ballot was re-opened, his plans might be rejected. He would be assigned to take part in other colleagues' visits. He dreaded to think who. Working on Martin's visit cycle to President Mason had been fine, but he couldn't stand the thought of visiting some useless place in time while Copil burned inside his head, waiting. So he had to make it work. He had to convince Hould that Sarai Tailor was worth visiting. And her son.

Figuring out how to actually make a difference to Copil's life was a barricade he would smash later.

Dyrne had stopped scrolling. He glanced at the time behind the glass. An hour had passed already.

"Still no date for new bids." Phoebe's chirping voice startled him. Dyrne whirled around in his seat to see her standing, arms full off bursting folders. "I'm working on a new submission though." She had a habit of launching into conversation without any sort of introduction. Dyrne smiled. No needless formalities had to be conjured, and he liked how comfortable she felt around him.

"I'm thinking of focusing on Jane Winstone," she continued. "She's been visited before, but not during her trips to the former USA, surprisingly. And I want to focus on her gender. Maybe it was a factor in how seriously her opposition to WMDs was taken. I know Charlotte's keen on female world leaders." She nodded in the direction of Hould's mezzanine office.

By now it was usual for Dyrne to have at least chipped in with a suggestion or witticism, often at Phoebe's expense. She nudged him with her elbow.

"You OK?"

He replied with a robotic smile. "Yes. Fine."

"Working on your bid?"

"Sort of."

She can't see this yet.

"Post-War?" She must have spotted a date on one of his documents. "Not like you."

"Yeah, well..."

She sighed, perching herself on the edge of his desk. "You know, I reckon that's the real reason they're so obsessively secret about this place. It's not the time-distortion technology, really. It's the fact that we're basically spying on people. Can you imagine the public's reaction?"

Dyrne knew she was right but said nothing. He couldn't now be a hypocrite.

"Anyway," she continued, "think you'll be accepted?"

"What?" He shrunk back into the chair.

"Your bid. Think it'll be accepted?"

"Mmm. Don't know." He offered a half-shrug before standing and manoeuvring away from the Net screen, encouraging Phoebe to follow him through the pathways between workstations. Arriving at the Hub, they met Yusuf studying a Net screen.

"Yusuf, do you know anything we don't about the ballot opening for visit bids? Or any updates on the new regulations?" Phoebe asked.

"Check your alerts." Yusuf smiled, nodding to the row of Nets in front of them.

Phoebe dove aside, face scanning into the nearest machine without another word. Dyrne's insides plummeted. Mirroring Phoebe, he skittered around the circular table and scanned into a screen.

Don't overdo it. Keep calm.

A new alert blinked at him.

He crouched down, wheezing, and pressed the message open. The white words that beamed out pounded his fluttering pulse like a hammer:

'Urgent meeting with Dr. Hould at midday regarding historian bids for visits. Attendance mandatory.'

10
JUNE 2265

After the second night of heat and restlessness, Dyrne chose the short path to the Line station. His upper back ached, and his puffy eyes squinted under the fluorescent station lights that glared at him. The previous week's warmth had faded to a murky, sunless sky, making the cocooned journey on the Line more appealing.

Sitting beside a window on one of the benches, surrounded by other wordless passengers, images from his broken dreams replayed in his head. He had been in the class again, hearing the insults and barbed jibes from the students, shouting and jeering toward the corner of the room. Except Copil wasn't there. Instead, it was Dyrne who sat at the far seat by the window. He hadn't been able to move from the chair, forced by his own inferior body to stay imprisoned by the loud, dark circle of faces and pointed fingers. The front of the tutorial room was empty with no professor in sight.

He'd managed a few years without nightmares until now. And it wasn't the students who smothered shame on him. He'd done it to himself.

Yesterday Copil hadn't come to class. It was the first thing Dyrne had checked for and the last thing most of the other students seemed to care about—only one or two of them appearing to glance around as the tutorial began, searching for the missing outcast. Dyrne had looked for him in the library after the class, even tracked down his dormitory room, but after knocking on the door several times, the unanswered echoes behind it told him Copil wasn't there.

Maybe he'd return today, or turn up in the library or in one of the usual lunch halls Dyrne sometimes saw him in. He could speak to the boy then. Apologise. Try to fix things. Somehow.

But what if he had dropped out of the class and transferred to another module altogether? Would he do this without telling Dyrne? Would other lecturers protect him in different classes?

With paranoia dropping its net over Dyrne and dragging him in, he left the Line at the University station, marching to the campus, avoiding the faces of the other students this time. Floating under the looming arched entrance, he became aware of a group crowded together at one of the doorways to the dormitory buildings on his far left; ants around an open jar of honey. The swarm comprised mostly students but some adults, too. He ignored the spectacle and continued with his head down, rushing toward his office in the main building.

Arriving at the tall, cloistered entrance between great, white pillars, a broad-shouldered figure shoved his way through the door in the opposite direction. He glanced up, making direct eye contact. Daniel. The perpetrator from Copil's class. His forehead was creased in a frown as strong, brown eyes glared at Dyrne for a second before passing by without words. Dyrne was sure he had seen something else, something sadder glimmering in the moment, but could only watch him go.

Pushing the door open, he stepped into the long, stone corridor of staff offices. The first person he saw was Herman, staring at him from his office doorway, as if he'd been waiting for Dyrne to appear in this exact spot. He held one hand up to his head, shielding himself from an invisible sun.

"Dyrne," he whimpered.

Shit. Copil's reported it. Or his mother.

"You need to... there are men here. Police." Herman raised an arm, pointing down the corridor.

He turned and saw them. Three men. Officers in dark suits and heavy boots, staring with cold eyes. Dyrne heard Herman exhale in trembles. Ice water washed over Dyrne's feet and crawled up his back. Beside the officers, the University rector swayed in her office doorway, one hand clenched, the other rubbing her red face with shaking fingers.

Then the clenched hand lifted, pointing to Dyrne. She mouthed the words 'he's there'—a silent mime from here. All other sound dissipated. Dyrne stood, trapped in a glass case, unable to do anything but watch the officers march toward him in unison, soldiers ready to carry out orders. Herman was lost in an enveloping blindspot.

"Dyrne Samson, history professor?" The vacuum split open, air flooding in, assaulting his lungs.

"…Yes?" Why would this need three policemen? Had lying about his birth status been discovered too? Was this the severity of such deceit?

"Tutor of Copil Tailor, the second year student?"

Fuzzy numbness seized him. Static electricity.

"… Yes." His voice was an unrecognisable whisper belonging to some other body he listened to.

"Perhaps we could move to an office?"

"No." His vocal chords croaked for him. "Just say it now."

"I don't know if you have been informed yet, Mr. Samson…"

The unfinished sentence was already swinging at him like a cannonball, all senses and awareness tumbling down and burying him.

"… I'm sorry to be the one to tell you. Copil Tailor was found dead early this morning." The cannonball froze. "We believe it to be suicide". And smashed him apart.

11
SEPTEMBER 2270

Dyrne squinted as light glinted off an ancient telescope into his eye. It was one of a few antiquities placed around Dr. Hould's office that all glared under the synthetic light tubes: a silver sundial; a torn piece of parchment encased in a glass block; a set of green, leather-bound books with gold lettering on their spines. He'd had a shelf filled with books like this at the university.

Any important briefings were always held in here, never in a separate conference or meeting room. Dyrne thought it was Hould's way of treating the historians like they were equal to her and should see her office as a sort of communal space. Except this time, there *was* a separation: no one had any idea what she was going to say. The air felt tight.

Some historians sat around the oblong table, while others crammed against the wooden-shelved edges of the room. The physicists had joined them, too, from the pods further underground, like miners who'd left a pit en masse.

Everyone sat in near-silence, around forty in total, shifting chairs and eyeing one another across the table. Dr. Hould sat at the head in front of her desk. A few seats from her, Dyrne squirmed, wishing he was further back. Behind Hould, where he always thought there ought to be a huge window, was another shelf-covered wall.

Just as Hould looked ready to speak, Phoebe flew in the door, last to arrive, interrupting the settled quiet. After reading the alert with Dyrne, she'd sprung off back to her workstation to gather notes which were now clenched in her hand. She bustled down the long table trying to find a seat close to him, rather than taking the empty one nearest the entrance.

Hould clasped her hands on the table. Her tailored black cuffs made her look neat and symmetrical. Dyrne heard Geraldine Schue—who now sat across from him—once describe Hould, with her short, grey hair as 'militaristic'. He rarely agreed with Geraldine, but this he could see.

"I want to get straight to this, everyone. I've had... concerns since I arrived at the Department two years ago. About what—or *when*—we're visiting. But after one or two incidents recently," she said, slower, her eyes flickering to Dyrne's half of the room, "I think it's time to reconsider the way we're operating. We need to change."

Fuck.

"We already know that our work is fragile. We are pioneers. What the Department embarked on in '62 was experimental to say the least. But one of our main questions, I feel, remains unanswered. And this question fundamentally underpins whether what we are doing is... appropriate, or not." Her hands unclasped and she tapped the tabletop. "Are we affecting the events we visit?"

Three or four staff members glanced at one another with unsettled looks. Dyrne held steady, fixated on his superior, feeling the first bead of sweat trickling through his hair toward his forehead. He couldn't see how Phoebe was reacting from where he sat, but imagined she'd be clench-jawed and desperate to interrupt already.

"It's the observer effect. Are we inherently changing the past just by studying it? We know we have transference. We know we are sometimes seen and heard. But how much is too much?"

Dyrne looked around to Phoebe's intense face, gazing at Hould. There was more silence about her than he'd anticipated.

"Looking over one or two recordings from this past week alone I cannot continue to ignore the alarming possibility that some of our high-profile visits are incurring more critical transference than I feel is... acceptable."

It was mine.

The withered President flashed in his mind. He had definitely seen Dyrne, or the effects he had caused at least: the radio interference, the thump on the bookshelf. Already he felt his plans for Tailor crumpling. Hould's confident stance shifted for the first time. Dyrne remained stoic but couldn't stop his eyes darting across to Martin in the seat nearest Hould. When he had arrived Dyrne noticed that Martin had already been in the office before any of the others. Had he messed up one of his visits to President Mason too? Martin glared back.

"Let me make it clear that this is not a criticism of any of you. I understand fully that sightings cannot be avoided; it is a by-product of the technology." She looked at the physicists, most of whom had clumped together at one corner of the table like glass magnets. "I know you work hard to avoid as much transference as possible."

Most of the technicians nodded. One or two others, like Alex, raised eyebrows and folded arms.

"My point, quite simply, is that we may not be able to continue to visit the eye of the storm. We don't always know the impact of our sightings, and we cannot afford to wait until history has been changed to find out—whether it is as far back as medieval times, or as recent as the War." She hesitated again, as though about to elaborate, but changed course.

Dyrne swallowed and pushed his shoulders back. He pictured his notes on Sarai and Copil Tailor, locked in his desk drawer, shuddering in an earthquake.

"What I propose is to begin integrating a series of precautions. The Department already prohibits visits to historians' personal events in their own lives, for obvious reasons. Of course, I trust all of you—"

Dyrne was sure he heard Alex smirk.

"—But I'm sure you all understand the danger of visiting your own past and being seen by a relative, or even your younger self. As of today, historians will no longer be permitted to visit *any* events occurring within their own lifetimes."

Dyrne twitched as a familiar drip scurried down his side. The desk lock in his mind disintegrated. Sarai and Copil tumbled out, the documents vanishing into a crevice.

Heatwaves emanated from Dyrne's body in shivers. Any minute, he was sure, those on either side of him would feel it too.

What the fuck is she doing? Does she know?

Underneath the table, he rubbed his fingers down his thighs. He saw two years of work, hope and patience stretching uselessly behind him sheared off by an enormous blade.

"I want to reassure you, visits to post-War events may still be permitted—in cases where no other form of research is available and the area of study is deemed essential. Taking all of this into consideration, I will inform you via alert of the new submission date for visit bids."

Quiet gasps. A cough. Darting glances.

The remainder of the meeting was spent discussing details and ramifications of the new rule change. The hot buzzing in Dyrne's head blocked out most of the words.

Phoebe was the first to ask questions, followed by one or two others around the table, but the overwhelming reception was one of quiet acceptance.

Hould brought the briefing to a close. The team rose and filed out of the office. Dyrne stood last, letting everyone else move around him as he stared at the empty table. He didn't speak to Hould. When he left, Phoebe grabbed his arm and led him down the stairs from the mezzanine office to his workstation.

"So what do you think?" she asked. Dyrne winced, hoping none of the others were listening. "Does this mean someone's been fucking things up? Causing too much transference? And what does it matter if it's ten years ago or a hundred years ago? She's obviously panicking about something, but why now? What's the next 'precaution' going to be? From now on are we observing through telescopes three miles out from the nearest human?" One hand still held Dyrne's arm while the other flailed every few syllables, sending one or two of her sheets flapping away.

"Firstly," he mumbled, "we technically already are observing through telescopes."

"So Alex keeps trying to explain to me," she waved the idea off with her hand. "I'm a historian, *not* a scientist."

"Secondly, nice grip you have there." Dyrne held his upper arm. She sighed, letting go and placing both hands on her hips, head tilted to one side. "And thirdly... I don't know what I think yet." As he lied, he continued watching the pages of research in his mind flap around and blow off into blackness.

"So what were you planning on visiting then?" Phoebe carried on. "Those notes you were looking over the other day?"

"... Doesn't matter now," Dyrne murmured, rubbing his face. "Can't visit. It was... stuff that happened when I was alive."

"But maybe I wasn't," Phoebe grinned. "I'm not as old and decrepit as you. Want me to visit for you?" She nudged him and winked like a kid.

"That wouldn't be allowed either." The steel voice interrupted from the other side of the glass wall. Phoebe and Dyrne both glanced at Geraldine, who turned away to face her Net, sitting down. Phoebe rolled her eyes before motioning for Dyrne to follow to her workstation instead.

"Is Hould even allowed to do this?" Dyrne asked, slipping his hands into his pockets as they walked.

"Charlotte can do whatever she likes. There aren't many people above her as far as I can tell. And those guys from the government who come in— no one even knows their names. God, we don't even know about the upper echelons of our own Department!"

"Secrecy at its most efficient," responded Dyrne, trying to lower the collective volume of their conversation.

Reaching her workstation, Phoebe grabbed her chair, whirled it around, and sat, letting her hands droop at her sides. Dyrne leaned against the desk, facing her. Green eyes looked up, bright as ever, despite her frustration.

To her left rested the news site holoograph of Jane Winstone. She smiled in front of a tall, black door with a white 'io' in the centre. Hould had a similar framed image on a shelf in her office.

"What do you think she meant by saying we can't keep 'visiting the eye of the storm'? Do you think she was talking specifically about... anyone?" He glanced at Phoebe sideways.

She twirled from side to side. "It means that instead of visiting the launch of the KEPLER Mission we'd be allowed to visit three weeks beforehand and observe the pet dog of one of the NASA janitors." She snorted at her own joke. But Dyrne was staring off at nothing again. Eventually, he blinked and looked back at her, still not laughing. A few moments passed before Phoebe spoke again.

"Anyway, look—Francis and I are taking a meditation session at our apartment on Threeday night. Would you like to come? He hasn't seen you for a while."

Dyrne had met Francis twice before and sometimes read his environmental articles on one of the news sites. He'd even been to one of their omni gatherings once but wasn't willing to describe himself as *being* omni, despite their insistence that the philosophy had migrated away from superstitions and the paranormal.

He asked a few questions about what time it would begin and if she was sure he was welcome, stalling to give himself time to consider without appearing rude. He also wanted to ask how many would be there and how long it would last and how many people from DOHR would be involved and how many people he didn't know would be there and what exactly they'd be doing. But he swallowed his anxieties back like dry pills.

"Yusuf is coming. You get along with him, don't you? And I've asked one or two others, but it's mostly a few other writers from Francis's work." Did she know him that well?

"OK then, sounds nice. I'll come along." He feigned a smile.

As he turned to leave, ready to return to his desk to face what had just happened in Hould's office, Phoebe spoke out again.

"Dyrne... do you think we *are* having an effect on the past?"

He looked back, his response instant. "Of course we are. People believe in ghosts, don't they?"

12

Dyrne waited until every other historian and physicist had left. Hould was still in her office, but at least she couldn't see his Net screen from there, even if she stepped out.

Re-opening Sarai's obituaries, he forced himself to read every sentence this time, as if he was swallowing disgusting medicine that he knew was necessary.

'Tailor was also an adoptive mother to son, Copil..."

The single mention of him amongst all of these articles still burned his throat.

"... a metaganic boy who died at the age of nineteen five years ago...'

Read it.

'accusations of bullying... found dead... suicide.'

The words branded his eyes. Every day it had remained with him yet reading it again in black words gripped him with a cold fist. His plan had been to visit Sarai. She was famous enough to warrant observations, wasn't she? Then he could fix it. Stop her from sending Copil to his university. Make her call him more often. Help show her the bullying. Something.

But not now.

No visits allowed within his own lifetime. The medicine hadn't helped.

He spent another half an hour staring at his desk, one arm folded across his torso. He chewed at nails and skin on the other hand. A timeline glowed from the screen; a codex of each key event and evidence reference for Sarai's life. The year Copil killed himself was saturated with Dyrne's notes and holographs and document references, blooming like mould behind the glass. Saving Copil from being tormented by other students wouldn't work; Dyrne couldn't visit anywhere near that. His lone option now floated toward him, like a body trapped under thick ice.

"*Historians will no longer be permitted to visit any events occurring within their own lifetimes.*" He replayed Hould's words yet again and stared at the year 2230 on the timeline in front of him: the year of his own birth. He was forbidden to visit Sarai at any point after this, any time within his own lifespan. Reaching out, he swiped the screen clear in an instant, erasing everything.

•   •   •

The grey stairwell stretched above Dyrne. As he craned up, the spiraling tunnel made him want to fall backward. Elevators were reserved for scrapers like DOHR—even if they traveled down rather than up. He had come straight from the labs, still wearing his same constricting shirt and trousers.

Walking here, he'd wondered why Phoebe would be having a party—or 'gathering' or whatever she called it—at such a crucial time. But approaching her apartment and hearing the chattering voices within, he realised the bids didn't have as much of an impact for her. She had an entire, separate life outside the cocoon of DOHR. Envy gurgled in his stomach.

He remembered the orange door from last time and rapped twice before Francis opened. He was older than Phoebe, or so he looked; Dyrne had never asked. He held a small green bottle in his hand, and his thick beard and moustache reminded Dyrne of his father. His seemingly permanent smile and tactile nature didn't.

"Dyrne! Great to see you!" The hug drew attention to his sweat, making him hold back.

Francis urged Dyrne into the small, humid apartment with a swooping arm, patting his back. A warm, floral smell filled the place. The décor was as simple as any other flat in the city, with white walls, few furnishings and one large window, from ceiling to floor, at the far end of the room. Eight other guests lounged around on oversized cushions and foam-filled sacks. From a quick survey of them, Dyrne was glad everyone looked to be around his age or younger. He'd worried about this since Phoebe had invited him. Older people's views on synths were unpredictable. Not that anyone would know just from looking at him, despite some people's claims that they could 'just tell'. Maybe it was the sweating.

A single canvas hung on the wall facing him. The image was a series of multi-coloured concentric circles that radiated from the centre, almost spilling over the edges of the frame and out into the room. These were the brightest colours he'd seen in a while. Except for Alex's shirts.

Phoebe bounded up from a cushion.

"Dyrne! I'm so glad you came!" She sounded surprised and led him by the hand to the kitchen area. "Do you want some relaxant?" She pushed a bottle toward him.

"Mmm." He nodded, feeling it would be an unappreciative start to say no, even though he was sure he'd told her he didn't drink relaxant the last time he'd come. He didn't like the thought of drinking something whose name instructed him how to feel, especially if it might loosen his defences. And it reminded him of the times he *had* drunk, back at the University. Taking the cold bottle, he let the condensation run down over his fingers. He wished he could hold it against his forehead.

Francis took the coat from Dyrne's shoulders and hung it by the door. As he took a reluctant gulp of the fizzing drink, Phoebe beckoned to him to come and sit beside her on the cushion-covered floor. Yusuf was next along, sitting cross-legged beside a tall, poised woman, Zaira, who smiled. Dyrne took another drink, sipping this time, trying not to let his face relay the bitter taste.

After the introductions, the conversation carried on around him. They referred to 'consciousness', 'energy', 'power of the mind' and all those other phrases that tasted strange in Dyrne's own mouth. He wasn't sure when the omni movement had begun. It seemed to have evolved more organically than any of the old organised religions—from what was known, at least— and he'd always been aware of it growing up, in the same way he knew there had been a War or the way he knew he was adopted. It just was. Only now, in adulthood, did people officially recognise themselves under the collective title. He didn't understand this willingness to be labeled— something he'd been trying to escape his whole life.

One of Phoebe's visit cycles had tracked omni's development from belief in the supernatural, psychic abilities and other ridiculously outdated notions of fantasy and magic to something founded in new, metaphysical and psychology-based thinking. But it was still something Dyrne had thought he could never subscribe to, even in secret. He listened to Zaira and Phoebe discussing an invisible set of forces holding everyone together, even past death. Something to do with dark matter or atoms. They sounded content enough, he supposed.

As time passed, he slid further down into the large, comforting cushion and let the calm, contented ambiance cradle him. It had been at least ten minutes since he'd thought of Sarai or Copil. Quite an achievement considering he'd thought of nothing else for five years.

He realised he'd drunk three-quarters of the bottle without wincing each time. He'd even grown used to the taste, having developed a technique of holding his breath and swallowing it in quick gulps. For the first time in months, Dyrne allowed himself to relax. Or at least let the drink he was holding do it for him.

Around the soft, pillowed circle, on the opposite side of the room, another two men and a woman chatted. The first man had short, black hair and a happy face and when he looked over Dyrne glanced down to his socks, avoiding eye contact. Only then did he realise that no one else was wearing shoes either and so bent forward and fumbled with his own, pulling them from his feet and placing them as neatly as he could against the wall. Phoebe told him that the black-haired man was one of Francis's fellow writers, as was the woman with long black hair and large, owlish eyes. She caught his glance several times and smiled. After a while, he stopped looking away.

Yusuf, Zaira, and Phoebe all talked beside Dyrne, laughing and sharing stories. He smiled when paying attention and gave brief laughs where he felt it right, without ever contributing. The room radiated heat and fuzz, and Phoebe handed Dyrne his third bottle. He knew he was feeling the relaxant's effects. He hadn't drunk like this in years, having always given up after a few forced sips and abandoned his bottle in a dark corner or on a high shelf somewhere. Now, his joints loosened and his back unrounded itself. He felt as if he had exhaled for the first time in five years.

About an hour had passed, or maybe it was longer, but the final member of the group was still unknown to him. The anonymous man sat cross-legged with his hands clasped in his lap, reminding Dyrne of images of the Buddha figure he'd seen from other historians' visits and rare holographs he had in one of his books at home. The man was dressed entirely in black and was the oldest guest, with curly grey hair and blemished skin. Dark-rimmed glasses—an oddity these days—were perched on his ruddy nose. Dyrne wondered why he hadn't had laser treatment as a kid. The man spoke to Francis and was closest to the door, somewhat separated from the rest of the group. It felt unusual to Dyrne to be enveloped by others in the circle when he would normally be the one on the edge.

As he stole furtive glances at the man in black, he listened vaguely to the conversation beside him. Phoebe, Yusuf and Zaira were discussing lucid dreams—the practice of becoming consciously aware whilst dreaming and mastering the art of altering your surroundings. Was this even achievable? For a minute he allowed himself to imagine such a luxury before Phoebe spoke to him:

"Having a good time?"

"Yes, I am," Dyrne grinned back. He had to tilt his head to look up at her, having sunk far down into the soft cushion.

"I realised after you sat down that you don't drink relaxant. You told me last time."

"I don't normally, no. But you were so insistent on intoxicating me." He held back burps. "Who was I to resist?" They both giggled.

In his giddy haze, he ventured loudly, "Who's that talking to Francis?" motioning with his bottle, a little off-target, in the direction of the unknown man. The stranger, still speaking to Francis, glanced over.

"Oh that's Antony. Haven't you met?"

"Nope. Another of your mysterious men, eh?"

Antony looked over at the mention of his name.

"Antony is Dr. Moth I used to tell you about."

The name was familiar and floated around Dyrne's head, bashing against a window trying to get in.

"I used to see him for my therapy days. He was my dream analyst. He's a friend now. Francis and I see him a lot."

The window opened a little and the moth entered.

"Oh… yes."

Recollections and stories from Phoebe about her sessions fluttered their way back to the fore of Dyrne's consciousness. The familiar discomfort of hearing her talk so openly about the subject began to rise again in him. Dr. Moth was the psychoanalyst who used to dissect Phoebe's dreams to cure her of whatever she thought was wrong. A common practice viewed as routine by many omnis, like dentist visits. Dyrne could think of nothing worse.

Moth had stopped talking, but was still looking over to Dyrne, who shifted up onto his elbows.

"Who wants to get started then?" Phoebe called out beside him, interrupting the murmurous hum of the room.

In immediate agreement, everyone propped themselves up, smiling, and began shifting around, forming a more perfect circle. Dyrne hadn't taken part in one of these meditations before. The last time he'd been at Phoebe's for one of these omni gatherings he had left early, escaping the embarrassment of such a contrived and exposing procedure. But now that it had sprung upon him—thanks to the bottle in his hand, no doubt—he had no option but to become part of it. No point in drawing attention to himself with awkward refusal. Instead, he would look at it as a case study. At least they weren't staring into crystal balls.

Dyrne watched them, unsure of where to place himself. Phoebe, who had now stood, crouched over and placed a hand on each of his arms, urging him farther along. Like Francis, she was always this tactile. She had even held his hand already tonight in the presence of her husband without hesitation. He had considered it before, but wondered again if perhaps she thought he was same-sex. She'd never seen him with a woman or even heard him talk about a partner. He'd never spoken about Maria; didn't tell Phoebe *anything* about the University. He didn't even mind what she thought now, though. It was another disguise to hide behind if she did think he liked men.

Now, as he assumed his place, tentatively taking his lead from the others, he realised that Dr. Moth was shuffling along beside him to complete the circle. Dyrne felt an instinctive uneasiness beside the black-clad figure. The whole point of sitting around, facing one another like this was probably to create a sense of unity and openness; that would be the omni view. But Dyrne felt the opposite—an invisible barrier between himself and Moth. Might that affect the dynamic of the operation?

Don't be an idiot.

Why would it?

"Sit upright, perhaps against a wall for support. Make sure you are completely comfortable and when you are ready, close your eyes." Phoebe began guiding the others, in a low, calm voice. Dyrne wasn't used to hearing her speak in this deep tone; she was usually so frenetic. The disciples followed their guru's command. Dyrne watched the others follow Phoebe's instructions one by one. He wanted to look to his right to check on Moth, but stopped himself. He glanced to his left to find Phoebe looking at him. He saw her smile before he snapped his eyes shut.

"Close everything else down, switching off your other senses one by one, and focus on the sound of my voice and on your breathing. Everything else fades out."

Dyrne listened to his own ruffled respiration. Was his breath always like this? His crossed, bony legs hurt a little, even with the padding of the cushion underneath. His body, as well as his mind, was resisting.

"Breath in through your nose as I count, one... two... three... and out, one... two... three."

He struggled to breathe in for three long seconds, let alone control his exhalation for as long.

"And again... The beta waves in your brain will soon begin to slow, focusing less on physical activity..."

It was still awkward hearing Phoebe speak in this unfamiliar way, like suddenly hearing a dog meow. He fought the compulsion to peer around, checking on the others. He was sure at least one of them would be staring at him, wondering why he was breathing like a broken humidifier. Probably Moth. Or perhaps they had done what he had failed to do so far and were focusing only on themselves and Phoebe's words. They were all more used to doing this than he was. Maybe it was better that Phoebe sounded so different; he could imagine her as someone else entirely.

He exhaled. He ought to try harder. Thoughts formed, unable to stay at bay.

It was funny how people needed ritual. Omni had no revered texts, no leaders, no messiahs, no buildings for congregation. Yet here were a group of seven people, not including Dyrne, who couldn't help but return to some form of ceremony and routine to hold themselves together. All of the lost religions had their masses and offerings and chantings and communions. Had Sarai Tailor belonged to a religion? Could he use that?

Push thoughts away. Focus on Phoebe.

He had seen Hindu meditation too. It was also a focus of Buddhism and many other old religions, or so he had read. And seen. Another thought sprang up—only three people here worked at DOHR and had any knowledge of the visits. They couldn't share this with anyone else, even their partners. Wasn't very honest and open. Didn't that fly in the face of omni?

Forget it. Focus on breathing like the others.

Maybe Phoebe did tell Francis the truth about DOHR. And Yusuf the same with Zaira.

An image of Copil painted itself behind the black of his eyelids.

He opened them, frustrated. He was now determined to take part like the others. Just moments ago he had looked at the meditation as a foreign practice to be observed. But now he wanted to be on the inside, to let himself be absorbed. Even if only to push away the thoughts of the boy. He closed his eyes again and inhaled deeply, straightening his back in a final attempt to start over.

"Consider the atoms and molecules that comprise your body. They are identical to those in everyone around you. We are the same, and we are connected."

Perhaps the relaxant helped too. After a few more interruptions and restarts, Dyrne's senses dimmed. His breathing wasn't quite smooth, but he continued, able to ignore it, allowing Phoebe's directions to guide his mind. Her words seeped into him. He was the same as the others. The presence of Moth was forgotten, and gradually, he let his thoughts settle and subside.

"Forgetting the physical room around you, you feel a faint breeze. Allow yourself to begin visualising. The chemicals your brain produces in this state can have a transformative effect. The sun shines warmly on your face. You are in the forestry preserves. The trees tower above you, swaying gently. The sky is bright blue, and there are no clouds. Continue to breathe slowly and steadily. Just imagining being in a calm place like this can open the same neurological pathways you might use if you were there in reality."

Dyrne could see the blue sky framed by swishing leaves overhead. But there were clouds that he couldn't imagine away.

This'll do.

"You see everyone else around the circle there with you and know that you are safe with them."

The image of the psychoanalyst observing him through his magnifying glasses batted into him again and again.

"You watch as they turn and walk away to their own private areas for now."

He was glad of this, before quickly feeling ridiculous, noticing his own silly reaction.

"You wander over to a large field with long grass and beautiful flowers all around. You hear birds singing and the breeze softly blowing, relaxing you. The field is surrounded by the tall trees, protecting you, keeping you safe. You sit down now. The flowers are soft beneath you, and you are completely comfortable. You are alone, with no one to distract or bother you. This is your time."

Men watching me. Heavy boots. Uniforms. I am not alone.

"You are happy and relaxed, and you stay here for a while to enjoy nature and the peace it has brought you."

They are going to ask me questions. They are suspicious.

"You look to your left. A beautifully carved wooden box has grown out of the earth. Inside it is a message just for you from your subconscious. It may be a note or a special object. Whatever it is, it will mean something only for you to understand."

They step closer. They know.

"As you move nearer to the box, you realise it has shining yellow edges. Your name is inscribed on the lid of the box in gold. Remember, the box contains something unique, just for you."

Not a box. A coffin.

"Carefully, you lean over and open it, looking inside."

Copil. Folded up and grey. Bruised and crusted with blood. 'LAB RAT' carved into his skin.

Dyrne felt himself falling and jumped upright. Blood surged through his limbs like gunshots. Phoebe looked over to him, still speaking. The others' eyes were shut.

"... as you leave the field behind. You feel the floor beneath you again."

How had he allowed himself to drift away like this, here, in front of others? Did he really dip over, or did that falling feeling trick him? He must have moved enough for Phoebe to notice him.

"Flex your fingers and toes. Become aware of the sounds of this room again. Take another deep breath in. One... two... three. And open your eyes when you're ready."

Dyrne was panting. The group opened their eyes one by one and began to stretch. No one else seemed to have noticed his abrupt movement. How much time had passed? The human circle flopped around and lost its shape. Quiet chatter began, everyone sharing their immediate feelings with one another in sleepy whispers. Dyrne could still see Copil's body blinking in front of him. He felt the relaxant taking its revenge, churning sloppily in his stomach, a burning grasp reaching up his throat.

"Does anyone want to share their thoughts?" Phoebe asked, smiling around the room.

He hadn't realised this was next. He thought the imaginary field was supposed to be "theirs to be at peace" and that the fantasy box was "just for them". Apparently, this included everyone else in the room. The others were all too keen to share their messages and devour one another's deepest thoughts.

The writer from Francis's office, Jackson, was the first to volunteer, explaining that he had opened the box to find his late father's old pair of glasses. He had decided that they signified how he should use his father's wisdom to see things in his life differently. Dyrne expected a round of applause from the others.

The other writer, Luna, revealed that her box had held a hand-written note on a piece of paper—something vague about fighting for what she believed in. She smiled at the others, pleased with herself. They mirrored her satisfaction back at her.

Zaira's box had contained a holograph of Yusuf, garnering a collection of syrupy sounds from the others, as if she had just plopped a puppy in the middle of the room for everyone to hug. Yusuf held her hand and beamed at her. Dyrne wasn't sure whether to feel that she had missed the point of the exercise, or something else. Envy again?

"And Dyrne?"

It took him a moment to realise that he was being prompted for his turn in the game. He cleared his throat.

"Well, when I was imagining the field I suppose I couldn't concentrate properly. I wasn't alone, see. These men kept popping up, surrounding me."

"The men here?" Phoebe interjected, nodding around the room.

"No. No. Officers. Strangers." Why had he told them this? "I must not have been doing it right."

"I thought you were falling asleep at the end. You were doing it fine."

He shifted a little, feeling the circumference of stares. His shirt stuck to his back as he moved.

"Maybe, then. I think I was just remembering the men from a ni— dream I had last night."

The mute room amplified every word he spoke. The others waited, expectantly. Dyrne shrugged again and tried to smile.

"And what was in the box?"

Why is she doing this?

"Nothing. I don't think. I can't remember. Couldn't focus at that point. Think I just opened my eyes then."

"That's alright," she smiled. "OK. Francis? Come on then, picture of me in your box was it?" Laughter rose around the group. Phoebe nudged Dyrne. Attention shifted.

He rubbed his forehead before examining his oily fingertips. It was then that he became aware of Moth, whose glasses flashed at him, magnifying his stare. Dyrne had almost forgotten the presence of the psychoanalyst.

Was that one of his skills—to make you forget he was there whilst he observed? He'd make a good historian. Now, even with Dyrne looking at him, nothing altered. He gawped right back, his chin resting on his fist as one finger stroked his cheek. Dyrne felt like a vulnerable animal, preyed upon by a much larger, more advanced creature.

Turning his head away again, he faced the rest of the group who were now laughing and chatting amongst themselves as before, some moving to the kitchen. Phoebe's dulcet notes rang out, no longer the solemn-voiced sage. The grueling feedback session was over. Dyrne joined his clammy hands, rubbing them together. He counted in his head. "One, two, three, four, five, six, seven, eight…"

After reaching two hundred and forty, he turned and and eased his shoes on. He rose, sliding his empty bottle against a wall, and slipped out of the flat, feeling the intense, violating stare of Dr. Moth the entire time.

The winding white metal staircase swiveled and swayed in front of him and he laid a steadying hand on the bannister. He began his descent, one step at a time.

It was only as he stepped out of the building into the cool, dark, welcoming air of the city that Dyrne realised he had left his coat. Tasting the relaxant on his breath, he chose to abandon it and continue wavering through the dark streets. His hot skin protected him anyway. An autochemist gleamed at him from the pavement with neon allure. He stopped. Perhaps there would be something in the machine that would erase the meditation images from his mind.

It wasn't real. Just made up. A stupid daydream.

But he knew this wasn't true. He'd seen Copil. Like every night asleep he'd seen Copil. And soon he might have the chance to make it stop.

13

The metal doors flew downward. Glaring light flooded Dyrne's bloodshot eyes. He grasped his frontpack with both hands and lurched out of the elevator, squinting.

His morning check of his half-reflection in the tiny apartment entrance had been no more than a glance and he couldn't remember sitting on the Line or who had been around him. He had floated here, like blinking in a dream and appearing in a completely new place. Dyrne hadn't even feigned acknowledgement of the receptionist today.

Historians shot across his path at random, faces busied in handheld Net screens and papers. No one looked at him. He traversed the maze of workstations, steadying himself on glass walls every four or five steps. Approaching the Hub, he heard Phoebe's warm laughter before seeing her and Yusuf. The familiar sound brought flashbacks of last night's brazen, stupid honesty. But Yusuf had glanced over—too late for Dyrne to change direction. He swallowed and straightened his posture, bracing himself for the first comment, either about his disheveled appearance or about whichever aspect of his behaviour last night Phoebe found the strangest.

She turned, wide-eyed and smiling.

"Goodbye, then!"

Dyrne winced, trying to figure out what he had missed.

"... Last night? You disappeared. We didn't even know you'd gone!"

"Oh... sorry. I don't remember so well myself." This wasn't true. He didn't know what *time* he had left, but photographically remembered doing it. He felt his face redden.

"I suppose you're not used to drinking so much. You need to be careful!" She joked. No further questions. No irritation. She turned back to Yusuf and carried on their conversation. Her nonchalance was admirable.

"You just getting in? Thought you had a bed in this place?" Alex quipped from behind.

Dyrne glanced back as the physicist approached. He felt Alex's breath as he leaned in, pressing warm fingers into his shoulder.

"Checked your alerts, pal?" Not one of his usual jokes. He patted Dyrne on the back, seamlessly joining Phoebe and Yusuf's conversation. Dyrne edged around the Hub a little, scanning into a Net. Leaning forward, he grasped the table with both hands, his fingertips rubbing the plastic underside.

An alert icon zoomed toward him on the screen. Sender: C. Hould. The date: today's—04.09.270. Holding his breath, he tapped it. '*New Bid Submission Deadline*'. His eyes skimmed down, a familiar nausea churning in his gut.

'*Following our recent briefing on regulation changes, the ballot for new observation bids from historians is now open. The deadline is 28.09.270. I look forward to reviewing your applications at this new juncture.*'

Three weeks.

     •   •   •

Dyrne had buried himself in his workstation. Around him, the other historians chattered and bustled from desk to desk, ignoring him. He was glad of it. After an hour or so, though, he sensed heads rising from behind the glass partitions as a hush fell all around. Edging around in his chair, he followed the collective stare of everyone else. Two men in black suits hurried goodbyes to Hould at her office door. They both descended the stairs—the second gripping the handrail and taking uneven, thudding steps—and headed to the elevator. They were older than Dyrne; older than everyone at DOHR, he thought, with white hair and wrinkled, pale complexions, the slower of the two hunched a little. Officials from higher up in the government. They had been here several times before. Neither spoke nor even looked at anyone in the lab, and halted side by side at the elevator doors with their backs to the historians.

"Government dictators."

The loud jibe came from the adjacent workstation. Martin stood, leaning back against the low wall with folded arms. From behind her desk, Geraldine craned her neck to squint at the men.

"Why don't they even speak to us? Aren't we important enough?" She rose, joining Martin.

"We don't even know their names. What are they hiding?" he continued.

Dyrne looked wide-eyed at the baiting pair, mentally willing them to stop and retreat, even ducking when it looked as if one of the men was about to turn around. Geraldine leaned over the glass—an easy task considering her height.

"What do *you* think of these two?" She screwed up her eyes as the elevator door opened and the men stepped in, facing the rear mirror without turning.

Dyrne wondered what it was everyone else seemed to know. He looked at Geraldine, dumbly. Her black hair, pulled back in a tight bun, made her thin face look even sharper than usual. She stared at him, lips pursed, her expectant look demanding a response. He could tell which kind she wanted. He said nothing—his specialty in moments of pressure.

The elevator door shot up and the men were gone. Geraldine slithered back down into her seat. Martin skulked off across the lab floor.

Within two or three seconds, the office returned to its previous state, as if the past minute had been a warped daydream. Around Dyrne everyone carried on with their work, the ever-present electronic humming of Nets buzzing across the floor and one or two historians and physicists walking between workstations, reading documents.

"Hi." Phoebe appeared at Dyrne's side.

He turned to her and saw that she held his coat. A burning cold rushed up through his chest and over the back of his head like a steel hood.

"Forgot to give this to you earlier. You left it last night." She offered it forward.

"Oh, yes, thanks." He took it, placing it on the desk behind him, listening for the paper crunch of the synth flyer in the pocket but hearing nothing. "Those men, the government seniors—do you know why they were here?" he asked, trying to shift attention.

"Another big secret. They were with Hould for over an hour though. I think there are more changes coming. Big changes." She leaned against the glass wall and sighed. Dyrne gazed across at the opaque glass of Hould's office door. "Anyway, how's your bid coming along?"

Dyrne spouted vague responses. He was only half aware of what he was saying. He observed his own body talking for him, swaying from left to right on the chair, hesitating and answering back "And you?" after everything asked of him. All the time the coat pocket signaled out to him; a beacon calling for his attention. He was consumed with the need to know—was the leaflet still there? Had she looked at it? Surely she'd checked the pockets to figure out who it had belonged to.

Why did I keep that fucking thing?

The obvious thought then occurred to him that she *had*, of course, found it, and this was why she was hanging around, asking these questions. He tuned in to what she was saying.

"... I mean, are you just tweaking the same idea or are you going for something else entirely?"

Was she making connections? Knew he was a synth now? Piecing it all together like Dyrne was research of her own?

"... I... haven't decided yet."

"Mm. Suppose you don't have to submit anything. We could always work together—if my bid's accepted."

Perhaps she wasn't trying to get anything out of him at all. And then he realised—if she did know the truth, she was still here talking to him. Maybe she didn't care.

"I'm going to speak to Charlotte now, actually," Phoebe added, as if it were just another ordinary task amongst her list of errands to work through by the end of the day. "I obviously wasn't alive when Jane Winstone was, so that's not an issue. But she was also yammering on about 'high-profile visits' being dangerous too. I don't even know how Charlotte's defining that. Isn't the point of DOHR to research what the hell happened before the War? How are we supposed to understand anything important without visiting important people? Do we just visit random citizens like spectres, floating around waiting to overhear something interesting?"

She turned and marched off. Dyrne stared off again, lost in some other place in his mind. But Phoebe's words had begun to penetrate his fog. He absorbed them slowly, forming a distant idea. Lunging back to his Net, he scoured through research, penciling notes on the scraps of paper.

Seconds later he snapped from his note-taking, suddenly remembering and reaching for the coat. He grabbed the brown, lumpy garment bundled on the desk and thrust his hand into the right-hand pocket, groping for the crumpled note that had blown to his feet in the dark of the city.

Nothing. Gone.

He felt his chest tighten, like he had been hoisted by the shirt in a vicious grip. He flipped the coat over, shoving his hand into the other pocket. Relief surged from his left hand spreading through his body, releasing the grip of paranoia. He pulled out the folded, yellow paper, opening it furtively for confirmation, before concealing it once more in the deep pocket, on the right this time. He always kept things there—he was right-handed.

So why had it moved?

•   •   •

"No more 'visiting the eye of the storm' then? Guess you guys just have to... I dunno... listen to the rain through the windows?" Alex leaned with both elbows on the metal railings, the pod control screens humming and flickering behind him. "Kinda ruin things for you up there?"

The blank, bright openness of the workstations had driven Dyrne down to the stone pod chambers.

"Hope not. So... do you think we can—*are*—affecting the things we've been going back and visiting?"

"Well, you're not going back anywhere, you guys still need to get that into your heads. Come on, you know this. You're *observing*. We're using the telescopes to show you things while you stand in the pods, basically looking at giant Net screens." Alex sat back into his chair. "And I can tell you about particles, but history..." he shrugged again.

Dyrne nodded and was about to ask another question when Alex continued.

"The way I think of it, though—if you are changing things, how the hell are you gonna know about it?"

"What do you mean?"

"I mean you're not gonna come out of a visit—which isn't a great name, by the way—and suddenly realise that things have changed. Oil is abundant again. Nobody figured out the world was round yet. The War didn't happen. None of those things would feel anything but normal. If you somehow change something in the past, would you even be aware of it the second you step back out of the pod? How do we know there isn't a parallel universe out there where the London attacks didn't happen, and that's how our universe is supposed to be? How do we know *you* didn't burn the painting of that Italian woman—the Lisa whatever-she's-called—when you went back to investigate it?"

"Well, because we wouldn't have gone to vis—observe in the first place if it hadn't already happened."

"Yeah, or maybe time runs in cycles instead of straight lines, and you're going back to observe but actually cause the event which makes 'future you' want to visit it which makes you cause it which makes you visit and on we go... Or maybe time works in an entirely different way altogether: one that our brains aren't equipped to understand."

"My brain's beginning to feel pretty unequipped already," Dyrne exaggerated, as if he hadn't thought endlessly about the theories already.

"My brain felt like that for seven years studying this stuff."

Alex continued to detail innumerable possibilities and implications of time manipulation, faster-than-light travel and quantum physics as Dyrne tried to keep up and work his way through the impossible intricacies of it all.

When he left, scuffing his way back along the stone corridor to the elevator, Alex's words still lingered, clogging up Dyrne's head. He'd thought about the nature of time for the past two years in a hundred different ways, but hearing it from a physicist made his insides shrivel. He remembered struggling with mathematics at school, once spending an entire lesson dissecting a complex equation. Then he flicked the Mobile to the next page to find he'd only covered the introductory example. Now here he was again, sifting through problems and hypotheses and imagined scenarios.

And saving Copil Tailor was buried deep in the last page of answers.

14

The next sixteen days became a tunnel, with one tiny exit far ahead. And headlights zooming at Dyrne flashed the same two words: Sarai Tailor. His colleagues had become a background insignificance, skirting by. All extraneous distractions were blacked out and every activity centred on crafting and perfecting the minutiae of his application. He'd scavenged all possible information on Sarai's birth, childhood, absent father, neglectful mother, schooldays as an outcast, University campaign work, visits to the synth birthing facility, government internships... Somehow it had to be moulded and manipulated to convince Dr. Hould that visiting this woman was a worthwhile area of 'historical' research. And he had to figure out how deliberately transferring on visits, making his presence seen and felt, could lead to Copil's ultimate safety. All without arousing suspicion from his colleagues. Impossible. The September deadline prowled forward, ready to swallow him whole.

After another morning of concentrated hibernation at his workstation, Dyrne eased back in his chair, straightening his stiff back and stretching his neck from side to side. His body creaked like old furniture.

"Boo!" Two hands landed on his shoulders.

"Fucking hell, Phoebe." Dyrne swivelled and shoved his chair against the desk, nearly toppling over.

"Bloody hell, you're tense." She grinned. "The applications aren't that bad, are they?"

He raised his eyebrows and looked away.

"Look, you've not even spoken to me in days. Let's get outside, take a break from this, get lunch."

"Phoebe, I really need to focus. My bid's... all over the place."

"Come on, I've missed you. And, more importantly, I'm hungry."

"I've missed you too, but... shouldn't we... wait until next week or something? I haven't finished any of—"

"—Neither have I, but I need a break from looking at it. We still have time, Dyrne. And you must know what you're doing with yours anyway— you're always so prepared. I've seen you looking over notes for weeks now."

Longer than that.

"Come on." She nudged him on the shoulder again.

Knowing that his refusal might invite unwanted questions, he sighed. "Sure. But a quick lunch."

Everything outside was tinted with a muddy yellow. Dyrne and Phoebe became part of the flow of pedestrians, moving from block to block along chalky pavements. Phoebe waited at crossings for glowing signs to tell them to walk while Dyrne powered ahead, marching out onto roads and urging Phoebe to follow.

They had left the DOHR building no more than three minutes ago and he had already looked at his wristwatch twice. He forced himself to stop it before Phoebe caught him. He even tried convincing himself that lunch might fuel him on, help him focus better. Maybe a break from staring at those Net screens would give him space to think of a new plan for visiting— and influencing—Sarai. Some spark of inspiration would hit him. Besides, he knew that he owed it to Phoebe to spend more time with her.

"Ugh, I hate those things." She nodded to an autochemist on the wall of a shop they passed. "Bloody dangerous."

"Mmm," Dyrne mumbled, memorising what street the machine was on.

There were only a few cafeterias dotted around, and after the first couple they chose one to stop at. It didn't matter which; the choice of food didn't vary much from place to place, but this one looked less busy, with empty seats and one person waiting at the counter. And Dyrne didn't want to walk any farther away from DOHR.

Dull lights gave everything inside an off-white coating, including Dyrne and Phoebe as they entered. It didn't even smell like food, just something floral masking bleach. A boy who looked about seventeen greeted them without smiling. Phoebe replied politely before choosing items from the touch-menu, asking a question about the ingredients of one of the liquid meals. Dyrne stared at the boy. He'd gone from teaching rooms full of these kids five years ago to avoiding all contact with them. Catching himself, he shook the thought off; a distraction he didn't need. The boy looked back at him, his gaze blank, but penetrating. Dyrne rushed a repeat order of whatever Phoebe had wanted.

They took seats beside a window looking out onto the street. On a building opposite, a large newsscreen displayed the time. Dyrne glanced out at it every minute.

"So are you still going ahead with the bid for Jane Winstone?" He broke his self-imposed rule of not talking about bids, mostly to distract himself from the clock and the counter boy who now circled in his brain.

"If I can."

"Doesn't she count as a 'high-profile visit'? Did Hould say anything else about that?"

"She told me visits '*generally*' won't be allowed to these kind of events but that there may be exceptional circumstances," she replied, picking at a loose thread on her sleeve. "It's all a bit malleable if you pick through her rules carefully."

"I suppose you are pretty 'exceptional'".

"Yeah, that's what I thought." She shrugged, grinning. "But really, I'm hoping it will get approved. I only want to visit her very early on—long before she was Prime Minister. I'll suggest just visiting her colleagues or relatives. Charlotte sounded pretty keen as soon as I told her what I was planning. Obviously, I need to officially enter the bid, but..."

Dyrne forced a smile. Under the table he clenched his palms together. How it easy it was for her.

Phoebe leaned back in her chair. "Anyway, what is it you're bidding on?"

The dreaded question. He had invited it.

"I'm..." He considered a vague answer, or even lying altogether. But today his bleary eyes and lagging body quit. She would know eventually, if the bid was approved.

"Well, I don't know if you noticed on any of the news sites in the past couple of weeks... I'm looking into the early life of, um, the activist—"

The heavy door of the cafeteria banged open, and a group of young teenagers swarmed in, shouting over one another's heads. Fifteen or sixteen of them in total, followed at the back by a teacher, trying and failing to gather them together.

Dyrne shrunk back in his seat.

Phoebe laughed. "Looks like we came in at the right time," she said, a little louder. Dyrne raised an eyebrow. "I wouldn't have wanted to wait behind them in a queue to order."

"Oh." He nodded.

"Antony's working with a couple of teenagers just now, actually."

"Antony?"

"Dr. Moth. Remember?"

"Ah." His name alone made Dyrne squirm. He knew it was irrational.

"Yeah, the problems kids seem to have nowadays is frightening. I mean, not that he tells me their names or anything too personal. Client confidentiality and everything."

Dyrne half-smiled, pretending he thought this breach of trust was normal.

"Didn't you used to work in a school?" Phoebe asked.

"No, um, it was University." He forced the words out. "I lectured History."

She raised her eyebrows a little, nodding. There was a moment of relative silence between them, save for the rabble of school students yelling orders and thrusting wristNets at one another. He knew he could either finish telling her the truth about his bid or talk more about the University: a choice between discomfort and pain.

"I worked at New London. I was a student there myself, too."

"Really?"

"Yes, I worked there for nearly six years. Started when I was twenty-nine. Eleven years ago now."

"So you felt an allegiance with the place? To go back and work there?"

He sat forward in the chair, leaning on the table, blocking out the growing mass of teenagers to his right.

"Not particularly. If anything it's kind of strange that I ended up working there. I enjoyed it, as a student, I suppose, but I didn't get involved in much. I spoke to a few people in my classes and I liked being in the city. But... I didn't make any friends."

Phoebe pulled a mock frown, tilting her head a little.

"I wasn't unhappy though. I liked what we were learning, as pathetic as it sounds." He looked off out the window again. "The lecturers themselves were pretty boring sometimes, but I did all the reading without a problem. I'd even go off and research extra areas I was interested in—based on the limited supplies in the library—whether the tutors had asked me to or not.

"There was one tutorial group run by Dr. Selby. Was she still there when you were a student?"

Phoebe shook her head, smiling.

"The class was on histories of some of the African countries; well, what was left anyway. It was fascinating discussing our theories on the remnants we still have, but I also had a bit of a thing for Dr. Selby. Erica. She had an incredible accent, Greek or something, I always thought." He laughed. "I know her name doesn't give that impression. And she was so passionate about history. Obviously beautiful as well. Surprisingly young for a professor." He looked back at Phoebe, grinning.

She gazed back at him, transfixed. Their meals had arrived at the table without either of them noticing. The teenage crowd had settled.

"I was always the first to arrive to our research classes, as well as the last to leave. I would be so engrossed in what she was discussing— imagine all the professors had made such avid students of us!" They both laughed.

"Well I had been working on my own project, something to do with Egypt, or Iran—lost countries—and somehow I'd managed to get a meeting with Erica in her office one afternoon so I could discuss my research with her. So I arrived, unthinkably early, desperate to impress. She invited me in, and I sat down ready to dive into my findings. And before I began she leaned over the desk and asked 'Sorry, remind me of your name.'

"My heart thudded to the floor. Devastated!" He laughed again, with less of a smile than before, then chewed his lip. "The holograph of her husband and child on the desk didn't help. I must have thought I had some sort of chance with her!"

Phoebe rested her head on her hand, fixated on every word. She didn't speak; only beamed up at him.

"She didn't even end up helping me out with my project either—wasn't that interested in what I'd found. In retrospect, I don't know how I let myself get so carried away. Silly of me. Maybe that's where my poor judgement began... Anyway, that's possibly why I went back as a tutor myself. Some kind of retribution!"

"So did you have any student admirers then?" Phoebe asked.

"No, no. Well, not that I know of." He felt his cheeks tingle and sat back in the chair, pushing his shirt sleeves up. The conversation was veering back to his own time as a lecturer. He needed to divert it.

Two boys in the school group were standing at Dyrne's side, shoving one another, one of them teasing the other about something on his wristNet. Without warning, one of them flew into Dyrne, a mini-avalanche of lumpy limbs and hair, pushing him half off the chair, up against the window. The boy stumbled back to his feet.

Phoebe leapt from her seat to reach over and help Dyrne, but he was propped back up in the chair quicker than she could do anything, stuffing his shirt back in, eyes cast down. She tutted at the two boys, who hadn't even acknowledged Dyrne, but whose teacher had come over to haul them away, apologising on their behalf.

"Are you OK?" Phoebe asked. "Stupid boys. At least you didn't have to work with students that age at the University. They must have been a bit more sensible by the time they reached you."

Dyrne shoved his hair back off his forehead, his cheeks red.

"They weren't that much older." He puffed his cheeks. "Sixteen isn't quite the height of maturity either."

He pictured those three boys back then, that day in the university grounds. Pointing and smirking. Copil on the ground with books scattered around him. Dyrne still saw the look in his face. Anger and humiliation and shame and sadness all at once, glaring out from the hair that always hung over his eyes. Dyrne hadn't even found out those boys' names. Hadn't done anything.

"I wonder if we'll ever go back to older school systems," said Phoebe. "I've seen it on visits: people still in school at seventeen, some at eighteen. I know they sped everything up after the War. Pump out workers quicker and younger. Bring in synths and everything. But aren't we good now? Can't we slow down?"

Dyrne focused on a single passing car outside. A piece of bread hit the window followed by squeals and giggles.

"And Francis still wonders why I never wanted any. I knew since I was a teenager I wouldn't have kids. Got stuck in an elevator with a woman in labour once. It was torture just watching her. Even then I thought, if they can cause that much pain before they're even born..."

Dyrne watched her as *she* looked off out the window now. He strained to tune into a secret frequency that Phoebe's words had whispered to him.

"It put you off having children? Even back then?"

"Pretty much, yeah," she laughed.

Dyrne nibbled his moist, processed bread, staring into the shiny tabletop like it was a crystal ball.

"So are you sleeping any better?" she asked, sounding peppy.

It took a few seconds for the daydream to break and for him to jerk back to life. "What?"

"Well, the other night, at my place, you mentioned dreams you'd been having—officers watching you... or something. Were you having trouble sleeping?"

The flashbacks of the evening he had dismembered began piecing themselves together again. The knowledge that he allowed himself to talk about the dreams made him clench his molars together and dig his fingers into his thighs.

"Oh. No, well, I don't even properly remember what I'd been dreaming about now. Not sure. But I've been sleeping fine. Been sleeping well actually; I've been so tired after work every night these past couple of weeks."

He hoped it was obvious enough that he didn't want her to press any further. She would probably know he wasn't being truthful. He wasn't *really* lying, he told himself. It was just a defence. Protecting the truth.

"Maybe we should head back now," he muttered. "We've been out for a while."

"Sure."

They rose from the table, Dyrne abandoning his half-finished meal and Phoebe shoving the last bite in her mouth. They left the cafeteria with the squabbling of the hyperactive students screaming louder and louder in Dyrne's ears.

But the break from DOHR had been worth it. Phoebe had helped him without realising it.

It was a tiny black rectangle in an exterior wall panel of Hould's office. Dyrne had to have it pointed out to him two years ago when he was bidding for the first time. He hadn't even spotted the thin slot each time he'd climbed the stairs to a meeting with Hould. But now it gaped at him.

"Goodnight, Mr. Samson."

He twitched at Yusuf's voice passing below—the last person to leave the labs. Dyrne didn't answer. Holding out his hand, the Netdisk didn't shake or shudder. Instead, his damp fingers gripped on as if cemented to it, steady as a Line carriage.

He wasn't sure why they continued to submit bids in this physical format. They hadn't even tried to justify it when he'd joined DOHR. Sending it via alert would feel more anonymous. Sitting at his desk he'd be protected behind glass and metadata. Instead, he must deliver a disk by hand; some exposing game like laughing at the smallest naked boy in the school changing rooms. Or the boy with the navel scars. That was why he'd waited until everyone else had left.

He felt he should mutter something. Some prayer. Some omni dedication. Finally, he thrust his hand forward, shoved the disk into the black mouth and listened to it tap against metal and clink onto the pile of other Netdisks lying in there.

Holding on for the weight to lift, he felt his shoulders crushed lower and his head drop. He heaved himself out of the building and into grey rain that lasted all night.

Damp sheets stuck to burning skin. Dyrne sucked in breath and unscrewed his eyes. The inconsequential temperature system whirred overhead. He eased onto his left side and scanned the small, dark room. While he looked at the blank windows and bare corners, the soundless images still swam through him. Knocks at the door. Black uniforms. Desperate fumbles. Officers searching his flat. His stomach gnawing itself.

The hidden body.

He lay for minutes, replaying the nightmare. The more he relived it, the further its potency faded; a chalk message washed away by rain. It would return, he knew. Tonight, no doubt.

Stretching a clammy arm across to the bedside counter, he checked his Mobile: 0510. It wasn't due to wake him for another hour, but he decided there would be no point in trying to sleep again. Partly because of the sodden sheets but more pressingly because he could now think of nothing but the day ahead at DOHR; a day of results. He was surprised he had slept at all. Before making the first awkward move, he glanced at the crumpled, yellow note stuck to the side of the counter by his head.

'Metaganic Support: Coming Together'

He didn't know why he had kept it, but as long as he had it he wanted to be certain of where it was at all times, where no one else could find it in a coat pocket or have any chance of seeing it in the flat, even if he *were* to invite someone here. That hadn't happened for months.

After staring at the comfortless, faded black words for a few final seconds, he propped himself up on the bed, swinging his legs around to meet the cold, wooden floor. The automatic lights brightened, and Dyrne used the waiting towel to dry himself. He crossed the near-bare bedroom to the living area, taking the Mobile with him and dropping the wet towel into the dryer beside the door, its quiet humming beginning automatically.

Still, with his eyes half-closed, he shuffled past the low, square table in the centre of the room piled high with books. Lining two walls were shelves with more books, journals, articles, compendiums and almanacs, covering just about every era of researched history possible: ancient mythologies and religions, world monarchies and political leaders, major conflicts, the War itself, pre-War atlases, lost countries. What was known and recorded about them all, at least. A lot was speculation and theory. Most of these items were incredibly rare. One or two were even pre-War originals. His private, clumsy library.

Dyrne's own published studies were stowed out of sight at the bottom of a box in a corner of the blue-grey room. He had never felt the need to repaint since moving in and hadn't bought any new furniture since before that. Everything here had been here for years. The only things new were the books he brought home whenever he could claim some from colleagues at DOHR to add to his ever-growing, overbearing collection.

In the corner kitchen, he made tea and bread, his habitual breakfast. Sipping from the steaming cup, he glanced at the lone holograph tucked in the corner, resting on the white tiles. A broad-shouldered man of around twenty posed in front of trees on a breezy, bright day, smiling. His black hair fluttered in the wind, and his hands rested in his pockets. Dyrne turned away from it without lingering.

He turned on his Mobile as he sat in the chair. Surveying the myriad of books around the room, he leaned his chin on clenched hands. He knew he could have digital records of all of these made but had never wanted to. He couldn't face the risk of losing it all in another terrorist Net attack. Besides, he liked being surrounded by them here, feeling the paper between his fingers and smelling the dust of time. When he read them, he imagined seeping himself in their knowledge. But it was a library of every important history except his own. No diaries or family heirlooms. Even the holograph in the kitchen was nameless, isolated.

Still waiting for the Mobile to function, he picked up the only other personal keepsake he owned: the small, wooden-framed hourglass resting in the centre of the table. Copil's gift. He remembered the green tissue paper it had been wrapped in. Remembered the smell of the dusty wood in the classroom and the broken window tint that made everyone squint in the glaring afternoon light. Remembered Copil's red cheeks as he handed the ornament over, before shoving his hands back in his coat pockets and murmuring a 'thanks, sir'.

Dyrne flipped the hourglass, watching the tiny grains slip through the gap, piling on top of one another. It took about thirty seconds for it all to dribble from top to bottom. He turned it again, watching the same grains slipping back through time. Useless, really. But more precious than anything else in the room.

Once the Mobile was ready, the remaining hour before his strict 0630 preparation routine was spent checking in on news sites, browsing through some saved academic research papers and scouring various New London University forums and recordings. He read aloud in mumbles, wittering his own thoughts and observations intermittently. But he couldn't stop his mind from wandering to the imaginary picture of his Net screen in the labs, the impending alert icon blinking boldly.

He knew he had ruined it, that he could have suggested more appropriate dates for his visits, given better reasons for wanting to visit this woman. He should even have asked someone to check his application for him—someone he wasn't close to. But nothing would have made a difference. A hundred years and it still wouldn't be ready.

I've fucked it up.

He left the apartment making sure not to even glance at his reflection in the glass entrance door.

•   •   •

His head vibrated against the Line window. Every twenty or thirty seconds the tunnels they shot through blindfolded everyone. Between the mini-blackouts, Dyrne focused on a young woman down the aisle, facing his direction. Her short hair was a rare red colour and her face fresh and pretty. She was much younger than Dyrne but wore a professional, smart suit and white tunic. The carriage passed through another tunnel, and as it emerged she was looking straight at him. And smiling. Instinctively, he shifted his head, looking in the direction of the window, but not through it. He remained in the position, counting for sixty seconds before stealing another glimpse of her. She was looking at her Net now, but Dyrne didn't dare let his gaze linger for long, in case she happened to glance up and catch him staring for the second time. Apart from how attractive she was, there was something else drawing him to her.

Familiarity.

He looked a third and fourth time before they arrived at his stop.

Choosing the exit behind him to avoid a further encounter, Dyrne weaved through the passengers on the platform. He stepped out into the sunlight of the Central Gardens ready to follow his path when he felt a brush on his right elbow.

"Mr. Samson."

She appeared at his side like a mirage forming out of air. Dyrne didn't lose stride.

"Yes?"

"How are you?"

"I'm fine, thank you." The standard response. The girl fell in step beside him.

"... And you?"

"I'm doing well. I work in Genealogies now—armed forces lineage, just up in the Mason Building." She gestured north with a nod of her head.

"Aah," he nodded, showing he knew the building, although he still couldn't place the young woman or figure out how she knew his name. He remembered that Alex's wife worked in Genealogies. The government had a department dedicated to tracing ancestors back as far as possible in an attempt to restore some sense of identity for civilians as well as to help piece together the jigsaw of the United Empire's history. Dyrne assumed there must also be some level of deception at work; they'd never let anyone know that their family's DNA had been used for the synth programme. And obviously, the department knew nothing of DOHR's existence. No one did. It seemed, to Dyrne, a complete waste to have this entire workforce digging away at what DOHR could unearth, and had probably already unearthed, far more easily, like one man trying to start a fire with wooden sticks while his neighbour secretly has a nuclear reactor. He also remembered wondering whether Alex's wife knew what Alex did for a living. Had *he* breached government confidentiality for Mrs. Myers?

"You must work nearby now," the young woman said.

Was she a friend of Phoebe's? Connected to Alex and his wife?

They traversed a street crossing. He couldn't now ask who she was. Too much had been said already. As he wondered how he could extract a clue from her, she spoke again.

"Are you teaching at a different University?"

He almost stumbled on the flat pavement.

"I work in Cataloguing. Keeping track of birth and death records, updating the census," he blurted, rushing to wipe the dripping bead of sweat from his forehead. "I'm going in a different direction from here, I'm afraid."

The girl stepped back from him, her brow creasing in confusion. Dyrne took a left turn down the street they had been about to cross. He craned back clumsily after a few paces.

"See you again," he muttered and waved, leaving her familiar face to melt away into the crowd.

. . .

After walking for an extra ten minutes through Central New London in the wrong direction, Dyrne doubled back down a parallel street and rushed toward DOHR. Marching through the foyer, he didn't even look at the receptionist. In the elevator, he checked the time on the display: 0841.

Fifteen fucking minutes late.

As soon as the elevator door slid downward, he sensed the change. Louder talk, pairs and trios at workstations skimming papers together with stupid grins, physicists bounding in and out of the sliding door to the pod elevator. Even the lights looked brighter. He trooped to the Hub, dodging two separate historians on the way. Upon arrival he found Phoebe, Alex and various others clumped together in groups. The bid results were in.

Dyrne's compulsion was to scan into the first empty Net he could find, but fear of appearing too eager in front of the others held him back like the shielding hand of a parent. He edged off in the direction of his workstation. As soon as he turned from the Hub, though, Phoebe caught sight of him.

"Dyrne! Hi!" It was already clear from her bright yell what the outcome of her bid had been. Dyrne swivelled back, feigning a smile. "Where are you going? Hey, did you check your Alerts yet? Was your bid accepted?"

He wasn't sure which question to answer first, but knew which to ignore.

"Um, I just arrived, was held up for a while. Just heading to my desk. How did your bid do?"

She smiled and bounded to him. "Going to visit Jane Winstone. Mostly before she was Prime Minster but still..."

"Great... And who's been assigned to the visits?" Asking this way would soften the impending blow of his own disappointment—if he'd been assigned to her visit cycle, he'd know his own bid had failed.

"Don't know yet, lists haven't been issued."

His jaw twinged, clenching through a smile.

"There's Yusuf. I'm going to see if he's heard anything about what visits he's coordinating. Alex doesn't know much, unsurprisingly!" Phoebe touched Dyrne's arm before rushing off again. "Let me know about yours when you find out."

While no one else was coming near him, he took the chance to slink off to his desk and sink into the chair without even removing his frontpack, despite the perspiration underneath. Scanning into the Net, his feet tapped the floor, his heart beating faster.

The Net activated. The blinking alert icon waited for him to touch it. He tapped with a shaking finger, biting the inside of his mouth at the same time. New alert. Sender: C. Hould. '*VISITS COMMENCING 4.10.270.*'

He tapped again and scanned through the initial pro forma sentences. Four lines in, he stopped reading.

Dyrne craned up at the glowing sign, his noose-tight collar strangling him: "Central New London 90000 seconds."

What?

There must be some malfunction.

"Dyrne? Where are you? Why aren't you here yet?" Phoebe's voice crackled through the Mobile.

"Sorry Phoebe, can you hear me at all? Phoebe?" He shook the device, trying to make the image clearer, but could only see some vague outline of Phoebe's features swirling and shapeshifting on the damaged screen.

"I know... you've done... Copil...need to tell... find out...your fault." her broken words faded in and out. Dyrne's head throbbed in a panicked fever, and he darted glances around him at the others on the platform.

"I can't hear you, Phoebe. I'll just meet you on the Line."

She probably hadn't heard him, but he didn't care, shutting the fragile, hand-sized rectangle down and trying to shove it in his frontpack. But it wouldn't fit. He wedged it in at different awkward angles, pushing every way he could conceive. Eventually, he abandoned the struggle and held it under his sweating armpit. His face grew hotter still.

More and more people filtered through the gates behind him and onto the platform, the crowd jostling him and the others near the front farther forward. He felt endless elbows and frontpacks press into his back but refused to turn around. He squinted up again at the announcement panel.

"Central New London 22302230 seconds."

Why can't they get the bloody display fixed?

He wanted to shout it, his head pulsing.

Within moments, though, the familiar high-pitched whistle echoed along the track and Dyrne felt the waft of muggy air blowing at one side of his face. At his sweating back, the crowd surged again, and his clumsy feet were forced closer to the platform edge. The carriage zoomed in front him, and he strained through the whooshing windows at the blurred faces inside. His Mobile buzzed under his arm. Phoebe again surely. But no time to yank it free just to hear fuzz and crackles. He knew she was in the train and he would see her soon. He ignored it.

The carriage slowed further in front of him, and he searched the crowd of faces inside. Phoebe sat at a window wearing an electric blue suit. He bobbed his head, smiling at her, but her marble eyes only stared out at him—through him—glossy and empty. Poison spread from his solar plexus.

As he prepared for the doors to stop and open, the carriage lurched ahead again. He shot quick glances around at the other commuters, but their gazes were glued in place, unblinking. All of them. The nausea grew. Looking back at the unfamiliar Phoebe he saw she was mouthing something to him, still with the same stoic look on her face. He squinted and leaned in to decipher the code of her mute wordings, but the carriage accelerated and sped off into the black tunnel, pulling Phoebe's frightening face with it.

A murmuring storm cloud rippled through the crowd behind him, starting far off at the back, before rumbling its way closer and closer to the front of the platform, where Dyrne waited, knowing somehow what was happening. The horror grabbed him in its talons.

"There! There he is!" A man hollered from the shoving mob. Without looking, Dyrne recognised it as the sneering, snake voice of one of the synthphobic men he had listened to on the Line weeks ago.

He couldn't avoid it any longer. Turning, he saw them there. Black-clad, slender but towering above all the others, slithering their way through the throng. Three of them. At the same moment, each officer slammed eyes on him, shooting toward him faster, unhuman. Their weaving through the mob—who now jeered and pointed—made the entire horde surge forward one final, fatal time.

Dyrne was pushed over the edge of the platform, yelping.

His last sight was of twisted faces sneering down, growing smaller.

Darkness. Heart drumming in painful beats. He inhaled noisily and bolted up. Sweat trickled from his armpits down to his elbows. The familiarity of the four close bedroom corners washed over him in waves of relief. The whirring of the temperature control unit comforted him.

0456 shone from the Mobile. Earlier than yesterday. Beside it, still stuck to the side of the bedside counter, the useless, yellow flyer taunted him.

. . .

He waited farther back from the platform today, standing with his back against a cool pillar, examining the brown tiles underfoot. A man coughed loudly as he walked past the other side of the column, making Dyrne wince. He heard the carriage whistle toward them from the tunnel and watched it emerge. He wondered how fast it was traveling.

His focus lingered on the platform edge.

He shuffled closer.

A woman standing beside him edged closer to him, eyeing him sideways. But the carriage glided to a stop. After waiting for everyone else to board, he wedged himself through a sliding door near the back.

Half an hour ahead of his usual schedule. After waking so early, he had decided there was no point in waiting around in the flat. He felt a duty to make up for lost time yesterday after abandoning his desk at noon. An early arrival would also avoid the looming certainty of curious stares and uncomfortable questioning.

Standing instead of searching for a seat, he bumped against the carriage wall, his thoughts doomed moths flapping around his head. He had overthought the bid, spent too much time staring at it, allowing the words to become meaningless and empty. And he had rushed it. Shouldn't have submitted this time. Should have waited another month. Enough time to make sure it looked balanced, innocent, normal. Surely it must have looked suspicious that he was bidding to visit a woman who'd only just been cremated? He had been so consumed, his thoughts so concentrated in the vice grip of the bid, that he hadn't even contemplated how morbid it would all seem. The woman's ashes had barely cooled, and he was already sifting through them for gold.

Could have saved him. And I've fucked it up again.

He shook the thoughts away as Central New London drifted into view.

Exiting the Line, he noticed the sun hadn't risen yet. Winter's dull navy spilled over everything. He allowed the almost-darkness to cloak him. Stepping into the Central Gardens, Dyrne set out on his route across the concrete path once again, puffing yesterday's rejection and last night's terrors away. With fewer people cluttering the way, he looked, for the first time since before working at DOHR, at the gardens around him, glowing under dim light posts. Long strips of greens, browns and reds ran in parallel rows along the quarter-mile passage, interrupted with cross-cutting walkways. A handful of dry, browning leaves fluttered across his path, making him stop. He watched them chase one another in invisible ribbons and circles before being lifted off by the cool wind, rushing into the bristling green bushes. Now that his feet had stopped moving, he gazed down at the topiary and saw something else—something he'd been blind to these past two years. A series of small, bronze placards embedded into the beige slabs lined the walkway. How had he forgotten these? Names of entire family lines wiped out in the War. Masses of people deleted from existence. Which of these families was *he* a descendant of? Whose genes did he share? Another missing piece that reminded him he'd never be like everyone else. He bent over, squinting to read an engraving. 'IN MEMORIAM.'

"Professor Samson." The woman's voice yanked him out of his temporary sedation.

He swung around, almost hitting her with his frontpack.

Her. The familiar girl from the Line. She had called him Professor this time. Her identity pressed at his mind, a face against a misted window, ready to shatter through.

Dyrne squinted back at the redheaded puzzle girl, analysing her features.

"Sorry to bother you again. You look like you were reading the memorials—never lost your interest in the past, I guess." She looked like she wanted to laugh.

How the hell is she here at this time? Is she following me or something?

She took a step back, her smile fading.

"Are you alright, sir?"

Somewhere in Dyrne's brain, a connection snapped, like two magnets hurtling at each other and clanging together. New London University. The girl who had questioned him; urged him to defend Copil from his tormentors.

Ember.

"I really must go," he uttered, angling his head downward, barging past her to get away.

"What's wrong with you?" She called, throwing her arms out.

"Wrong with me?" He mumbled, before turning to shout, "Don't talk to me again!"

She stared and stepped backward. He mirrored her, horrified at himself.

"Don't come near me!" he kept yelling, before storming ahead, desperate for breath. His face shuddered with heat, and he exhaled in rasps. Fleeing the Gardens, he hurried North through the channel of scrapers, chewing his lip and muttering. A suited man walked by, looking at him with alien eyes. As the stranger passed, Dyrne caught sight of his own reflection in a ground-level window, showing him what the man, and anyone else around, must see—a frail, hunched wreck, angry and sweating. A rat.

18

Yusuf led Phoebe and Geraldine through the opaque glass door. It closed with a snip behind them. The dark metal crate they now stood in, lit by two overhead strips of blue lighting, descended to the real heart of DOHR. The caged elevator rattled around them. Geraldine folded her arms and sighed, flopping against the bars.

Metal shutters lifted, presenting them with the narrow catacomb corridor, much darker than the open office space they spent most of their days in. They marched on in single file. Phoebe felt the familiar flutter of adrenaline, knowing she'd be back down here again to use the pods in the coming days.

When Phoebe let Geraldine know that Dyrne would be the other member joining the visit cycle, she had paused with raised eyebrows before giving a quick nod and asking where Dyrne was, glancing exaggeratedly from side to side.

"I haven't seen him since I arrived today and he… was ill yesterday, I think." Phoebe left the explanation at that, not even understanding for herself what had happened to Dyrne. After he'd vanished from DOHR, she'd Netcalled him four times with no answer. Geraldine nodded with a knowing smile as if understanding the excuse for Dyrne's absence perfectly.

Reaching the end of the passageway, they glanced down either length of the T-junction. Peering to the left, Phoebe heard Alex's accented voice emanating from one of the open metal doors. They arrived at the pod chamber to find him leaning against silver railings that protected the intricate machinery, control panels and screens. Dyrne sat on the stone steps leading to a deactivated pod. His resting position in front of the impressive, looming orb made him look like a pensive man in the moon. He looked up as they entered.

"Here you are! I didn't even know if you were in today." She readied herself to barrage Dyrne with questions. But knowing him well enough, this tactic wouldn't help. And she was supposed to be uniting her new team. She stopped herself. Dyrne leaned his head on both hands with elbows on knees. He said nothing.

"Hi, Alex. Dyrne, Geraldine's going to be working with us. You know that you've been assigned to my visits?"

Alex rolled his eyes. "Observations!"

She ignored him, still looking at Dyrne. "Have you even checked your Alerts?"

"Yes, I did. I was going to come and see you soon..."

"Well, we obviously all know each other, so I don't think introductions are necessary."

Dyrne stood up straightening himself, as if it required extreme effort. He looked like he was unsure whether to wave, shake his waspish colleague's hand, or do nothing. His eventual reaction was an awkward swaying, nodding in Geraldine's direction without looking her in the eye. Geraldine watched statue-like, hands clasped behind her back. Phoebe continued, already irked that this wasn't the beginning to her visit cycle she'd envisaged.

"So, this is our team, folks." She smiled, almost sarcastically. "I think we can really do this cycle justice together. Shall we start assigning individual visits?"

Yusuf offered a polite smile and a nod. Geraldine coughed and remained static. Phoebe began listing her visit plans: Jane Winstone's first electoral campaign, her advances as part of the America-Britain Bridging Council, key speeches to government, her anti-WMD movement. As Phoebe talked she paced back and forth in the small chamber, her hands whirling as she bobbed her head. She stopped when she caught Geraldine yawning. Then she looked at Dyrne. Hands in his pockets, one leg crossed over the other, his gaze focused on a random spot on the smooth, dark floor, unblinking. Phoebe stopped pacing. Her hands fell.

"I thought you might be a bit happier to be working with me on this, Dyrne. It's been a while since we were on a cycle together." His eyes met hers but maintained their blank look. "And I thought you would understand how much this research means to me."

No answer.

"And what the hell happened to you yesterday?" An angry whisper now.

"I'm going to head back up," Geraldine interrupted. "I'll start looking over the notes and the schedule you've given me before anything else."

"I'll come with you," Alex added, pushing himself from the railings. The pair left, their footsteps and mumbled words echoing down the corridors. Phoebe realised she must look like an angry mother, chastising her child for not coming home on time.

"I'll just wait outside. Breech of protocol to leave you down here unaccompanied, I'm afraid." Yusuf edged out backward.

"So, what happened to you? I tried to contact you."

Dyrne straightened his back to look at her, as if having to force himself to speak.

"I... didn't feel well. I took the day off. Headache."

"Headache? And you're better now? Because you don't look it."

"I'm fine. I'll deal with it."

She stepped closer to him, folding her arms and sighing.

"I was worried about you, you know. You disappeared in a bloody hurry. You could have told me what was going on." She had softened her voice, trying to sound more sympathetic. She expected him to give in, accept her counsel, offer a truce.

"Why are you so bothered? I left for the day, so what? You weren't my first port of call. Sorry." His shoulders were raised like ramparts, his eyes squinting. She opened her mouth to argue, before blinking and shaking her head.

"Fine. I was just concerned about you. Forget it." She spoke without looking at him. "Can we get back up to the office to start going over my visits?"

"...Yeah." He cleared his throat.

Turning, Phoebe left the chamber and strode back down the dim corridor as Dyrne followed behind at an awkward distance. She heard the clunk of the pod chamber door being closed and locked behind them. Yusuf was correcting Alex's mistake.

19

Winter had eased its fingers around the mornings, the shapes of the bushes all merging into navy silhouettes. As Dyrne trod through the frost-tinged pathways of the Central Gardens he couldn't even recognise the various shadowed figures milling by whom he used to have memorised. Glancing down, he caught sight of the memorial plaques lining the walkway again. It had become a new habit on his route to cast a look toward them, sometimes counting them in his head as they glided past. "One, two, three, four, five, six...". He never stopped to read the inscriptions, though; not even on late nights home when no one else was around. He dreaded anyone stopping to speak to him about the plaques. Any discussion of those killed by War could lead to a discussion of synths. Dyrne's DNA could have been extracted from one of these families. Must be.

"Hey, Samson!" The American voice called out from somewhere unseen, making him jump. "Hold on!"

Still walking on, Dyrne turned his head awkwardly to find Alex, wrapped up in a thick scarf, gloves and coat, jogging to catch up with him.

"Hi, Alex," he mumbled, slowing a little. He resented his last moments alone being splintered by unanticipated conversation, even if it was with a friend. If he could call Alex that.

"You got built-in insulation?"

Why is he asking that?

Dyrne looked back, wide-eyed, unresponsive. Alex waved his gloved hands in front of Dyrne's face.

"It's cold! They don't have scarves where you're from?" His voice was loud but the words were muffled through the woolen, black scarf that he had pulled up around his neck and chin. Dyrne let out a noise— a half-laugh, half-cough, trying to guess if Alex was making fun of him.

"Just kidding, pal."

Dyrne wore his most convincing smile.

"Too bad about your bid, huh?"

The feigned smile lingered for another few seconds before he understood. Alex had seen the Sarai Tailor obituaries on Dyrne's screen that night weeks ago.

"Hey, come on, it's freezing!"

Dyrne realised he'd stopped walking as Alex turned to call back to him. He picked up the pace again with an awkward skip, his mind still stuck.

"So things any better with you and Rush?"

"Better?"

"Yeah. Pretty obvious she's kind of mad at you for something, the way she was going on the other day down at the pods."

Dyrne threw a quick glance around. Why was Alex talking about the pods out here?

"Relax, no one's listening. So, you and Rush...?"

"Oh, yes, that was nothing. It's fine," Dyrne shrugged, lying badly for a change.

The silver doors of the elevator revealed the labs like a tired eye opening to bright sunlight. The men went their separate ways with Alex giving Dyrne one of his pats on the back. Shooting straight to his workstation Dyrne didn't even glance at Phoebe's desk. Not that he didn't want to. But neither knowing nor not knowing where she was or whether she was around would make him feel any better. Ignorance wasn't quite bliss, but it was preferable to churning thoughts and unintended eye contact.

Dyrne wasn't due to take part in another of Phoebe's visits until tomorrow so prepared for the irksome process of sightwriting his most recent visit—an observation of Jane Winstone. He hadn't even spoken to Phoebe about it.

Preparing both screens and stretching his back, he settled into position, shifting his gaze between the pod recording and the waiting, blank screen.

10.10.2270
VISITATION REF: E001009
COMMISSIONED BY DR. C. HOULD ON 01.10.2270
HISTORIAN: D. SAMSON
VISITATION DATE: 11.02.2148
LOCATION: PHILADELPHIA, FORMER USA
SIGHTINGS: 0

Despite everything consuming his mind, the sightwriting was flowing with relative ease. Ironically, this effortlessness worried him. It had never worked when he was feeling this uptight. Was this a manifestation of something? Perhaps, at some point, part of him really had given up on his own bid.

The images on the screen crackled. Dyrne remembered being in the pod yesterday. He had watched Jane Winstone in a meeting with members of the USA government, almost yelling across a table at one another about military strategy. He had admired her confidence but at the same time knew she would have intimidated him, had they ever met.

The mention of synths came next. A copy of the Synthetic Repopulation Programme had rested under the chubby pink hand of one of the American men. Winstone was resistant to the entire idea, claiming that cloning new humans from the dead would be "ethically questionable" and that its long-term implementation would result in "chaos". Dyrne had shrunk back against the conference room wall, wincing. Even now, watching this section of the recording in his chair, heat prickled his cheeks.

During the observation in the pod, he hadn't heard part of the conversation, too distracted at one point by a pile of papers on a desk.

Pressing the audio piece to his ear, he listened to the next part. Roarke Preston, the official chairing the meeting, seethed: "Miss Winstone, you are one single female representative from an island the same size as Florida with overly ambitious ideas about how the rest of us who know better should be doing things."

It was inescapable. Dyrne looked at the pixelated image of proud

Jane Winstone, now withering back into her chair, absorbing every pejorative word. Dyrne smiled. Not a smile of sympathy or even admiration for Winstone. It was a smile for Phoebe. She'd been right.

Dyrne pushed the chair back and strode across the office toward her desk, flexing his hands open and closed. He spotted her dark brown hair over the edges of the partitions, loose wisps sticking out from the small knot tying it back. As he approached, he could see a recording playing on her Net screen.

"Phoebe, hi," he called out, still a few steps away from her station.

As she turned around, another head rose over the edge of the glass panel from behind her.

"Oh. Geraldine." He stopped walking. She stared at him. "Sorry, I didn't realise you were both working on something."

"We were just reviewing some of the visit recordings so far." It was Geraldine who spoke first. Phoebe turned back to face the screen before talking.

"Done your report yet?" she asked, without sounding especially curious.

"Yes. Just finished. That's what I was coming to talk to you about." He took another few steps forward. Geraldine continued observing him the entire time.

It was then, standing beside the seated pair at the opening to the workstation, that Dyrne could see what the women were looking at on the screen. His visit. The recording of the same observation he had just been reviewing. His nerves seized.

"I... didn't realise you were watching me. My visit I mean. Is everything okay with it?"

"Fine. We're just looking over everything we have so far," Phoebe responded, again without looking Dyrne's way.

We.

Dyrne hadn't thought Phoebe knew Geraldine well before this. In fact, he was sure she disliked Geraldine as much as he did. Were they both leading the visit cycle together now? When all three of them were last together, he hadn't thought Geraldine was interested in any of it. The two turned their heads to look at Dyrne in perfect unison, like a pair of cats responding to a sudden noise.

"I just wanted to tell you about some of the things I heard in this meeting that I knew you'd be interested in including in your study." Dyrne was barely aware of what he was saying, instead focusing on avoiding on Geraldine's staring eyes. "Although... I suppose you've heard it all for yourself now."

"Some of it," Phoebe replied. He didn't recognise her like this, but forged on, refusing to be dismissed like an annoying child.

"It's incredible the way this guy Preston is speaking to her. I mean she's the only sane one there, trying to avoid a cataclysmic nuclear event rather than plan for its aftermath, and she's accused of, sort of, stirring up trouble. Well, not that he really believed that, I don't think. Probably."

He knew he was rambling. The two pairs of eyes continued looking in his direction.

"And did you hear him getting frustrated with her? 'You are one single female representative'—I couldn't believe it. Well, I mean, I suppose I could believe it—you knew some of this already; that's why you wanted to visit her. She's being treated like shit just because she's a woman."

Geraldine turned back to the screen. Phoebe propped her chin on her palm, resting an elbow on the edge of the desk. Dyrne couldn't tell if she was taking it all in or was bored with him.

"Yeah." Her sole response punched Dyrne in the chest.

He flexed his fingers again, desperate to clutch Phoebe back for himself.

"For my next visit, do you want me to go back to this Preston and scare him a bit? Throw some things around and terrify him into thinking there's a poltergeist? An angry, female poltergeist." He felt ridiculous as soon as he had said it.

"Not ideally, no," she responded flatly, ignoring the joke bait.

At this, Geraldine rose, taller than Dyrne.

"Phoebe, I'm going to get down to the pods early."

"Thanks for your help." It was the warmest thing Phoebe had said so far. Dyrne pressed himself against the corner of the glass panel, allowing Geraldine to march past without a glance in his direction.

An invisible, silent wall wedged itself between Phoebe and Dyrne. She seemed unaware, glancing between her Net screens as if he wasn't even in the building. He stared through the barrier, trying to figure out the best way to smash through. What had Geraldine told her? Why were they watching his recording?

"Phoebe, is there—" But before he could formulate his next thought, he was cut off at the starting line.

"—Look Dyrne, I need to get through all these recordings and start making my own notes. Can we leave this for another time?" She finally looked at him, her expression devoid of the connection they normally shared. No frown or glistening eyes or creased brow. Just a blankness. Empty.

"Sure... sorry."

He had seen Phoebe irritated with him before. They had even argued once. But the detached words and glances were unmistakable and unlike any version of her he had encountered. He had a feeling of déjà vu and could hear the whistling of the Line in his head as he turned away.

20

Blinding winter light glared off the scanner panel so that Dyrne couldn't even look at it. Face scans didn't work without eye recognition. A short monotone buzz emanated from the speaker. The doors refused to budge.

"Let me help." The authoritative voice startled him.

A large silhouette moved in, brushing against him, blocking the light. As he drew back, adjusting to the shade, he made out short, grey hair and deep brown eyes set into dark skin. Like a schoolchild in front of the headmistress, he fumbled with his frontpack.

"Oh, thank you, Dr. Hould." He turned back to face the scanner, unlocking the sliding doors with a chirruping beep from the wall panel. They stepped through together, out of the icy glare into the dim foyer. He could see Hould better now, with her long, thick coat and old-fashioned, leather briefcase.

They passed the receptionist, Hould saying something to the young man who answered, smiling, and waited for the lift doors to slide open. It occurred to Dyrne that Hould was always here before anyone else every day. He had planned his own schedule precisely and knew he wasn't early. There must have been a reason she was late.

"… Mr. Samson?"

He realised she was looking at him, awaiting a response.

"Sorry?" Dyrne asked.

"I was just asking how you were this morning. Tired or just preoccupied?"

"Oh. Tired," he smiled back, nodding his head too much, "and thinking through some ideas for my next bid, too."

The lift opened, and he shuffled in behind Hould. They plunged downward, and Dyrne anticipated an uncomfortable silence. He needed to fill it. He turned to ask some mindless question when

Hould's deep voice took control again. "And will you be bidding with the same proposal as before, or something new?"

Silence.

What?

Same as before? Could he do this? After his bid was rejected and he'd spent the first week submerged in defeat, his alternative had been to visit someone else. Someone with a connection to Copil. Affect some change in the past that would ultimately lead to his safety. How? He had no idea yet. Every seed of a plan so far was pathetic. He switched between answers he might offer Hould, and sighed into the stifled air of the elevator. He looked up at her for some kind of sign. A wink, a smile, a nod. What answer did she want? Instead, she looked ahead, chin raised, briefcase clasped in both hands. But was there a subtle smile at her lips?

"Well... I'm not sure yet."

Dyrne felt the lift come to a halt.

"Sorry you missed out on the last round, Dyrne." This time she glanced sideways at him. He looked back, saying nothing. Hearing her use his first name was disorientating.

"A very tragic life," she then said. Dyrne's eyes widened. He opened his mouth to stutter something in reply before Hould clarified. "I'm sure she had a child who died. Faded into obscurity after that. Very sad."

'Faded into obscurity'? Was this her way of telling him Sarai Tailor wasn't important enough to visit? And she was probably horrified that he'd bid to visit a woman who'd only just died. It was morbid. Sadistic even. The stupidity of this punched him in the stomach again.

Electronic buzzing and busy murmur filled the stifling carpeted box as the lift doors slid away. "Have a good day, Mr. Samson."

She marched through the workstations to her raised office. Dyrne watched her go for several seconds before putting his hands in his coat pockets, lowering his head and gliding straight to his station.

He hadn't spoken to Phoebe since their cold encounter two weeks ago. Their one form of interaction was through alerts on the Nets, with formal and curt updates to one another about visits and reports. Avoiding the Hub each day amplified how awkward their next inevitable meeting would be. But putting it off was all he could manage for now.

Arriving at the relative safety of his glass cocoon, he exhaled and pulled off his frontpack, hanging it on a glass magnet hook beside his desk. As he did, he caught sight of the back of Geraldine's narrow head over the cubicle wall, her black hair pulled back in the usual tight ball. Sliding into his chair and avoiding his Net screen, he glimpsed through a slit between papers stuck to the glass wall. Like a few other historians, Dyrne had managed to cover much of his workstation partitions in notes and sheets now, subtly defying the 'open' nature of the office. He reached out, peeling back a brown sheet, widening and perfecting his viewpoint. Geraldine's screen glowed through at him, inviting him to look. She was reading an alert. Squinting, he could make out Phoebe's name as the sender at the top of the message. Pulling himself in even closer, he pressed his forehead against the glass, trying to scan the contents of the brief message. He couldn't make out most of it at this distance. But was that his name? In more than one sentence? As he craned in even further, a harsh cough made him jump back as Geraldine swiveled in his direction.

He shoved his chair back and lunged toward his desk, leaning over an indiscriminate piece of paper, pretending to scour it, wincing. He waited for Geraldine to leer over the dividing wall and demand to know what he'd been doing. But turning back carefully, he saw her sauntering off. Perhaps to the Hub, or to see Phoebe again, more likely. The thought of crawling back to resume reading the alert through the glass occurred to him. Instead, he allowed the sheet of paper on the wall to fall back into place; a curtain shielding a forbidden backstage.

The lights were dimmed, and the historians began closing Nets, gathering their belongings and migrating away from the secrets of DOHR back to their pretend, ordinary lives. By the time Dyrne spotted Yusuf stepping out of the elevator crate from the pod chambers, the office floor was deserted. He watched the physicist stroll across the coolly lit white floor, glancing around. The geometric shining glass cubicles looked like crystal formations on a cave floor.

"Yusuf?" Dyrne bobbed his head above his workstation wall, hermit-like.

Yusuf looked back over his shoulder.

"Mr. Samson, everything alright?"

"Yes, yes... Just getting to work on my next bid... want to make a head-start. I saw you walking out and... was just wondering how you were."

"Working on anything interesting?"

"Well, I hope so..."

"Your observations for Mrs. Rush's project seem to be going well." Yusuf had approached and now leaned against the glass edge of the workstation.

"Yes, they are. Well, I think Phoebe's happy with what we've unearthed, anyway."

"Not too many sightings either."

"No, that's right. I'm usually so clumsy on visits. You're obviously very good at controlling things. I'm not sure all of the physicists are so concerned with it."

"All of the physicists? You wouldn't be referring to our mutual American friend?" Yusuf grinned. "To be honest, there's not a lot we can do to avoid transference; apart from advising historians on their movement and trying to be as accurate as possible with our co-ordinates and settings. Sightings are an inevitable part of the process, as much for me as for Alex."

"And people still talk about seeing ghosts now. We aren't going to figure out how to stop it for quite some time."

"Yes... I suppose that must be true. If we believe people who say they've seen ghosts at least. I'd never thought of it that way." Dyrne watched Yusuf's eyes—not suspicious, but surprised.

Behind Yusuf, a door opened. Both men looked across the rows of shining glass edges to see a white-haired man in a black suit leaving Dr. Hould's mezzanine office—one of the men Dyrne had seen weeks earlier.

Dyrne lowered his voice. "Someone from the government. He was in here with another man a few weeks ago, speaking to Hould. Most of the historians didn't exactly seem pleased to see them."

"Wonder what he's here for. And so late at night," Yusuf whispered back, watching as the white-haired man vanished into the elevator. It was unusual to hear Yusuf speculating like this. Anytime Phoebe and Alex had gossiped about others, he tended to busy himself on a Net or wander back to the pod chambers.

"Not sure why they've been here," Dyrne continued. "Checking over Hould's new regulations on visits I assume. And he's probably here at night because of the reaction he got before." But as Dyrne spoke, his brain tightened, burning through ten other theories, all involving being hunted down. He'd seen more of these government officials in the past month than he had in the previous year.

"I wonder what *their* families think they do. What area of government they are in charge of. Do you think they're trained for alibis like we are?" Yusuf asked.

Apart from unwanted encounters with ex-students, Dyrne didn't have to think about his alibi training too often. There was no one at home to have to cover up to and his few friends worked at DOHR. He looked back at Yusuf, wondering again, as he had done at the meditation group at Phoebe's—did *he* lie to Zaira about his job? Or was he honest with his wife?

"Suppose so." A non-committal answer was best. "What do you think of all the secrecy though?" Dyrne asked. Yusuf looked at him, squinting a little. Panicking, Dyrne picked his way ahead carefully. "I mean—as a physicist. Those original scientists worked for decades on time and light-distortion, everyone knew that. But for it to become a reality but not be able to share that success with the public, with anyone—it must have been difficult not to be acknowledged."

"Well, I'm sure any difficulties were made easier with the enormous payoffs they were given for their silence... apparently."

Yusuf then bowed his head, as if knowing he had revealed a secret. Dyrne had heard these rumours too.

"I suppose it's for the best, really," Yusuf continued. He still whispered even though the labs were deserted again. "I wouldn't normally agree with the government keeping secrets from the public, but can you imagine? This technology in the wrong hands—what people would use it for? What people would try to go back and alter? It would be catastrophic."

"...Mmm," Dyrne nodded, gazing at an empty spot on the glass wall.

"I'm surprised it's been kept controlled for this long, that the government haven't used it for their own means in other ways."

"As far as we've been told. How do we know every other scraper on this street isn't housing secret facilities underground, using the pods for... well, who knows what?" Dyrne continued staring, fixated on nothing. "Yusuf." He swallowed. "Do you ever feel guilty?"

Yusuf tilted his head.

"I mean—about the visits. Observations. That sometimes we're seeing people's deaths and we're just... letting it happen. Don't you ever wonder whether we could prevent some of it?"

Stop talking.

"I admit, it can feel uncomfortable, Mr. Samson. But we are scientists. Observers. It's our duty not to allow sentimentality to affect our research. And anyway, think of the consequences of changing past events. Who knows what it would cause in the present? What chain reactions alterations like that might result in."

Why did I even say anything? Too much.

"And above that, what about the moral implications? Who are we to judge who should be saved? Whose lives should continue? At what point do we decide to save one person and not another? It would be like introducing some sort of reverse capital punishment."

Dyrne pursed his lips together, forcing himself not to say another word.

"There's no point in fixating on it, Mr. Samson. Besides, I doubt the transference we sometimes cause could even make a difference."

"Mm. Although... I've seen people react like animals when they think they're seeing a ghost..." He looked off again in a daze. "Yusuf, do people bid for the same things repeatedly?"

"I'm not sure. You mean if their applications are unsuccessful?"

"Yes."

"I don't see why not. As far as I know there isn't a ruling against it. You'd know better than me, really. I'm a physicist—I just co-ordinate what cycles I'm handed. Wouldn't you be better asking Dr. Hould or Mrs. Rush?"

Dyrne nodded, sucking on his lower lip.

"Although I'm not sure why yo—a historian, would want to, if their idea had been rejected the first time."

"Perhaps they only get rejected because there were marginally better applications at the time to choose from. Maybe in a different pool of choices, the same bid *would* be more successful."

Dyrne's waterfall thoughts tumbled, ignorant of Yusuf's presence.

"Or maybe there were just small, trivial features of the application that needed altering here and there. You know, Hould should give us feedback explaining why our bids have missed out."

Dyrne had begun scratching his earlobe, looking off at papers lying in an open drawer.

"I'll leave you to your work. Goodnight, Mr. Samson." Yusuf touched his shoulder, shocking him back to attention.

"Oh, yes. Goodnight, Yusuf."

He watched the physicist traverse his way through the gleaming workstations to the waiting elevator. "Thanks for your advice," he said, just loud enough for Yusuf to hear.

"Try submitting the bid again. See what happens," Yusuf called, before disappearing into the elevator, leaving Dyrne alone in the labs. Again.

• • •

The electric glow cushioned him. He wasn't sure why he had stopped here tonight. Other nights had been worse than this. Today had been another lap of an endless circular marathon, the same as every other. Two or three people had passed him, none stopping of course, although they'd probably given him odd looks—some dazed, sweaty man standing on a kerb staring at an autochemist well after dark wasn't a normal sight. He'd been there for ten minutes now. The array of pain relief pills beamed back at him. He doubted there was anything in there that could be too dangerous and there were surely limits on how much you could buy at once. But there must have been a reason for so much debate about the existence of these things; must be some truth to the stories of people scattered around UE hospital units overdosing on tablets vended from these machines.

Squinting sleepily at the flashing prices, he swayed on the kerb. The numbers blinked in and out of order and rearranged themselves to form dates and deadlines in his mind. Hould must be releasing the next bid deadline soon. He had spent hours one night staring around his own museum of books and flicking through pages of scattered pieces of recovered histories searching for something to reel him in and ignite a new idea for a bid. But the stories, ideas and legends that once captivated him and invited him in were now just words on pages that couldn't help. How could Copil be replaced by any of them? Copil was part of him.

Blinking and shifting his focus, he spotted his reflection in the autochemist glass. The flat, ghost image gazed back. His side-parted, dark hair—greasy and disheveled. His white shirt—clipped in place; but baggy and unkempt around his belt. His eyes—puffy and bloodshot.

As he blinked again, his attention latched onto something else. This time it wasn't his own reflection he refocused on, but someone else's. A white face floating in the dark behind him, across the street. Curly black and grey hair. Pink, pocked skin. Round, dark glasses. Eyes focused on him.

Moth.

Dyrne jerked his head away from the machine, pulling a muscle in his neck. Dr. Moth from the omni gathering at Phoebe's. The psychoanalyst. The watcher. What the hell was he doing here? Did he live nearby?

Or was he spying, sent by Phoebe?

Dyrne refused to feed Moth's greedy stare. Swiveling around, he bolted off in the direction of his flat.

Copil flashed in his head again like lights switching on and off. The same dreams from the past several months. Years. That was no doubt what Moth had latched onto, analysing and dissecting what he had been tricked into revealing at the meditation. He couldn't believe he had managed to take part, unlocking himself like the imagined box in front of strangers, never mind those he knew.

Dank melancholy seeped into him as he thought of it, and of Phoebe, and of his bid, and of being watched and of reacting this way. Images and memories bubbled to the fore as he stumbled through the dark, cold streets. He saw Phoebe and his colleagues from the University and the students like Ember all fade away like a distant Line stop being left behind.

And his family.

He knew that his stubbornness had worn away all of the other precious stones in his life, leaving him with one tiny diamond—the bid.

The harsh, glowing screen shone at Dyrne uselessly as he cradled his head in his hands. He felt like a scientist whose radiation-sickness cure had been stolen. The application and its screeds of notes and research existed idly on the Net. For a while, he was tempted to erase *everything* with a spiteful wipe of the screen. But it wouldn't fulfill him. Within days he would begin to reformulate and regret and become consumed once more. He needed this to work. And now Hould had practically given him permission to bid for Sarai again.

He sat back, breathed deeply and began scanning his initial notes, looking at significant events in her formative years, the University enrolment records, Netcall trails, the synth birthing facilities, adoption procedures, news site interviews. Precious, floating cargo rose through the debris of a shipwreck, worming its way to the fore of his mind. Hadn't she once described herself as omni, even back then?

Snip. Light was gone. Darkness gulped the labs whole. A woman close by yelped. A siren blared from somewhere overhead, and electric blue sheen flashed on the ceilings across the entire office. The main elevators boomed out a thick, metal clunk. Neon cobalt figures shot up from workstations. Elongated shadows blinked on and off, blue and black. Heart thumping, legs frozen, eyes widening and searching. Dyrne's brain unclenched just enough to form questions. Were the government officials back? What had they found? Had they looked through his desk and figured it out? Looked into his background? Found the connection between him and Sarai?

Then the wailing siren cut off. The heavy door of Hould's office flew open as she rushed out, arms swinging, head down, almost breaking into a run as she descended the staircase. Two or three others had already drifted to the white door of the pod elevator—Dyrne didn't know why. Hould, though, was also flying in that direction, fidgeting with some small object in her hand. Dyrne floated toward the gathering group.

Approaching the doors, above which one of the fluorescent blue lights still swirled relentlessly, Hould pushed through the gathering and stepped to the face scanner without saying a word. She held up the small, black object to it. A tiny green light flashed, and she pressed the glass, entering some sort of code. Dyrne glanced around at the frightened faces of his colleagues. Geraldine was there, looking the most vulnerable he had ever seen her, gripping onto Martin Daley's arm. Turning in the other direction, he saw more faces he knew less well, but who all looked similar now; frightened animals cowering. And Phoebe. Flanked by two pairs of shoulders further back: her eyes screwed up, trying to see, her mouth making a silent O shape. He felt the need to go to her—for her sake or his own, he wasn't sure.

Then a long blare whistled from the lift door, followed by scraping metal, as it yawned open.

"We have an emergency in the pod chambers, everyone," Dr. Hould called, struggling to keep her voice steady. "DOHR is currently in an automatic lockdown and will be for some time. No one can enter or leave the facility for the time being—"

Echoing from the elevator shaft, the unmistakable frightened shout of a man shook Dyrne's entire body.

Who the hell was that?

The sirens and flashing lights were insignificant now. The knowledge that they were working underground at an unknown depth suddenly felt real and pressing. Even Hould looked unsteady and turned to face the dark elevator cage.

A sickening silence settled over the horrified group, who stood around her in a curve, the swirling blue light illuminating them like a frantic, twirling hand on a clock. Hould intended to go down there, despite the obvious reluctance in her stance. There were a few small movements as the historians shifted and twitched furtive glances at one another. Dyrne wondered if they were all thinking the same thing—that someone else ought to go down there as well. The blank seconds continued like endless sand through his precious hourglass. No one spoke. Someone, surely, would volunteer and step forward, perhaps even taking Hould's place. But rather than searching the group, Dyrne looked down at his concrete feet. His heart pumped blood into his ears, filling his head with a high-pitched ringing.

"Stay at your workstations for now. I'll debrief with you as soon as I can. Your safety is not at risk, though, I promise you. A security team is automatically alerted via the government in case of an alarm like this."

Like this. We've never had anything like this.

He didn't even know there was an alarm system. Or what 'this' was.

Hould stepped into the looming, black elevator cage, looking out at the spectators again. The last chance for someone to volunteer, be a hero. But no one budged. The semi-circle of men and women held steady, doing their job—observing, like some mass visit with Hould as the subject.

She pressed the black square in her hand to the interior scanner, and the juggernaut door clunked shut on her, devouring her in its jaws.

The small crowd waited, listening to the mechanical clicks and whirring signaling the lift's descent below them. Dyrne wasn't sure if it was just coincidence or if Hould had initiated it somehow with her electronic card, but low-level, emergency lighting flickered on. The historians murmured amongst themselves, congregating in pairs and threes, eventually dispersing back to the workstations as ordered. Swallowing a dry lump, Dyrne turned to see Phoebe standing alone as the others around her drifted away. He was surprised Geraldine hadn't scampered to her. Phoebe caught his eye and allowed her gaze to linger. As he inched closer to her, she hugged herself and lowered her head. Anticipating her launch back to her own area, Dyrne took a longer lunge toward her, his knee wobbling under him.

"Phoebe..." Her round, emerald eyes looked up at him. "Are you okay?"

She nodded, and what even looked like a smile appeared.

"I think so." She exhaled. "I just hope Yusuf is, too."

"Yusuf?"

"Yes. He's down there. That was his voice shouting."

Perched on the edge of Phoebe's chair, Dyrne watched her as she sat with bent knees on the floor leaning against the workstation wall. The emergency lighting made a dull glow around the zigzag outline of her body. Fear of saying the wrong thing prevented him from saying anything at all. She had led Dyrne over here with the fewest of words, explaining that she had seen Yusuf just minutes before the alarms rang, ambling toward the elevator cage with Charon, another physicist.

More than half an hour had passed since the siren. Dyrne wanted to ask more about Yusuf, ask about how her visit cycle had been, ask what she was bidding for next, and apologise for how unsupportive he'd been. But each time he thought of something to say, he swallowed it back down, thinking it better to appreciate the fact that he was even in Phoebe's company again for now. She sat, childlike, clicking her fingernails in a daze, sighing every now and then.

"What could go wrong down there, apart from a mechanical failure or an electrical fault?" she finally asked, still not looking at him.

Dyrne shrugged. "I suppose there could be a fire or something. But then they wouldn't be keeping us in the building, and Hould certainly wouldn't be going down there."

More empty seconds.

"I've missed talking to you," he said, his eyes closed. Opening them, he found Phoebe looking up at him. Loose strands of soft, brown hair framed her face.

"Well it's taken you long enough," she responded with a smirk. The barrier he had felt for weeks began to thaw.

"I'm sorry. About what happened. I was too caught up in my own problem... selfish." With every word spoken, Copil and Sarai lurked in the back of his throat, waiting to spill out. "I didn't even think about your bid and how great it was for you. I should have."

"Look Dyrne, I don't even remember what happened. Let's just forget it."

He didn't know whether he was surprised or not. Or if she was being honest or not.

Testing ice on a frozen lake, they continued talking, tentatively at first, venturing guesses about the alarm and Yusuf. They returned to the notion of technical problems with the pods or the telescopes, but ruled these out, surmising that alarms and an automatic lockdown felt too extreme a sanction for something of that nature. Their speculations then turned to more severe possibilities. Had someone injured themselves? A historian already down in one of the pods on an early scheduled visit? A problem on a visit? But what? It was normal for the physicists to get coordinates or lens settings wrong and show historians the wrong places, the wrong times—hence apparent "ghost" sightings in the most unremarkable of times and places. But it was always rectified within seconds. Even transference on visits was usual, expected even. Unavoidable, Yusuf had said. They all knew this.

"So something more sinister?" Phoebe suggested. "Some sort of confrontation or fight down there?"

"Not likely with Yusuf is it?"

"Guess not," she shrugged. "It must be connected to a visit then. Something going wrong. But how?" Dyrne watched the floor, pretending to think it over, before Phoebe spoke again, quieter. "Someone messing things up? On purpose? Like that historian Alex told us about?"

"I don't even know if that was true."

"Hmm, I suppose, just another of Alex's mad stories..."

"Yes. Remember he almost had you convinced that he had an identical twin going around the city who took his place some days."

"Ha! I think he might have even believed that one himself."

Dyrne smiled, glad he had thrown Phoebe off track.

"What are you bidding on next anyway?"

Shit.

"Well... I might talk you through it a bit later. Maybe ask your advice. But were you happy with your visits? Everything okay with my reports? I still didn't ask you properly."

He leaned forward, hands clasped, smiling naively for approval. But she flopped over again, looking into her lap.

"Nothing changes, Dyrne."

Just as quickly as it had dissolved away, the uncomfortable clouded blockade rebuilt itself between them.

"Always avoiding really *telling* me anything. What is it you can't, or won't, say to me? It's just a bid, Dyrne. I'm not going to steal it."

Opening his mouth to justify himself, he spat out empty gasps.

BLEEP. The rattle and clunks from across the lab sent tiny vibrations through the floor. At once, the historians rose like meerkats, their heads drawn to the white elevator door. All talk dissipated to whispers. The whirring sound of the elevator machinery came to a stop and the seconds filled with silent anticipation.

The lift opened its jaws and dribbled out three figures. Hould. Charon. Yusuf.

Trooping out, Hould led the other two through the most direct route across the lab floor to her office, squinting straight ahead, avoiding everyone's stare. Charon raised her bowed head every few seconds, glancing with wide eyes at those she knew. Yusuf lagged behind, gripping a folder to his chest, shoulders hunched. He looked at no one.

Leaving nothing but a trail of questions, they ascended the stairs to Hould's office and disappeared behind the swiftly shut door. The confusion and speculation flew across the lab floor in hushed tones. Dyrne surveyed the others, but was haunted by Yusuf's blank face wherever he looked.

"I'm going to speak to some of the others. Geraldine might have some idea of what's happening." Phoebe rubbed her arms as if feeling cold and turned to wander off.

A red balloon expanded inside Dyrne, pressing against his ribs. "It's Sarai Tailor!" He called out. "The synth rights campaigner. That's who I want to visit." His heart throbbed and his head coursed with blood. He had vowed not to let anyone except Hould know about this. But his tongue had spoken the confession for him, without conscious thought. He felt lighter somehow, unbelievably; the balloon lifting him.

Phoebe looked back at him. "Okay." She paused. Something melted from her expression and was replaced with an almost-smile. "Sounds great, Dyrne."

Despite everything, her smile was contagious.

ALERT
Sender: C. Hould.
28.10.270
'All staff: as a result of a major incident in the pod chambers today, operations at the Department of Historical Research will cease until further notice.
Leave immediately.'

22

With his hands stuffed in his coat pockets, Dyrne shuffled on the spot, watching his breath puff out in clouds that floated off and faded into the air. He tried thinking back to the last time he'd been above ground at this time of day, but couldn't remember. White daylight filled the misted sky, and people strolled instead of marching to offices. Being this far out of the centre of New London made him glance around more often, watching anyone who passed by, visualising the quickest route back to his flat. It felt wrong to be out here in this way, serving no purpose, filling time with wafer-thin patience. But this is where she'd wanted to meet. And returning to DOHR wasn't an option.

At least the past two days had been spent indoors at home reading and scanning his Mobile for any further scraps of information that might turn out to be useful. It had meant he could pretend he was getting somewhere; that he was still working on the bid. But meeting with Phoebe in the middle of the day was making the shutdown of DOHR far more difficult to ignore. Still, he was grateful she had asked him; a sure sign that their broken connection could be healed.

The cold air nibbled the end of his nose, and he nuzzled into the upturned collar of his jacket, trying to find some relief from potentially watchful eyes.

"You look like a secret agent!" Phoebe called out from across the empty road.

"Aren't I one?" He had waited until she was a little closer to deliver his retort, having spied two men further along the pavement.

Wrapped up in a long olive coat, Phoebe skipped up onto the pavement, hands in pockets, still a full foot shorter than Dyrne.

"So where do you think we should go?" he asked, trying to sound nonchalant. He still didn't know why they couldn't have just spent the day inside. At *her* apartment, of course. There might be clues at his own place. Too many questions.

"Relax, I wanted to meet here so we could wander out a bit. There's a nice route I have in mind. We can talk about work—no one will hear us."

Turning like a soldier, she strode off. Dyrne followed her lead.

"So what have you been telling people about your sudden time away off?" she asked. "Have you used the story they suggested for us?"

Dyrne was warmed by the idea that Phoebe thought he might have someone in his life to give the alibi to.

"I haven't seen anyone the past few days, so it hasn't come up. What about you? What did you tell Francis?"

"Pretty unoriginal but I just went with the 'emergency building maintenance' idea. What have you been doing with your time anyway?" She had shifted the questioning back onto Dyrne, rather swiftly he thought. Had she told Francis the truth?

"Well, apart from fostering a new obsession with my bed," he joked, lying, "just catching up on some reading, researching the election candidates a bit more, cleaning the flat, other thrilling things of that nature."

"So who is it you're going for then?"

Does she mean Tailor? Is she asking already?

"Going for...?"

"For the election in December. Who you're voting for."

"Oh... I'm still undecided. Who do you think?"

"Well, would've thought you'd be going for Louis Apol. He's becoming very popular. Seems to be quite... liberal," she smiled.

"Yes... yes, he is."

"Heard anything from Yusuf?"

Again, she had assumed that he was in touch with people outside the walls of DOHR. Rather than endearing, though, this time he realised the sad truth—she didn't know him as well as either of them thought.

He shook his head. "Have *you?*"

"Nope. He won't answer my Netcalls."

"I don't suppose he's allowed to talk about it. And Yusuf isn't one to break the rules, is he?"

"No, I suppose not. I wonder how long he and Charon were kept there. I mean they took long enough letting *us* go anywhere, after the hours of waiting around. And what was the point of the last-ditch five-minute window to take whatever files we needed. Did you do that by the way?" She asked with abrupt, childlike curiosity. Dyrne was used to Phoebe's directness, but still no better at dealing with it.

"... I did. Just wanted to finish my bid application off. Who knows when we'll get submit next."

"Yeah, could be weeks before we're allowed back in."

"Weeks!" He hadn't meant to shout. Or stop walking.

"Well, yeah, that's my guess. Something pretty big's obviously going on in there, don't you think? Doubt we'll be back to normal anytime soon."

The cold wind blasted his chest for the first time.

"I suppose. Yes. I just thought... might be a few days or something." He forced himself to keep his voice level, unfased. He could work through what this all might mean later, when he was alone.

"What about Geraldine? Will she be submitting a new bid?"

"Geraldine? No idea. What makes you ask that?"

"Nothing. Just thought you two were pretty good friends now."

"Well, not exactly friends. Is that a hint of jealousy I detect?"

"No, no. Just wondering. I didn't mean anything," he answered, shaking his head and waving a hand.

"I know, I know. Relax. Anyway—DOHR. What the hell's going on?"

"I have no idea. And I doubt we'll get any honest answers even when we go back."

"*If* we go back!" Phoebe laughed. Dyrne ignored the quip.

"What's confusing me most is why there was even an alarm at all."

"Well, because every building has fire alarms and security alarms."

"Yes, but that wasn't a fire alarm. And security alarms for what? Why would there be an interior alarm fitted so far underground? It's an incredibly high-security building—a government building. Scanners at every door, that man in the lobby giving us elevator entry, recording equipment everywhere. What kind of breach did anyone ever anticipate?"

Phoebe shrugged. "Maybe it was just a safety thing, then. Something wrong with one of the pods."

"So wrong we had all had to be banished without a word of explanation?"

As they had walked, the scrapers had lowered in height and spread themselves out, dying off block by block. They passed through an area of grubby apartments and shut down shops, passing rattling wire-fenced gardens containing nothing. Dyrne's nose had warmed from its red, nipping state and he could smell more out here—stale smoke and weeks-old rubbish. They wandered on for a while in silence, both absorbing the surroundings, spying from the corners of their eyes every now and then as a sole wanderer walked by. Dyrne followed Phoebe as she took a sharp left through a thin alleyway.

It was the smell he sensed first. The stink had washed away to reveal something fresh and invigorating. As they emerged onto the main street, he looked at what lay ahead, where she had been leading them.

"What do you think, then? Recognise it?" She asked, beaming.

Walking closer, Dyrne slowed, as clumps of grassy greens blossomed out ahead all the way to the horizon, peppered with tall, dark brown spikes, rising higher and higher into the distance, touching the white film coating the sky. The fresh scent he had sensed wafted over him now with a cold wind. The extraneous sounds of New London faded away behind an invisible closed door. The forestry preserves spread for miles up and down this edge of the city boundary.

"Thought you'd like to come out here. It seemed to help before," she gave him a wry smile, before crossing the final road separating concrete from trees.

Before?

He followed on, checking for traffic, even though he hadn't seen a vehicle all day, and was about to ask what Phoebe meant. But then he remembered. The meditation. This is what she had induced the group to imagine. Isolated in one of these fields, cocooned by the trees. Of course now that it was winter, the real image was starker.

Caught in the memory and everything it brought—Moth, the nightmare, throbbing sickness in his stomach—Dyrne trailed along behind Phoebe with blind steps as she hopped up onto the small wall before squatting and leaping down over the other side. Bounding onto the soft earth, they skittered several feet down a grassy slope together and submerged themselves in the enveloping dark green thicket, leaving the dreary grey and brown city at their backs. Gazing up at the towering, barren branches ahead, Dyrne barely paid attention to Phoebe's ensuing question.

"So what is it you want to find out about Sarai Tailor?"

"... I want to go back quite early, to when her campaigning started. She was a bit of a loner at University apparently." He answered slowly, too busy looking up and around him and thinking back to the omni visions to be self-aware. His thoughts poured unimpeded, protected by the trees. "For one thing, it'd be interesting to know how she managed to get people to support her... or why she was even interested in synth rights in the first place." He spoke as if dreaming, still staring upward while they stepped through bushes and bracken.

"And what about her son?"

He stopped breathing. Quicksand feet.

"I know why you didn't want to tell me about all this."

Hot waves radiated from his torso. Everything pulsed. He finally inhaled, staring at Phoebe who continued walking straight ahead, as if oblivious to what she had just said. He swallowed knives and squeezed out words.

"Well... it's a big issue, isn't it? I think a lot of people would want to know." He gulped again, his heartbeat shaking him. "There's a lot that we—I mean, society—can't ask her in person. You know she died recently?" He'd blurted the last part thinking he might as well say it first, knowing she was going to mention it.

"That's not what I mean, Dyrne." She stopped and turned back to face him with a dipped head and knowing look. An expression that reminded him of his mother. He felt the usual perspiration trickle down his side, like an insect invading his shirt.

"You're metaganic. It must be important to you."

A whistling in his head. Acutely aware of his own breath. The vibrations stopped, and the frozen air locked everything.

She said it. She really said it aloud.

"I know that you'll be worried about other historians' reactions. It can't be easy."

Phoebe walked on, saving him the embarrassment of looking his way. It was as if the words had meant nothing to her, like she had mentioned his brown hair or pale skin.

"But fuck them," she yelled out, head lolling up to the treetops. "If they're synthphobic it's *their* problem!"

But it isn't.

After fifteen seconds of nothing but twigs breaking under Phoebe's feet and wind rushing above, she turned to look back at him. He still couldn't move. They watched each other as moments blew by.

"Dyrne. It's OK. You think I didn't know?"

He tried to answer but only made soundless shapes with his lips, shifting his gaze between Phoebe and the foliage they traversed through.

"I... don't know."

She closed the distance between them, treading back to touch his forearm. "I've known for months, years even—since I met you, basically. And I don't care. Well, actually I do care—it makes me worry about you more!"

As he continued staring down to the forest floor, she snapped him out of his daze in the same way he would always do for her. "Oh stop moping; you're not that big a deal; my world doesn't revolve around you, you know!"

He glanced up, feeling his lips curl into a smile he couldn't help.

"Now get a move on." She giggled, hooking his arm with her hand and yanking him forward.

He walked with her, feeling the tension in his body melt away while Phoebe talked about the synth movement, probably trying to cheer him up. While he half-listened, he realised he'd been wrong all this time. Phoebe did know him.

He shook the feeling off, along with the threatening lump in this throat. The conversation continued, and soon Phoebe moved on from Sarai Tailor to metaganic equality before veering into post-War conservatism. Feeling an unfamiliar and unexpected sense of missed opportunity, Dyrne then dove in, before the topic had changed too much.

"What I said before is true, though; it is an important issue that isn't really being tackled by anyone. Unfortunately…"

"Oh, Dyrne," she said, leaning into him. "I absolutely agree. And I think this is an important visit. If Sarai Tailor had the sense to challenge perceptions forty years ago, why are so many people still synthphobic now?"

"Mm." Just as quickly as the urge to speak had encroached, a pang of regret tugged at him. Talking openly about this was perhaps too big a step too soon. Too early.

"And for you, I suppose, it must mean something even more personal."

Fuck. She does know.

He grimaced again and opened his mouth to stop her, but she spoke first.

"And I know this isn't why you're bidding, but if Hould does accept it, you'd be able to see someone who's done so much for people like you. It would be a real validation."

His stiff shoulders relaxed, he exhaled and gripped back at Phoebe's hand with the crook of his arm, giving her a happy bounce. She didn't know anything. He smiled at her as they meandered on into the cool enfolding arms of the forest.

23

Witness Interview Transcript #2

28.10.270
Subject: Dr. Yusuf Sarin
Occupation: Physicist, Department of Historical Research, Central New London
Transcript begins: 1436

I: We're going to begin recording again, Dr. Sarin.

...

Just to reiterate—we need to clarify the level of contact you had with him.

YS: I've told you the only way I can systematically explain it to you, sir. I barely had any contact with him.

I: Just talk us through it again so we can have as complete an understanding as possible.

YS: We've already told this to Dr. Hould and those other two men in as much detail as possible. And where is Dr. Zimiris, if I can ask?

I: Charon Zimiris is being spoken to separately, in order to corroborate the accuracy of both your accounts. Something Dr. Hould should have had the wherewithal to facilitate herself.

YS: Just check all the security recordings. You can see for yourselves.

I: We'll get to that in due course. For now—your version.

YS: ... I can't tell you anything differently from before, sir.

I: All the same, we need to hear it through again. Begin from your entry into the lower level.

...

YS: Dr. Zimiris and I exited the elevator and walked down the corridor together. We were each due to oversee separate visits later that morning. You can check for yourself—I see you have the schedule there.

I: Yes. Continue.

YS: I made my way to pod chamber 4 and Dr. Zimiris went to number 6.

I: You went straight there?

YS: Well, yes, like I already explained moments ago.

I: Dr. Sarin...

YS: ... Yes, I went straight there; there is nowhere else to go down there.

I: And you saw Zimiris actually go into pod chamber 6?

YS: Well, no, I didn't *actually* see—my back was turned to her. At the end of the main corridor, pod chamber 4 is on the left and 6 on the right; we turned in different directions. But I can be fairly certain she went straight there! As I said, there is nowhere else she could have or would have gone first, except to one of the other chambers, but there'd be no reason to.

I: ... Continue.

YS: I began setting up the system. I wanted to calibrate the telescope lenses and run the standard startup checks on the pods.

I: And Dr. Zimiris was doing the same?

YS: I don't know, she was in a different chamber! I'm sorry. It's just that I know Charon—Dr. Zimiris—very well and I have to say I resent the implication that she has done anything suspicious... I would assume she was carrying out the usual procedures, just as I was.

I: Yes...

YS: Anyway, only a few minutes in I heard... I heard her scream—Dr. Zimiris. I immediately—

I:—And nothing had been unusual leading up to this? Zimiris hadn't been acting any differently, saying anything unusual? Nothing wrong with the pods?

YS: No! Dr. Zimiris was as always. Friendly, happy. Professional. It was no different than any other day.

I: And the pods? Everything as it should have been?

YS: Yes. Well, there was a glitch in the system when it was powering up, but that's nothing significant.

I: That's for us to determine.

YS: With all due respect, unless you have a working knowledge of this technology sir, I believe Dr. Zimiris and I, and the other physicists, are whose judgment about the pods you will have to rely on. Or have you also studied quantum physics and engineering for nine years?

I: ... Continue.

YS: The issue with the system was minor. It has happened once or twice before—seems to be caused by an error in one pod affecting the entire network, but again, only a glitch—an anomaly that can be fixed instantly. It has no working effect on the operation.

I: So you heard Zimiris scream...

YS: Yes. Of course, I dropped what I was doing and ran to chamber 4... and when I got there... he was there.

I: Where?

YS: Standing in the pod. The sheath open. Wearing the operating suit. Our suit. Unique to DOHR.

I: And what was he doing?

YS: Nothing. Well, just standing. He looked as horrified as us.

I: And Zimiris?

YS: Behind the console, backed against the wall, terrified out of her wits.

I: And you don't know—

YS:—I don't know who this man is! He does not now, nor has he ever worked with the Department, and I have never met or seen him in any other capacity!

I: But you said you spoke to him?

YS: Yes, of course I did. I asked him who he was, how he got there. I mean, once I was over the shook and after I'd pressed the alarm—it's hidden behind one of the console railings; you can't hear it down there.

I: And his response?

YS: He wouldn't respond. I asked two or three times. He just looked at us both. He seemed... not scared, but... shocked... trying to keep calm.

I: You could tell this just from looking at him?

YS: Well yes, that was just my impression, I suppose.

I: ... Your colleagues in the upper level have reported they heard a male shout. Was that you?

YS: I think so, yes.

I: You think so?

YS: Yes. Well, it's difficult to remember, I was shaken... Yes, it was me.

I: And why did you call out like that?

YS: After he stood staring at us, he staggered out toward me. I... was frightened.

...

I: Dr. Sarin, do you have any idea how an unknown man ended up in a machine that is kept so secret fewer than sixty people in the world know it exists?

YS: Well isn't that what you're here to figure out?

I: Mm, but you did just remind us moments ago that you are the expert on this technology. So indulge us.

YS: ... I have no idea.

I: None? You couldn't even hazard a guess?

YS: ...No.

I: And Dr. Sarin, could you clarify, for the record, where he is now?

YS ... He's locked in the chamber. We left him down there.

...

End Transcript
Time: 1442

24

'DOHR Re-entry 08.11.270

Following the suspension of operations, the Department will resume function for employees as of Twoday, 08.11.270. Report directly to Dr. C. Hould's office at 0830. Attendance is mandatory for all staff.'

•   •   •

The air felt different. The lights even beamed brighter, like rescue flairs. Historians had been instructed to remove all paper and coverings from their glass workstation walls. Every eye turned to anyone emerging from either of the entrance elevators, which were now both patrolled by tall men in grey suits with wristNets shining from the edges of their sleeves. Even above, in the foyer, the familiar young receptionist had vanished, replaced by a hulking, vacant-eyed man. Dyrne had thought he was having another of the dreams when he arrived, seeing the concrete figure lurching down at him. No familiar smile. No courteous nod. Standing in the lift waiting for the door to close, Dyrne had also glimped a metallic glint from a lump at the man's hip.

As 0830 approached, the staff of DOHR drifted to Hould's office in pilgrimage. Remembering the last meeting, Dyrne waited back until 0829 to join the tail-end of the swarm, spotting Phoebe just ahead of him. He wanted to avoid sitting too close to Hould.

"Our last moments of government employment then?" Alex's gravelly voice uttered over his shoulder.

Dyrne shrugged without laughing as the physicist followed him up the short staircase and into the packed coffin-office. All the seats were taken, and Dyrne lined up with Alex and some of the others along the shelf-covered wall at the back, trying not to lean back and knock any of the antique books off. Two other historians dithered in after them before Hould, seated at the head of the long wooden conference table wearing her most funereal suit, indicated with a nod of the head for the last entrant to close the door. The stuffy room and its secrets were sealed. Dyrne spotted Yusuf sitting halfway down the table, hands underneath, head bowed.

"Let's get straight to it," Hould began, her hands clasped in front of her in the standard position, but speaking faster than usual. "I want us to return to as normal a routine as possible. Of course, there will have to be changes in light of the events two weeks ago. You will have seen the government officers on the premises... They'll also patrol the pod chamber." Her pause made it obvious that she had already anticipated the physicists' raised hands and loud whispers. Beside Dyrne, Alex tutted. Dyrne turned back to watching Hould, though, wondering how long she would take to spit out what had actually happened.

"I understand the problems this raises," she continued, louder, ushering the hands down with a calming gesture. "I am, of course, aware we need to keep the pods free from any outside interference. But under the circumstances, my hands are tied by higher authority. I have been assured that the officers will not be intrusive and that they will not tamper with any equipment under any circumstances. They don't even know the details of what we do here. But we do need more extensive surveillance down there in some capacity." The room had quietened. After staring down and rubbing her thumbs together for several seconds, Hould looked up at her staff again.

"An intruder managed to enter one of the pods."

This time the response was an electric static of silence. Dyrne didn't even dare swallow.

"Someone got in here and I have no idea how. In all honesty I'm grateful we're even being allowed to carry on at all, never mind so soon."

Dyrne noticed Hould wasn't looking anyone in the eye; more skimming the room as if she was practising and no one was here. Sensing Alex leaning toward him, about to whisper something, Dyrne coughed, blocking him before he could utter a word. Hould eyed both of them before continuing.

"Please go about your daily business as always. In fact, to ensure we return to some sense of normality as quickly as possible, I would like you to submit your bids for the next cycle of visits. By 1700 today."

Dyrne's heart pounded his chest, and he stifled another cough. Halfway around the ring of chairs, Phoebe glared at Hould.

"I will assess this round of bids by Fiveday to move things on as swiftly as is feasible. I assume there will be fewer bids with such short notice."

Fewer bids. Should make it easier.

He sucked in counted breaths through his nose and exhaled through his mouth—the technique he'd been taught as a child—trying to cool himself as inconspicuously as possible.

"Dr. Sarin is here, ready to move on from the aforementioned events, and I would appreciate if you could attempt to do the same."

Yusuf remained still, staring straight ahead to the shelves on the opposite wall.

"And where is Charon?" Phoebe then piped up, a hint of worry in her words.

"Dr. Zimiris will be taking extended leave for now," Hould replied, sounding oddly chirpy, as if she didn't want to cause more worry.

"Is she implicated in this?" A second, harder voice cut in like a butcher's knife. Searching out its source, Dyrne saw the others around her shrink back from Geraldine who remained unmoving, staring at Hould, waiting to be fed an answer.

"Absolutely not. Charon fully intends to return to DOHR in due course."

Yusuf glowered across the table at Geraldine, who paid no attention, looking unfased by her own appetite for blame.

As Hould cleared her throat and continued explaining new building entry and safety procedures, she returned to her ambiguous mention of the presence of the officers.

"What I do now have to tell you about the intruder is... that he has not yet been removed from the premises." She allowed the gasps, questions and horror to fill the little room as she sat back, nodding. Dyrne stared ahead, half at Hould's taut face, half at nothing, lost. Eventually, she held up parental hands to the group again.

"He obviously needs to be detained and confined by government authority. In their wisdom, though," she said, pausing, "they decided that the most secure facility in the capital to hold him in was here, of course." More disgruntlement and outrage around the table, except from Alex, who gave a loud and unashamed "Ha!" Dyrne tried not to react.

"The irony is not lost on me, I can assure you," Hould called over the din. "He will remain locked in pod chamber 6 for the time being, constantly patrolled by agents. When in the lower level, you will not come into contact with him." Dyrne wasn't sure if this last sentence was a reassurance or an imperative. There was something different about this speech from Hould. Her words were too prepared. Her body language stiff and rehearsed.

After several questions, which Hould did her best to control and abate, she added one final note, as if she had deliberately kept it until the end of the meeting.

"As a matter of procedure, the investigating body may be researching your work and careers... and personal history."

Dyrne felt himself fall back against the shelves, shoving his hands behind him, steadying some of the books he had almost tipped over. Alex looked at him, saying nothing. Dyrne avoided his stare. Luckily, his reaction was matched by others as the room filled with tuts and murmurs.

"This is a routine precaution, everybody. I have no doubts about anyone's integrity. You wouldn't be employed here if I did." The mumbles rumbled on, quieter now. "If anyone feels they need to ask me questions or... share anything with me, then please do so today. Other than that, it's time to return to your stations and continue the excellent work we do here." Her clunky, obvious compliment fell onto the table like lead, left behind by the group who rose unanimously and shuffled their way out of the office, sharing wide eyes and shaking heads.

Dyrne lay like a corpse against the shelves as the others passed by him. He would have been the last to leave had it not been for Geraldine, who remained seated at the table.

•　　　•　　　•

Peering through distorting layers of glass, Dyrne saw the huddle of Yusuf, Alex and Phoebe across the lab, gathered at the Hub. He turned back to his

Net screen, re-reading the new version of his bid for Sarai. He still hadn't had the courage to speak to Yusuf yet. He had convinced himself that he didn't want to harass the man and that it was probably best to allow him to just return to the routine of things for now. In truth, he was afraid, like seeing someone whose parent has just died, not knowing what to say, so instead saying nothing.

But guilt squelched inside, growing with every line he read. He might not even be re-entering his bid had it not been for Yusuf's encouragement, and here he was selfishly obsessing over every choice of word and turn of phrase, ignoring one of his few friends who was experiencing the aftermath of trauma.

Dyrne pushed back from the desk and drifted toward the trio. Approaching them, he caught Yusuf's large, brown eyes first. He sat perched on the edge of the circular table, hands gripping the rim with Alex and Phoebe standing in front of him, mirroring the guards who flanked the elevators.

Dyrne offered a nod and a comforting smile. It sounded like Yusuf's two protectors were doing most of the talking. Not wanting to seem obtrusive, Dyrne passed by them and stopped at a Net a few paces around the Hub, scanning in pointlessly. He lingered, listening to the three, knowing he must look either suspicious or more awkward than ever.

"You're probably sick of talking about it." Phoebe frowned, rubbing Yusuf's arm.

"Well, a little, yes," he answered. "Although I don't mind being asked by friends instead of being accused by strangers."

"Oh God, did they really think you were to blame?"

Yusuf shrugged.

Phoebe shook her head, still touching his forearm. She looked up at Dyrne, biting her lip. Dyrne didn't know whether to look away or not.

"So what's up with Charon? You're back, why isn't she?" asked Alex, hands on hips.

Phoebe glared at him.

"She was held for even longer than I was." Yusuf's voice wavered. "I've spoken to her briefly on a Netcall, but she's definitely shaken."

"Sounds a little weird to me," said Alex. "Maybe Charon's had us all fooled, huh?"

The joke was met with blank glances from both Phoebe and Yusuf this time.

Dyrne counted ten silent seconds while staring at his empty Net screen before Phoebe asked the question.

"So, who is this man? I know you don't know him... But what did he look like?" Yusuf dipped his head. "Although you don't have to talk about it anymore. Sorry, I shouldn't be asking."

"No, no. It's quite alright. Well, he looked... average. Nothing remarkable. Caucasian, medium-build, in his forties I reckon. Curly, dark brown hair. Blue eyes, I think. I didn't recognise him at all."

Dyrne found himself piecing the description together, creating a holograph in his mind of what this man looked like.

"No, of course you didn't recognise him," Phoebe jumped in with.

"But he was wearing one of the pod suits."

Dyrne's eye twinged. The words snagged at him like a thread caught on a ragged fingernail.

"So why the hell is he still down there? What's going on?" Phoebe had asked what Dyrne wanted to know.

"I have no idea." Yusuf still stared down at the tiled floor. "It doesn't make any sense to me."

"We're obviously being lied to," said Alex, folding his arms.

"For once, I agree with you," Phoebe responded. "This is the most secure place they could think of to hide him? Bullshit. What's the point of that max-security prison just outside the city? Why not throw every criminal in New London down here? Let them all hang out around the pods!"

"Just one more thing we know nothing about. But *she* knows something." Alex nodded to Hould's office. "And I doubt they're telling us anytime soon."

"But what? I just can't understand why keeping that guy down there—" Phoebe motioned to the floor, her face contorted, "—is the solution they've come up with."

Dyrne looked back to Yusuf, now rubbing repeatedly at his forehead.

"Look, I'm going to have another gathering one night next week if you'd like to come," said Phoebe. "You too, Alex."

Yusuf waved a 'no thank you' hand.

"Another one of your 'gatherings'?" Alex asked. "You trying to recruit me to your funny omni ideas again?"

She didn't bother to reply, rolling her eyes.

"I don't think I should be doing much socialising for the time being," Yusuf began. "I have a feeling I'm being monitored by the people who interrogated me. I wouldn't want to bring you under anyone's scrutiny, Phoebe."

"Ha, makes a change, eh? *You* being 'visited'." Alex laughed, but only saw Phoebe's glare again. "Ah, you'll be alright, pal." He patted Yusuf's back, urging him to his feet.

As the group of three looked ready to disband, Dyrne buried his face in the Net again, waiting until they'd left to return to his workstation.

•   •

After hours of seclusion, revising the bid reapplication in minute detail, checking the dates, the locations, the events, the 'motives' for the research—to discover more about the origins of the synth rights movement—he knew he could do nothing more. This time it would work, though. Must work. Hould had practically told him to try again. She wanted this.

He thought back to Phoebe and what she'd told him in the café: that seeing a woman give birth in an elevator decades ago had been enough to suppress her desire to have children. Even still. So that's what he'd do. Visit Sarai before the year of his own birth. He might not be able to trap her in a lift, but he'd find another way.

She'll never adopt. Never want to.

Minutes before 1700, Dyrne approached the bid submission depository once more. Its black slit hooked him in on a poisoned wire. The new Netdisk was shiny. Gold. Slipping with sweat in his curled palm, he shoved his hand against the slot, hurling it in. Fewer clinks than before.

25

"I saw a ghost once."

"Really? Where? Who do you think it was?"

"I think it might have been the man who died in our flat before my family moved in. I was a teenager at the time."

Three empty bottles of relaxant lay by Dyrne on the woven mat. A fourth was held in his damp, clumsy hand. He slouched in the corner and had been half-listening to Phoebe and Francis's friend, Jackson, laughing about some private joke. But now his animal ears pricked up on alert, tuning into the conversation gliding over from the other side of the living area. Phoebe's younger brother, Theo, leaned closer to Luna, the wide-eyed writer.

"And what did it look like?" he asked. At twenty, he was sixteen years younger than Phoebe, although taller, but with the same dark brown hair—shoulder-length; very unusual for a boy. After meeting, Dyrne hadn't spoken to him once.

"Well, I heard something move and then just for a couple of seconds saw a white, shimmering outline of a figure over in the corner of the room, looking in my direction," Luna explained. "Then it vanished."

Her words reached out, gathering the attention of the five others in the room.

"You must have been terrified!"

"I got a fright, seeing something there," she nodded, "but I didn't feel intimidated or threatened for some reason. That's why I thought it was someone friendly, watching over." She spoke with a naïve smile.

Phoebe glanced down at Dyrne, a silent communication passing between them, even through his lazy-eyed cloud.

"Hm. I'm still not sure I believe in ghosts, though," answered Theo.

"So you don't believe me, then? Hey, your brother's calling me a liar!"

Luna called to Phoebe. "Almost as sceptical as you! You sure you're both omni?"

Phoebe gave a nodding "Ha!" in return, raising her bottle.

Dyrne's head lolled down to glance at his watch. 2214. Peering up again, he surveyed the scene from the distance of his fizzy isolation, examining the others through a fisheye lens in his mind like he was in a pod, visiting. What would this tell him if he was from the future? That people still believed in ghosts? That no one was any wiser than people a thousand years ago?

His eyes fell to the floor. He saw the Net screen again, the memory staring at him.

Eardrums thumping. Scroll. Usual preamble. Scroll. Perspiration running. There.

'Your visitation bid, title: **Sarai Tailor**, *has been unsuccessful. You will be assigned to a colleague's visits in due course.'*

The message had stuck itself to his eyeballs.

Around him, the omni group continued a discussion of the concept of lucid dreams again. They'd talked about this at the last omni night Dyrne had attended, too. Two or three of them—he couldn't be sure how many were really talking—shared their own experiences and spoke about how they'd learned to understand when they were in a dream state: becoming more aware of illogical events, recognising their own unique recurrent dream happenings, noticing times changing suddenly on Nets. Once aware, the dreamers had been able to manipulate their surroundings, feel complete freedom, change things with a simple wish. The words floated at him like bubbles, popping on his face, seeping through his pores.

Conversation soon swerved to politics. He heard voices on the other side of the room discussing Louis Apol and his booming popularity. Phoebe leaned in, whispering "He's very supportive of metaganic rights, Francis has been telling me." Dyrne wondered if she really was whispering or if the insulation of the relaxant was muffling the sound of her words. He didn't respond but continued tuning in to soundbites detailing that Apol was 'also omni'—someone had read an interview with him on one of the newssites.

Omni. British. American. Physicist. Historian. Metaganic. Even the idea of political 'parties' had been creeping back into recent news articles, rather than candidates campaigning based on their own individual principles and merits. Some apparently felt it would be easier for them to club together and assign themselves to shared party labels. Easier or lazier, Dyrne wasn't sure.

His head swung around and down, a useless appendage he was half in control of. The picture of the alert in his mind changed. Now he saw a silhouette. The intruder at DOHR. Dyrne felt a cold pain stabbing his stomach and imagined the man locked in there, trampling around inside him. Who the hell was he? Dyrne hadn't even discussed it in detail with Phoebe yet.

But he lost grip of these thoughts too and his eyes refocused on his legs. New blue trousers. He stretched unsteady arms out and looked at them too. A white woolen top he was wearing for the first time. He had ordered them from a Net, sitting on the Line on the way home from DOHR after bid result day when he'd left at 1700—early for him; normal for everyone else. The clothes had cost an inordinate amount. He would normally never feel able to justify spending this much on luxuries like this. His hair was different too. He hadn't bothered fixing it in place the same as every other day, instead letting it flop around in dark greasy strands. It hadn't been cut for months now. He'd even begun turning up to the offices without his frontpack.

Working on Martin's visits to Italy in some mysterious BC decade didn't require anything of Dyrne except his presence in the pods and his pitiful attempts to sightwrite. What use was bringing anything to work? No one had noticed, anyway. Except Phoebe.

After his bid was rejected a second time, he had slipped and warped, an actor who had slid inside his skin to fulfill the role of Dyrne Samson. He hadn't discussed his bid in detail with her, nor did it seem likely he would in future. She'd asked him about it after seeing the list of successful applications and the omission of his name. He'd shrugged it off and pretended he wasn't surprised or upset. The insincerity must have been obvious, but she hadn't pressed him.

But tonight he had appeared at her door, earlier than any of the others.

And he had asked for the relaxant himself, grabbing it with a smile even after Phoebe asked if he was sure. She'd sat with him all night so far, though.

Eventually, Phoebe left Dyrne with Jackson—knowing the writer would initiate conversation—and could already hear vague small talk as she traversed the stepping stone guests around the room. Entering the kitchenette, she found her husband leaning against the rear counter, facing her. He was in the midst of what sounded like a deep conversation with Antony Moth.

"What are you two philosophising about?" She slid toward her husband and wrapped her arms around his neck, giving him a quick kiss.

"Just telling Antony about some of the dreams I remember having lately," Francis answered, smiling back at her.

"Yes, I should have started charging you twenty minutes ago," Moth added, the three of them chuckling.

"Anything I should know about then, Doctor? Any racy dreams about other women?" Phoebe asked, switching to stand beside *him* now and facing her husband with hands on hips.

"Client confidentiality I'm afraid, Phoebe," Moth replied.

"But you said he's not paying you! Not a client yet!" They laughed again. Phoebe grabbed another bottle from the countertop and unscrewed the lid.

"So what have you and Dyrne been talking about all night?" Francis asked. "He hasn't left your side."

"More like I haven't left his."

"Is something wrong with him?" Moth then asked, rather oddly, Phoebe reckoned, seeing as he hardly knew Dyrne.

"No, no. Well I don't know, really. He's just been acting a bit strange for the past couple of weeks."

"Mm, I thought he seemed a bit... off, when he came in earlier," Francis noted. "Well, more so than usual for Dyrne anyway."

"Francis..." Phoebe gave him a chastising look.

"Hey, you could have asked if I wanted another."

Phoebe whirled around at the sound of Dyrne's voice. He had half-stumbled, half-crept into the room behind her.

"Sorry, Dyrne, I didn't realise you'd finished your last." She rubbed her hands together, assuming he'd heard them talking about him. But looking at his glazed expression and dim grin, she just as quickly dismissed the worry.

Francis picked up another bottle, half-reaching out with it as if he wasn't sure he should. Dyrne stepped forward to grab it, but his hand stopped midway. His gaze shifted and locked onto the dream analyst.

"Dr... Mouse... Month...?" His words slurred like syrup.

"Moth."

"That's right, you met Antony before," said Phoebe.

"Yes," said Moth, "at the meditation."

"And you're the psychoanalyst, dream analyst, whatever you call it. Pretend doctor," Dyrne grinned again, taking a sip from the new bottle. Phoebe, blushing, looked to Francis.

"Mm," Moth nodded. "And what is it *you* pretend to do?" He sipped from his bottle.

"I, um, same as, uh, Phoebe. Population cataloguing. Census and..." Dyrne faded off.

"We were just discussing dreams. Apparently, I have issues," Francis cut in, trying to lighten the atmosphere that had fractured like cracked glass.

Moth hadn't broken eye contact with Dyrne yet.

"Weren't you telling us about your dreams, or nightmares, last time we met, Dyrne?"

Phoebe noticed Moth's odd use of Dyrne's first name. Again, it felt overfamiliar.

"I'm... I'm not sure I remember. Hey, I saw you the other night, when I was at the autochemist. You saw me, didn't you?" He scratched an armpit.

"Something about officers." Moth continued, ignoring Dyrne's attempt to change the subject. "You said they kept appearing in your meditation, from a nightmare you'd had."

"That's... that's right. I'd forgotten."

"You couldn't block them out and imagine being alone."

"... Yes."

"And is this a recurring dream?"

"... I've had it more than once, I suppose. Yes."

"Officers surrounding you. Do they hurt you?"

"No. No, they don't hurt me."

His eyebrows began to glimmer with gathering sweat.

"How *do* they interact with you?"

Dyrne gulped. "They want to question me. I've done something they want to find out about... that they already know about."

Phoebe and Francis felt as if they were intruding on a private session.

"So what do you think it is?"

"What?"

"What are you repressing? What are you keeping from them?"

Dyrne's eyes flickered. He wiped trickling perspiration from an eyelid. Phoebe shifted a little, opening her mouth to speak, fixed on Dyrne.

"What is it you feel guilty about?"

He looked down and around blankly, shrugging to no one, a confused animal caught in a trap.

"It's just that that's what your dream scenario seems to suggest, especially if it's recurrent. Either that or they're purely erotic dreams. Being dominated is a common fetish."

Francis snorted.

"I'm not same-sex." Dyrne's voice cracked. Phoebe held her cheek and shook her head.

"So I was right the first time—there's something hanging over you. Something you are hiding."

The air froze, Moth squinting at his unwitting patient, Dyrne blinking back at him, the relaxant slipping in his damp palm. Phoebe swayed on the spot, ready to dive between them, while Francis darted bemused glances between all three.

The clear glass bottle exploded into tiny fragments on the tiled floor. A wet fizz bled out, seeping into Dyrne's ice-white socks.

"Shit!" Phoebe leapt forward.

"I'll get it!" Francis followed, grabbing a towel and diving to the floor.

As the pair scrambled to the floor neither Dyrne nor Moth moved.

Sitting beside him on the edge of the bed, Phoebe didn't know how to begin. Glad he hadn't slunk off in secret like last time, but unsure how to coax him out of silence, she clicked her nails together, trying to make sense of the episode in the kitchen. Her brother and Francis were the only other people left in the flat, still cleaning up after everyone.

"So I think calling your friend a pretend-doctor was my first mistake," said Dyrne, finally.

"I think you could be on to something." Phoebe gave him a sideways glance and a half-smile. "So do you think there's any truth in what Antony was asking you? Not that he should have been asking you in front of us. Or at all."

"Everyone must feel guilty to some extent about things they've done. Doesn't everyone have something they wish they could change?"

"Well, yes, probably," she responded, thinking that this wasn't *exactly* what Moth had asserted. "But not everyone has recurring dreams about being stalked or interrogated or whatever it is." Dyrne's expression changed, the lines in his forehead deepening, his eyes focused excruciatingly on one tiny point in the carpet. "Do you think it's your feelings about... being metaganic?"

"No, no, no." He still didn't look at her.

"Sorry, I know it's not my business."

Muffled laughs and banter between Francis and Theo emanated from the half-open living room door. A bedside Net hummed. The room was lit by a dim tube-bulb in the corner and moonlight from the window. Faint silhouetted clouds drifted past. Phoebe watched Dyrne gazing out like he was a stranger sitting on her bed. Knowing he was metaganic meant nothing. There would always be something hidden about him.

"What do you regret, Phoebe?" he asked, still watching the sky.

"What do *I* regret?" She sighed. "Only getting out of the city once this year to visit my mum. Not focusing on Francis as much as DOHR. Letting you drink so much tonight." She saw Dyrne's shoulders heave and heard him give a little laugh. She thought for another few seconds, before adding, "And children. Maybe. I could have at least filled out the parental licence. More for Francis than me. He says he doesn't mind, but..." she left the sentence unfinished. "I think we need to learn from our mistakes, though, instead of letting them 'hang over us' like Antony suggested. I can see my mum next weekend, start coming home earlier, never let you drink again, that's for certain! And I suppose there's still time for applications. We can't alter things so we hopefully just develop from what we've done, try to do better. Isn't that the point of DOHR? To look back at—"

"—Nobody learns from the past, Phoebe. As a society I mean." He coughed. "We won't learn from our mistakes. You heard your friend out there earlier; people still see ghosts."

She squinted at him, trying to understand.

"If people are still seeing ghosts then DOHR, or something like it, still exists and functions in the future. We'll still be looking back on the past 100 years from now, trying to figure it all out and find where we went wrong. It's either that, or some other bloody War happens and history's lost all over again. And if we've let that happen, then we definitely haven't learned a fucking thing."

"Only if people really are still seeing ghosts. Luna gets a bit... carried away."

Dyrne shrugged, looking away again.

"Well maybe society doesn't change so easily, but as individuals—" She stopped as the close sound of Francis as his shadow flitted by the door.

Dyrne lowered his voice. "Look, just ignore me, I'm saying too much. Talking nonsense tonight."

"It's not just this though, is it?" She held up an empty bottle. "I know there are other things... affecting you right now."

He pushed sweaty hair away from his forehead and looked down at the bed.

"Since the bid results," Phoebe continued, "it's had such an impact on you." She gestured with an open hand, scanning him up and down. Dyrne glanced up through dark brown strands of hair that shielded him.

"The past couple of cycles you've been so affected. This never used to happen. What's changed?"

His eyes flickered from side to side, like he was reading pages filled with thousands of words, unable to pluck the right answer from the midst of it all.

"Is it because of this guy they've got locked down there? And Yusuf?"

Dyrne dismissed her suggestion with a quick shake of his head.

"Then is it because this bid is more personal? Visiting Sarai Tailor? I suppose it must feel like quite a responsibility."

He nodded.

"Yes, it is a responsibility I have." She squinted at his odd phrasing. "Different from other visits I've made."

She squinted at him, seeing the beginning of a skin peeling itself back.

"Phoebe... how do you always get Hould to accept your bids?"

"Not always."

"Well, not every single time, no, but 99 percent. You don't even like her."

"Yeah, well... I just figured out how to play to her interests. Make connections."

Dyrne raised an eyebrow and tilted his head. "Make connections how?"

"What do you have in common? Or at least, what can you pretend you have in common? I made sure she knew I had an interest in pre-War feminism. You've seen that holograph of Jane Winstone in her office, right? I spent twenty minutes with her talking about it one morning."

"Yeah but that *is* your specialist area. You didn't make that up."

"No, but I might have let her believe a few other things that weren't true."

"Like?"

"Going back to dorms now, Phoebe! Thanks for inviting me." Peering his head around the gap in the door, Theo's young face beamed in at the pair, filling the room with more light.

"Glad you enjoyed it, Theo," she replied, snapping away from Dyrne's hunched figure.

"Bye, Dyrne. Nice to meet you!" Theo gave an eager wave.

"Yes." Dyrne half-turned toward him.

As Theo ducked out behind the door, Phoebe called him back in.

"Theo!"

He reappeared.

"When you next go home to see mum... make sure you tell me beforehand. I'll come with you."

"Yeah, OK. Bye!" She turned back to Dyrne, a grin brightening her face in the gloomy room.

In return, Dyrne smiled wanly. She expected him to acknowledge what she'd done, see the change she'd made, even laugh. But his expression faded and he returned to the window, the moonlight casting him in black and white like an actor in one of the ancient films she'd researched. She left him there, giving up on understanding tonight, leaving him to rehearse the right lines for another time.

26

He sat on the identical floor beside Phoebe. The same faces surrounded him. He even smelled the stagnant aroma of the relaxant in his breath and felt his backache dully, slumped against the wall. Same position.

"I saw a ghost once." The words replayed. He watched Luna through the same orb of muted yellow. But here it changed. "I must have been visited. Was it you Dyrne?" A distorted smile stretched across her face revealing crooked teeth that threatened to swallow him.

He remembered the same feeling of wanting to forget, to let go, to exist without constantly pushing and holding and pretending, so he sipped again from the little glass hole. He glanced at his watch. 2214. Déjà vu that made him swallow hard. Looking up, he caught a glimpse of Phoebe's legs trailing off to the kitchen. Jackson murmured without break beside him, even as Dyrne rose to follow her, his departure making no difference to the voice. Entering the kitchen, the trio confronted him, Phoebe wearing the electric blue suit again. Something shifted in his brain, a tuning fork hitting a new frequency. He lifted his wristwatch again to check. 2246. The suit. Luna's words.

"This isn't real," he mumbled as the others looked on at him. "This is a dream."

"Weren't you telling us about your dreams, or nightmares, last time we met, Dyrne?"

The conversation skipped ahead as if they were part of a visit recording someone had scrolled through with the stroke of a finger. He rubbed his armpit again, unwillingly following the routine, yet recognising it at the same time.

"Something about officers," Moth carried on, without mercy.

Dyrne watched the scene unfold in front of him in third-person on a Net screen. He was sightwriting a report on himself. Moth's words still bore into him.

"And is this a recurring dream?"

I don't want to see this again.

"Officers surrounding you. Do they hurt you?"

I am dreaming.

"What are you repressing? What are you keeping from them?"

I can change this.

"What is it you feel guilty about?"

Screwing his eyes shut and deciding it should happen, Dyrne watched Moth implode in a cloud of dust that settled in tiny mounds on the floor, replacing his spilled relaxant. Phoebe and Francis collapsed on their knees, rushing to clean away the debris.

Fearing he would wake at any moment, Dyrne seized his new-found power. Taking Phoebe by the hand, they were instantly in the bedroom, perched on the edge of the bed as before, the moon still glowing on them through the window.

"Make connections." Phoebe smiled.

"Make connections with Hould how? How do I convince her?"

The door burst open. Again.

"Going back to dorms now, Phoebe. Thanks for inviting me."

The familiar terror of nightmare filled Dyrne. Where the bright face of Theo should have been, the grey, spectral image of Copil looked in on them. This wasn't right. He shouldn't be here. Can't be here. Mustering the energy from somewhere outside himself, Dyrne gripped the bed and blinked. He was gone. That easily. Simple accomplishment blossomed into euphoria. Dyrne spoke to Phoebe, emptying his truth to her—Sarai, Copil, the bid—like water into a vase, cascading everything she would never know in reality, containing it within the dream.

He woke without being stuck to the sheets. His back didn't ache. The cool air wafted over him.

After one taste, control had given him a craving.

•　　•　　•

Dyrne knocked on Hould's door—far too quietly at first, before adding an extra few louder thuds. After she'd invited him in, he stood, swaying at the head of the conference table, rubbing his palms on the edge. His stomach swilled. He had grown used to suppressing the hangovers of his nightmares, but this time he had allowed the fire of last night's dream to fuel him here. He could still smell the relaxant on his breath and taste it on his lips— remnants from the bottle he'd consumed in his apartment this morning. He'd returned to combing his hair this morning, the new blue trousers abandoned.

"Mr. Samson?" Hould glanced up from the Net on her desk arching a grey eyebrow, still tapping the screen. "Is there something you wanted to speak—"

"—Why was my bid rejected?" He dabbed his lower lip, as if he'd spluttered down his chin.

Hould stopped, waiting a few seconds before she spoke. "It's generally not procedure for me to justify my choices about the outcome of each visitation bid, Mr. Samson. If I did that for every historian, I wouldn't have time left to do anything else. Especially not under current circumstances."

He watched her, the oversized table a giant wedge between them.

"I'd just like to know if my application has any merit, or any chance, you think, of being accepted at some point. It adheres to the new regulation changes: out with my personal lifetime. I just want to clarify whether or not I'm wasting my time altogether—if it's the idea of the bid itself that's... flawed." He could feel himself raising his voice to be heard from his end of the room. Hould didn't seem to have to do this. The stakes of this gamble were piling on top of him with every word. One push too far and she'd either start asking the wrong questions or dismiss him and his bid completely. But the two rejections had warped all sense of caution. This was his last frantic roulette spin.

"You are an experienced historian Mr. Samson," she continued curtly. "If you feel your bid has academic merit, you are entirely free to resubmit during the next ballot."

Again? Is she fucking kidding?

She turned away, filing a pile of the folders on a shelf behind the desk. He was witnessing a new, hidden facet to Hould—colder and more ruthless.

The lucid dream's bright flame of success had burned, faded and fizzled, but its aroma still lingered. He edged along the right-hand side of the conference table now, moving step by step toward her.

"Doctor, I got the impression after our last conversation, in the elevator, that you were... encouraging me to resubmit. I thought I had a strong chance of being accepted—my bid, I mean. But..."

He was sure he heard her sigh.

"I don't want to waste another cycle bidding for the same visits again when I could be... changing things." He shrugged his last words.

He had played out the scene in his mind, rehearsing his lines, trying to predict Hould's understanding, calm reaction. He had fantasised that she would be malleable. The reality of it felt different, the lucid dream no longer a burning ember but a near-invisible stream of distant grey smoke, floating off.

Stopping to look at him without fidgeting with paperwork, Hould leaned forward, pressing the knuckles of each hand against the desk.

"Mr. Samson, what would we learn about the synth programme from your intended observations of Sarai Tailor that we don't already know?"

He couldn't tell whether this was an invitation to debate or a rhetorical question to shut him up and send him off.

"Well... it's not just the synth programme itself, but rather the development of the synth rights movement."

"Again, what don't we already know about this? Yes, we do investigate post-War events but only when there is an incentive to discover something genuinely unknown or something that absolutely cannot be unearthed in any other viable way. If not, we border on simply spying on people. That is not what DOHR is. What is *unknown* about Tailor and the metaganic rights movement?"

Dyrne took another few small steps along the edge of the table, an infantry soldier crossing a field of hidden explosives.

"It's... it's not that we don't know a lot about the movement itself, which we do, of course. But... we don't know why she cared... why she fought so vehemently for it, even to her own detriment. Her personal motivations are undocumented." Fearful of how far Hould's knowledge of Tailor extended, he fought hard against the impulse to squeeze his eyes closed. One more probe into Tailor's personal life could bring the detonation he dreaded. Sweat tickled his scalp. Hould shoved folders around her desk, inadvertently shoving a holograph askew.

As Dyrne edged forward another step, he caught sight of it—the picture tilted toward him. An image of a grinning Hould beside another woman, with lighter skin, gleamed back. Hould wasn't wearing a suit for once, but a milky-white dress. She held flowers. He didn't recognise the other woman, but could see how closely they were pressed together, their faces touching cheek to cheek.

Phoebe's advice flickered back to him.

Make connections. What do you have in common?

He squeezed each thumb in a fist.

"I... I want to find out more about... prejudice."

She glanced up.

"Discrimination. I know how it feels to be treated differently." The last words were forced past a gulp. He looked to the holograph, then back to Hould. She mirrored his movement, looking from the wedding image back to him, squinting.

He stepped closer, touching the edge of Hould's desk with one finger.

"That's why I want to observe Tailor's life. I want to learn about prejudice. We already know about Sarai and the metaganic programme, like you said. What many *still* haven't learned, though, is how to accept it. Embrace it even." Hould stared back. No more fidgeting with folders. No swiping through the Net. "We need to learn why Sarai Tailor was different."

"Mr. Samson," she said smoothly in her deep voice, "this all sounds very noble now, but the reasons for your bid as stated on your application were, to be blunt, so... cold. 'Record her first meeting with Edom Morrigan.' 'Catalogue lists of those who she encountered at the birthing facility.' 'Detail numbers of those in attendance at protests and rallies.' It was too clinical. Missing heart.'"

You don't know.

"DOHR is not merely in operation to find out facts, numbers, details. If it were, I wouldn't have taken this role. The purpose of DOHR, the opportunity we have been given, is to learn something bigger, something that names and dates don't teach us. Yes, many observations are in place to gain empirical knowledge," she conceded, "but for something as sensitive, and relatively recent as the metaganic issue, we have an obligation to do more. Your application didn't intimate anything concerning the nature of discrimination or Tailor's real motives."

She touched the holograph and tilted it back, away from Dyrne. She turned to her shelves again.

A throbbing in his neck. Face burning. His bladder bloated.

Dyrne closed his eyes.

"I'm metaganic."

Nostrils flaring. Loud breaths. He pictured boys at school laughing; classmates' parents squirming; Dr. Moth analysing.

Peering again, he saw Hould had turned. Her hard glare had melted, hands loose by her side. A nod.

"Why Sarai Tailor, though? I understand she was one of the foremost metaganic rights pioneers, but why not visit earlier, to the inception of the programme?"

No sudden step back from him. No questions about his birth status. No sneer in her lip. She was no longer referring to an unsuccessful bid but instead speaking about it as an almost-concrete 'visit'.

"Because you can't learn anything from hate. The inception of the programme came in the middle of the War. No one but the politicians wanted it, just to boost population numbers. The public hated the idea when they found out. Visiting oppression and discrimination teaches us nothing. *She* marked a change. *She* is who people need to learn from. Her actions are what can teach people the most."

He watched Hould lower her head again. Contempt? Revulsion? Laughter?

"Yes, Dyrne." She looked back.

A smile.

Lightning crackled through him, like more relaxant in his veins. He wasn't even sure what he'd achieved. Perhaps only the approval of one person who'd do nothing else about it. But an optimism he thought he'd lost long ago filled him. He spun around, striding to the door.

"Thank you for your time, Doctor."

On his way, she spoke again.

"Just unfortunate that Miss Tailor died just months ago." Reminded of the precariousness of his situation, Dyrne paused at the door and stole a brief glance at Hould before leaving. "You could have saved a lot of time by meeting her in person, although I'm sure she became a recluse. Shame."

"Mmm," Dyrne mumbled. "Shame."

27

Hours had floated past unnoticed while the adrenaline finished its pulsing course through Dyrne's body. The inevitable comedown melted in, leaving behind the stark debris of his dishonesty.

What if someone had seen him enter or leave Hould's office? Whispers would multiply and infect the workstations. No one could know about his repeated attempt at this same bid. It would draw too much attention. Why the obsession with Sarai Tailor? Why the metaganic cause? Hould and Phoebe knowing was enough. And Alex—who had already guessed for himself, if he even cared. And Yusuf? Geraldine? Moth? Even Ember.

He gripped his desk as if trying to cling to the empty high he'd felt hours ago. Two new guards—one at the main elevator and one at the pod elevator doors—radiated authority from a distance, perhaps watching him. Notes on Martin's visit he was supposed to be taking part in that afternoon shone at him from the Net screen: an observation of a group of Italian senators conspiring to assassinate their leader. Dyrne couldn't even remember his name, only that it was an incredibly early period to have any record to begin with. Apparently, they'd found a fictionalised account of the man's life and used this to begin tracing back to the truth. Dyrne had yet to read the several detailed reports from Martin, let alone the specifics of today's visit. With two hours to go, his head was too saturated with the ongoing loop of his conversation with Hould to begin reading.

He glanced back up to her office. Blurred, grey shapes floated and shifted behind the misted glass. Someone else was in there now. No doubt the government officials. Perhaps their investigations of historians had begun. He'd managed to force himself to forget this but now wondered who they'd begin with. If it was those whose bids had been accepted he had nothing to worry about. If they were working their way through alphabetically by surname, he'd have a while, too. But what if they were working through forenames? 'D' wouldn't be far away…

Deciding that sitting in the glass cube—with Geraldine's relentless sightwriting through the pane to his right—was doing nothing more than magnifying his manic thoughts, Dyrne pushed the chair back and walked to the pod elevator. He could rely on Alex's advice for the visit.

Approaching the doors, he prepared for the waiting officer, looming by the face scanner. As he stepped to it, the guard's gaze shifted a little toward Dyrne. The white glass door slid away, and he zoomed inside, urging the lift to descend quickly. As the view of the agent was sliced out of sight, he exhaled, leaning back against the heavy wire cage that trundled and whirred around him.

The cold, echoing air of the concrete corridor pinched at him as the shutters opened at pod-level. Already he could see two more officers, as severe and indistinguishable as the robotic man above, filling every edge of their bulky dark suits. One stood only a few feet in front of Dyrne, hands behind his back, staring in his direction but not *at* him. The other was a smaller black, block shape at the far end of the corridor. Dyrne edged past the first, compressing himself against the wall, as if trying not to wake a sleeping giant. Reaching the split path at the end, he avoided the face of the officer in front of him and turned right, head bowed. But a firm palm pressed against his shoulder, stopping him dead.

"Chamber?" the guard's voice summoned.

Dyrne looked up to face his square head, screwing the fingers of one hand against the palm of the other. "Uh, pod 8," he answered, before clearing his throat and repeating himself unnecessarily, even pointing to his right. The man stared back at him, his hands still on Dyrne.

"I'm Dyrne Samson, I have a scheduled observation with Alex Myers— he should already be down here."

The agent remained static for three or four seconds, his mass dominating Dyrne's vision, before releasing him and giving a nod. Dyrne surmised that he had either been listening in to an invisible earpiece for some sort of confirmation, or was just fulfilling a duty to be as intimidating as possible.

A few paces ahead loomed another officer, guarding pod chamber 6: the chamber of the intruder. This guard watched Dyrne squirm by with sniper eyes. He was sure the agent could incapacitate him in an instant at the slightest hint of anything suspicious. The matt grey door behind the guard was, of course, closed and had a thick, black bar laid across it. The chamber exuded secrecy; a black hole behind a sheet of metal.

Trying his best not to stare, he slid forward to the open door of pod chamber 8, where Alex sat behind the console in the left-hand corner wheeling from screen to screen, scanning information and tapping in commands. Dyrne knew Alex shouldn't have left the door open like this and was surprised the government officers hadn't closed it already. Something told him Alex had deliberately left it ajar, though: a stubborn protest.

"Samson. You're a little earlier than expected." Alex's coat was half fastened, revealing another garish, patterned green shirt underneath.

"Thought I'd come down now and go over a few things before we're due to start. Ask a few questions. If that's OK?"

"Sure! Catch up on all the stuff you didn't read yet. Not like you, Dyrne."

"I've, uh... I haven't managed to find the time lately..." He looked up at Alex who chuckled and wheeled back around to type something.

"So the observations are set for Rome, the capital of what used to be Italy. Yours is going to be hitting around 40BC—if Daley has it right." Alex talked Dyrne through the basics, still with his back turned, while Dyrne worried about the distant date. The further back, the less precise their pre-visit research tended to be. Trial and error played a part in these ancient observations, trying to track down events, often glimpsing several different years before they found what they were looking for. This was one reason, it was assumed by DOHR, for the increased belief in the supernatural the further back in time they delved—more accidental sightings in more places in more years.

Alex continued, confirming this. "Might have to vary that estimation for a while if we end up in the wrong time—so you'll probably be a ghost for a bunch of people 2000 years ago." He swirled around and grinned like a ten-year-old. "So this senator was apparently assassinated by the advisors around him. Shame we can't save the poor bastard, huh?"

Dyrne blinked and looked away.

"Hey, why am I telling you all this when you can read it perfectly well yourself?" He tapped on a Net screen behind him that displayed text waiting to be read, before inviting Dyrne up to the raised concrete platform with a wave. Feeling like a schoolboy allowed into the headmaster's office, Dyrne gripped the cool, metal railing and climbed the few short steps to the level of the console, surveying the array of screens and panels before hunching over to read the notes he should have studied long before now.

As the pair worked in silence, an echoing clunk boomed through the still-open door from down the corridor, followed by deep mumbles and the noise of shuffling movement. Both men shifted their eyes in the direction of the sounds, although Alex returned to what he was doing a second later, giving the impression he was used to whatever it was.

"Is that... the man? Chamber 6?" Dyrne asked, still looking to the open door.

"Yup. They usually feed him around this time."

Feed him.

Dyrne winced. "I suppose I never thought of that. What about... you know, biological functions? Surely they need to let him out at some point?"

"Well, I've never heard or seen him go anywhere. And all the toilets are up on your level." Dyrne raised an eyebrow. "Yeah," said Alex. "I don't think we'll be using chamber 6 until long after he's outta here." Dyrne who looked away, back to the glowing Net screen, as Alex continued talking. "It's funny what's happened to it, though—in there," he gestured, nodding his head to the wall, indicating the direction of pod chamber 6. His voice softened. "They've taken the most advanced facility on the planet, a tool for observing the furthest reaches of unrecorded time... and turned it into a prison." Dyrne stopped reading, the words hitting something buried in his consciousness. "That's people, I guess." Alex sighed, before swiveling back to key in numbers.

Seconds later, before any more reading could be undertaken, another noise reverberated down the thin hallway toward them. Hurried, deep mumblings followed by brisk footsteps growing louder and nearer until Martin Daley strode into the room with clenched fists. Dyrne jumped upright.

"Martin, hello. I was just going over everything again so there aren't any hitches in the observation and I find what you're hoping for." He wasn't sure but thought he could hear Alex snigger behind him.

"There's a pretty big hitch already," Martin responded, standing too close, hands on belted hips now. "The visit's off."

"Observation!" Alex called from behind Dyrne.

"What?"

"Observations. Not visits."

Martin shook the comment off with a jerk of his head. "You're not on this cycle anymore," he continued, looking at Dyrne again.

Dyrne felt blotches itch at his neck. Had Martin seen him stepping into Hould's office and gone snooping at his desk? Had Geraldine found about his bids? Or had Hould canceled the whole thing?

"...Why?" Dyrne gulped, fingers fidgeting by his side.

"Don't know. Ask Hould. Her decision. She just sent an alert reassigning my visits right before I begin the cycle. You're out."

Fuck.

"Oh. Sorry," Dyrne muttered.

"Alex, someone else'll be down at some point for the visit. No point in wasting it. Either Geraldine or me, no doubt."

"Thanks for the specifics," Alex added, before turning to Dyrne. "Ah well, guess I'll be spying on Caesar with someone else."

Martin about-turned and stepped to the door. "You shouldn't be leaving the chamber doors lying open like this, you know." He marched back out, his sharp feet echoing into the distance.

Dyrne was already trapped in his own churning head. Hould hadn't been fooled by his false epiphany. He had either been removed from all visits for the time being... or worse. The prospect flooded his mouth with salt, and his sponge-body squeezed sweat. Swiveling to face the Net again, he scanned into his own account. The white corner-icon blinked ominously. One new alert. Jabbing at the screen, he skimmed the message with unblinking eyes:

'VISIT ALTERATIONS 21.11.270.

Due to recent changes in circumstances, your visitation bid, title: Sarai Tailor, has been reassessed.'

His sticky throat dried and his breath pulsed out in quiet rasps.

'Your bid has been successful and will commence shortly. Colleagues will be assigned to you later today.'

Dyrne padded back out into the gloomy hallway. He looked at the concrete floor, noticing his shadows cast from the small series of lights echoing his tentative movements back at him. He leaned a hand on the wall as if the world were about to tilt sideways and send him tumbling. He'd left Alex behind with a series of vague mumbles and backed away from the words on the Net screen, suddenly afraid. His focus was now realigned by the tangled murmurings he could hear ahead: the back of Martin's tall figure speaking to the bulky official who Dyrne had been questioned by not long ago, and other, nearer, muffled utterances. Staggering forward, he realised the third officer was missing. The prison guard. Another pace ahead, the half-open silver door of pod chamber 6 lay vulnerable like an exposed diary without an owner in sight.

Another lucid dream? Five seconds of standing statue-still, left hand still holding the cold concrete wall as a crutch, and the very real heartbeat he could hear told him otherwise. Glancing back to the outline of Martin blocking the agent down the corridor, Dyrne knew he hadn't been detected. He edged an unsteady foot closer and peered into the open chamber.

Jumping back in fright, he saw the sturdy silhouette of the officer in his black suit. But the guard was looking *into* the chamber, his back facing Dyrne. Frozen and numb, Dyrne continued staring in, unable to pull his gaze away or to keep walking.

The bulky body stepped off to the side, speaking words that Dyrne no longer heard, and as he disappeared from view to some other edge of the cell, *he* was there.

The intruder stared right back at him. They locked together, reflecting one another, as if he'd been waiting for Dyrne to step into place just at that moment. The warped mirror-image had loose, dark brown curls hanging over his ears, framing a broad, white forehead. The eyes were sapphire blue. Wearing the pod suit as Yusuf had described, he lay like a child's toy on the floor, back pressed against the short wall in front of the pod, legs splayed out and arms restrained somehow behind his back. He showed no sign of struggle or resistance, though, even in this position. He had accepted his punishment, Dyrne knew.

They remained for what must have been mere seconds, watching one another.

"Oi! Keep moving." The commanding order from further down the corridor beckoned him away. The officer in the chamber swiveled around and barged to the door, slamming it behind him as Dyrne stumbled backward. The intruder was concealed inside once more, the connection cut like an umbilical cord.

Dyrne sprang on through the corridor, head down, a chastised child passing the aggravated titan. But the sapphire eyes remained when he closed his own.

28

Dyrne powered through the dark streets. He wasn't desperate to get home to work or read or plan but to stretch toward tomorrow; rushing through the night to speed up time. Looking forward to sleep felt strange, but there was some ironic consolation in knowing that the more nights he could force his way through, the more chance there was of putting the nightmares to an end. Fear had melted into impatience.

The prisoner's face flashed in his head.

What had started after reading the Alert—rising heart-rate, body heating, shaking breath, smiles creeping onto his face—now morphed into something else, realising that the long-awaited news meant more than just achieving a lucky payoff. After his endless search, something far greater was glimmering at the end of his tunnel. Copil might really be saved. If Dyrne could stop the adoption by Sarai, the boy might never encounter those persecutors. Or at least might have a tutor at a different university who would protect him. How he would achieve any of this, though, he still didn't know for certain. Could he cause enough transference to ruin her adoption applications? Push them out a window? Break her Net screen?

The sapphire eyes of the prisoner looked at him.

The first pieces had already begun to slot together like the perfect concrete squares beneath his feet. No one else had ever had a rejected bid reviewed mid-cycle. Surely this was a sign. Positive energy materialising for him—that's how Phoebe might interpret it.

Before leaving DOHR Dyrne had returned to Hould, thanking her without appearing too desperate. Fearing the possibility of somehow making her change her mind, he didn't ask questions. Instead, riding on his high, gliding over his nerves, he requested Alex as his physicist. After the arrival of the still-unexplained intruder, Dyrne knew Yusuf would now, more than ever, be paying attention to every minute and specific detail, letting nothing slip by unnoticed. Alex, on the other hand, was always less scrutinising, practically nonchalant. He was the one sure choice. The only chance of making this work. And besides, surely any visit Yusuf was working on was being scrutinised by those government officials.

When Hould asked why he wanted Alex, Dyrne explained that they worked well together and that Alex already knew a little about the bid—not entirely untrue. She hadn't confirmed it aloud, but her miniscule nod of the head and quiet goodbye suggested agreement.

Now Dyrne realised the extent of the disguise he had created for himself, unwittingly or not. Years of never speaking out, keeping quiet, waiting, submitting ordinary bids, taking part in predicable visits and working incognito to present himself like any of the other indistinguishable historians had made him trustworthy and reliable. Hould would never suspect him of a thing. He had walked out of DOHR more himself than ever before, as if having pulled back a dark hood that had been covering his face for five years.

He closed his eyes, and the handcuffed ragdoll man stared at him still.

Shaking the image off, he thought again about the government investigators. Somehow even this failed to rattle him. If they *were* manoeuvring their way toward him, perhaps it would be too late to find anything by the time his visits were underway.

Cocooned in his bubble of virgin emotions, Dyrne didn't even notice how many people were around him on the Line. It could have been crammed full or empty. He sat in a rear corner running through images of what might be ahead. For the first time in years, his future was unlike his past; he couldn't anticipate or prepare for what was to come. It was no longer a cycle to be replayed over in his mind. Every day spent waking from the same dreams, motoring through his routine, traveling on the Line, walking the memorised path to DOHR, speaking to the same few colleagues, working hours beyond every other historian and returning to his flat at night killing time before the loop began again the following day. The few differing flavours in his life were the visits, which were already contained adventures—thrilling for a time, but with no meaningful consequence anymore.

And Phoebe. The thing he had pushed from his consciousness during his planning now tumbled on him, thumping at his throat. Guilt was something Dyrne was convinced no one could ever become accustomed to. Like death. The blue eyes of the prisoner were replaced with the bright green irises of Phoebe, whose blinding disappointment was all he could see and feel. Even after all the time spent with her, he still wasn't sure why she was friends with him. He didn't give or offer anything and only took from her: relying on her company, but never asking anything about her life; seeking out her thoughts on his bids, but never asking enough about her own; befriending Francis, yet never divulging anything about his own family, let alone introducing her to them; and using her gatherings as a testing ground to break his shell. He had never once invited her to his flat. Tonight, he hadn't even told her his bid had been accepted before he scarpered from DOHR. Hadn't even looked in her direction. He wondered if their friendship was even that, and wiped a fast-running tear with the butt of his hand, a black vacuum returning once again.

Suddenly aware the carriage had halted at his stop, he sprang up and leapt through the moving door that bit at his foot in warning as he hopped onto the platform. The journey had passed in moments. Skimming along the dark, cold street with hands in his pockets, he delved back into his mind, thinking of the unknown tomorrow, trying to lock down and quantify the intangible, like measuring silence.

Phoebe still glimmered in his brain behind salt water as he tried again and again to sink her away. Arriving at his building, he almost didn't notice the ominous shining shape of a car parked metres away from the entrance—the only one on the entire street. His district wasn't particularly central or affluent, so the sight was rare, threatening even. Frost had begun to varnish the glass; it must have been there for at least an hour or two. He stepped toward it, trying to glance in the black windows before spotting his ugly, distorted, moonlit reflection and retreating.

After scanning into the building, he climbed the wide staircase, hauling himself up, grabbing the metal banister with one hand and loosening his grey tie with the other, breathing in the heat emanating from his own clammy chest. Pushing through the stairwell door at his level, he turned to his apartment, head still down.

"Finally!"

Thinking he was imagining the strong, warm voice, it took Dyrne a few seconds to look up.

"I didn't know when or if you'd be back," it said. "Almost gave up! Come here." And with two wide arms, Dyrne was embraced, his bulky frontpack pressing against the solid chest of his waiting brother.

29

With Mann at his back, Dyrne scanned into the flat entrance worrying what might be lying around inside that could be too telling. He still hadn't spoken.

"Sorry to turn up unannounced like this but I can never contact you—I don't have your Net ID."

"I don't have a Net at home." Dyrne's first words were cold, muted. "Still using my Mobile," he mumbled.

"Well, I'm just down here for work. Last minute arrangement. I wanted to come and see you while I'm here."

Mann slipped his hands into the pockets of his shiny, black jacket and followed Dyrne. The pair passed through the small entrance vestibule and into the square living area. Mann had visited Dyrne here twice before: the first time when he'd moved in seven years ago; the second after he fled his job at the University. On both occasions he'd commented on the size of the place; his own family home in Edenborough was far more spacious. Even now, he looked like he was surveying the four corners of the room.

"You're still working with the government?" he asked, as if to clarify the oddness of Dyrne's chosen habitat.

"... Yes."

"Census stuff, yeah?"

Dyrne nodded dumbly, almost forgetting the alibi.

He remembered Mann's last visit. Isabella had been with him too. The children left with Dyrne and Mann's father for the day. Mann's blonde, elegant wife was friendly enough, but being from a wealthy family, Dyrne always thought she must be looking down on him. They had called to 'check in' on him to make sure he was okay after his sudden departure from the lecturing job he had worked toward for so many years. Of course, Dyrne was even less likely to divulge information in front of Isabella than he would have been in front of Mann. No secrets were shared, the whole truth never told.

As he removed his burdening frontpack and laid it in a corner behind a pile of books, he turned to look at Mann, who leaned on the kitchenette counter, scanning the place. At the same moment Dyrne thought of it, Mann glanced over at the holograph on the worktop: the handsome, dark-haired young man.

"Hey. I didn't know you had that," he smiled. "My first day at University, I think."

"It was," Dyrne confirmed.

"And last day with—well, for all of us, together."

Dyrne said nothing else about the single-family memento. Instead, he looked down at Mann's expensive green shoes, noticing for the first time the bulky, black bag plopped beside them.

"I was going to ask to stay tonight, if that's OK," Mann said. "If not, I can rent a room for the night in the city. I can do that for the rest of the week, too."

"Um, yes, that's fine. You can stay tonight. Of course." Dyrne still stood limp, his long, brown coat hanging over his hands, fingers jutting out while he glanced down at his own fading, brown work shoes.

Then Dyrne's periscope mind shot through to the bedroom. The Metaganic Support flyer, still clinging to his bedside counter, lay waiting, begging to be discovered. He would have to make sure Mann slept on the couch without even glimpsing the adjoining room. He could just imagine the questions.

Why are you going to a support group? What do you need? Why haven't you spoken to me if you're unhappy? Or Dad?

After several static, silent seconds, he defrosted and rubbed his forehead. He invited Mann to sit down with a loose gesture of his other wilting hand.

"Can I get you some tea? I don't have anything else, sorry."

"Sure, tea would be great, thanks." Mann moved to the brown couch. One end of it was worn and faded, with one cushion dented and misshapen. The other half was firm and plump, as if had just been delivered and its packaging freshly removed. Mann rested on the arm so that he didn't have to turn away from Dyrne.

An elastic quiet filled the room, disturbed only by Dyrne's soft footsteps treading toward the kitchen counter. After that, the clinking of kitchen utensils and cupboard doors sliding open and closed. Mann asked about how 'things' had been: work mostly, questions about friends, spare time. Dyrne delivered feigned, brief responses, never asking questions in return.

As he watched the bubbling, steaming water in the relic glass kettle, he spotted his own lurid reflection—bony-framed and pale. His gaze shifted to his brother behind him—who still looked bigger despite being farther away—his physique bragging vitality and confidence.

Visions of school events swirled in the hot water. Sports and physical competitions prefaced by teachers' surprised faces, laughing even, when finding out the boys were 'related'. Broad, athletic Mann standing tall beside Dyrne—short, skinny, flushed, looking down. Mann, handsome even then, only defended his younger sibling from time to time. Dyrne would say nothing, assuming his brother resented the connection of a surname. He wondered now if Mann's insistence on keeping in contact was some act of atonement.

Maybe we do have something in common.

The inevitable question cracked his daydream open:

"Have you spoken to Dad recently?"

The water had boiled, but Dyrne kept staring at it.

"No." He knew the question was rhetorical. There was no point in fabricating any excuse or false reasoning.

"You do know he'd like to hear from you more often? We all would."

Dyrne tried making some sound of agreement, suspecting this was why Mann was here after all. All that came out was a loud gulp.

"Here's your tea."

He handed Mann the burning cup.

"I don't ever know how you are, Dyrne. Fuck, I didn't even know if you still lived in this building."

Sighing, but unwilling to give in this soon, Dyrne met his eyes. "I know, sorry. You're far away though. I just get busy. I'm fine. Nothing changes much for me." Each sentence was a new barricade. Mann shrugged and sank into the couch, sipping the hot drink and stretching back, retreating.

"Good to see you though, Dee."

Dyrne's instinct-smile was powerless to the childhood nickname. He eased himself into the other unused chair and observed his brother toying with the little hourglass from the table, watching the sand piling through to its last grain before flipping it again in the other direction. Dyrne let his hands nestle into his sides, looking on at the sand slipping around in its glass case, willing it to make time pass faster.

"Mm, this is good. Tastes of fruit. What is it?"

"I'm not even sure. Something expensive Phoebe gave me."

"Phoebe? You mentioned her the last time I spoke to you too, I'm sure."

"Yes."

"You haven't thought about living together yet?"

Dyrne saw his brother's boyish grin flashing over at him.

"Oh. No, no. Phoebe is married."

"Bloody hell, Dyrne." Mann pushed himself upright with his elbows. "How'd you get into this mess?"

"I'm not in a mess! I'm not in a relationship with her. She's a colleague, that's all. A friend."

"Oh... oh." Mann sank back down again, taking another gulp of tea. "So you're not... seeing anyone then? Last time I heard you talk about a woman was a Dr. Keller back at the University." Dyrne shook his head, mumbling and looking to the floor. "So Phoebe—she works with you on the census then?"

"That's right."

"You don't have any plans for a career change? Back to what you know best?" Mann gestured around the room at the stacks of history books. Now that the subject of their father had come and gone, not much more time could have passed without *this* topic arising.

"No," Dyrne swallowed. "I'm quite happy."

He had been passionate about history since they were children, excelling in it at school. Their mother had been the one to encourage the interest. Dyrne's father had always maintained this was one of the reasons he clung to it after she died when the boys were teenagers. Studying it at University had been the obvious path; the lecturing position a dream achieved. Which was why leaving it so abruptly had surprised Mann and their father as much as it had.

Mann sipped again. "You still have all these books, though." He pointed at a couple lying on the short table in front of them: *Post-War UE Human Rights* and *NLU Enrolments 2220—2230*. Dyrne edged from side to side in the chair. "You wouldn't like to, one day, go back to lecturing? Maybe another university?" he asked without looking at Dyrne, gazing down into his shallow cup.

"Mm-mm." Dyrne squeezed his lips together and rose from the chair. He wasn't even in control of the action. It was automatic, innate, his animal instinct to escape danger seizing his body. Moving back behind the kitchen counter, he pretended to move and tidy away objects to unnecessary new locations around drawers and cupboards.

"Did you hear that Sarai Tailor died?" Glasses clattered on the counter. "The synth woman?"

Why is he asking that?

Dyrne's eyes darted around the room.

What is he reading? How has he seen her name?

But Mann only sipped from the cup, looking straight ahead at the wall. "Dee?"

"No. No, I didn't know that. I don't think."

An obvious lie. He shuffled to a pile of books on the floor and crouched to rearrange them pointlessly.

"So doesn't it get monotonous?" Mann asked. Dyrne craned around to see his brother looking over at him now. "Keeping track of births, deaths, people moving to other cities—that what you do mostly?"

Dyrne pushed both palms into the floor, grateful his brother had changed the topic.

"Sort of, yes."

"Is that a yes to the first or second question?" Mann asked, laughing a little.

"I don't know. Both," Dyrne replied, still unable to smile.

"And is the population in New London increasing much?"

"Gradually, yes."

"Is that because organic births are on the rise or because of metas still?"

Metas. This new abbreviation must be popular in Mann's city, thought Dyrne. He still winced hearing him speak so overtly about the subject and knew he would never get used to it, like hearing parents swearing.

"I... I don't know. Both probably."

Mann turned around further, leaning his thick arms over the back of the sofa.

"Are you even listening to me? 'Probably'? You don't sound too certain for someone cataloguing the city's population."

"Well, I—it's just that we don't keep specific records on metaganics."

Mann raised an eyebrow, a few lines gathering on his otherwise smooth, tanned forehead. Dyrne shrugged and spoke faster, his words tumbling and tripping over his tongue.

"We don't—we don't record metaga—meta births, really. I don't think. No, we don't. They don't get their own numbers. They just—they don't... they don't count."

Mann looked at Dyrne, his brown eyes unblinking.

"Well," he drawled, before taking another sip of tea and turning away again. "You haven't changed, Dyrne."

Resolving to end the conversation as quickly as possible and hide in his room for the rest of the night, Dyrne took a few final seconds to observe his brother from a distance, who had put down his cup and was now rubbing his temples, crouched over.

"You just haven't changed."

30

Remembering everything the way it had felt on his first day, Dyrne crept into the shiny, white secret labs, anticipating turning heads, scrutinising eyes, perhaps even whispers. Here was the man whose twice-rejected bid had been overturned. But no one said a word. The only person to react to his presence was a pre-occupied physicist who almost walked into him, her head buried in a Net screen. Even then she hadn't looked him in the eye.

Glad of his unchanging anonymity, Dyrne walked to the Hub, ending each recent morning's pattern of hibernation in his glass cell. Reaching the wide, circular table, he scanned into the first Net he arrived at, wondering if his visit might be canceled at the last minute.

No alert.

Then he noticed the shadowed, lowered face of Yusuf on the other side of the desk. Since the arrival of the subterranean captive, they had become estranged. Yusuf looked up to meet Dyrne's eye. He must have become astute about being watched since his ordeal, Dyrne supposed.

"Hello, Mr. Samson."

"Morning, Yusuf. How are you?"

"Very well, thank you." Yusuf didn't return the question. Had they now traded places, Dyrne wondered? Yusuf the secretive introvert instead?

"I hear you're beginning a new bid cycle of your own today, Mr. Samson."

It was worse. Perhaps Yusuf had heard that Alex had been selected, by request, to monitor Dyrne's forthcoming visits. More guilt piled on like a snowdrift. Dyrne shook his head, trying to empty the nagging thoughts.

"Yes, I am," said Dyrne. "Hopefully things work out." The vaguest answer he could concoct.

"I'm sure they will. Be ready for any questions, though."

Questions?

"Government investigations have begun. The officials are here."

"Big day!" A new voice from behind—the sudden and unmistakable dulcet call of Phoebe.

Dyrne twisted around. At first, he thought she, too, was announcing news about being investigated before realising that she must be talking about the new visit cycle. Hould had assigned Phoebe to Dyrne's project. A perfect conclusion.

"Big day indeed." He wanted to add some quip or sarcastic joke, but preoccupation with Yusuf stopped him.

"Let's get together afterward and discuss how the visit goes today," said Phoebe. "Then we can think about where you want me to take things from there." Anyone listening in might assume the bid was hers. "We could even go for lunch, if there's time."

He knew, of course, her suggestions would be pointless. His plan was set in unalterable motion.

"We don't need to discuss where to take it. It's all mapped out for now."

The smile slid from her face.

"But we can go for lunch. That would be great." His forced buoyancy did nothing. As she sighed, looking ready to turn away from him, new words spilled out from his mouth like fizzy relaxant froth.

"My brother's here. Came down from Edenborough last night."

"Oh." She didn't look at him. Had he ever mentioned his brother to her? He knew he had told her about his mother's death long ago. But never this. Now he was a little boy showing off at school, brandishing a new toy.

"Maybe... you could meet him," the eager words continued pouring.

"Sure. Sounds great."

She wished him luck, touching his shoulder, before skittering back off through the glass maze to her own area. Dyrne turned back toward Yusuf, realising the lost-looking physicist had vanished. Instead, across the lab space, Dyrne spotted Martin ascending the short staircase to Dr. Hould's office door just as it was opened by one of the elderly government officials. Martin was ushered inside as the door smacked shut behind him.

Daley. They're already at 'D' then.

Dyrne's eyes fell, and he checked his silly expression in the Net screen reflection. Remnants of a grin were stuck behind but slipping off like melting plastic.

As the shutters lifted to reveal the dim stretching corridor, Dyrne trembled, and the quick heartbeat that reached up his throat made him want to be sick. He hardly noticed the ever-present watching security officer at the elevator exit as he paced past. Experiencing every unsure footstep as if the act of walking was new and unnatural, he felt himself pulled along on an invisible conveyor belt. The small glowing bulbs flanked him like tiny candles leading the way and a cool, quiet air puffed around him. Reaching the junction, he glided to his right, past the second guard who, this time, nodded in slow-motion without asking any questions. They had anticipated Dyrne's presence.

Chamber 5 swept by innocently. Chamber 6 approached as if it was the heavy silver door and accompanying officer floating past and Dyrne who was standing still. He felt the magnetism of the prison room and was sure this time the suited guard threw him a warning glance. It was bolted firmly shut today revealing nothing of its secrets. Chamber 7 barely registered on Dyrne's radar as it slid past; just another tiny compartment in the long row of confessional boxes.

Pod chamber 8 had been selected again for his first visit, and he arrived at a slow halt to find the door ajar. Alex obviously hadn't taken on Martin's stern advice. Pushing it open further, he took a final look back down the long aisle, gathering the image for a moment, holographing it in his mind. Inhaling, he stepped through the doorway and pulled it closed behind him with a thud. Alex stood in front of the raised, opaque sphere adjusting something, his back to Dyrne, a priest in his temple.

As Dyrne approached the altar with reverence, Alex spoke, sage-like, knowing the entrant without effort:

"Just can't get enough of me, huh?"

Dyrne wondered if Hould had told Alex that he had asked for him specifically. Perhaps this flattery could help. He replied with a muffled laugh. Deception had begun already.

"Well, everything's set," said Alex. "Just checking on a couple of the motion sensors. You can go ahead and suit up."

Shuffling to the corner, Dyrne slithered from his shirt and trousers into the stretchy pod suit in swift, practised movements, facing the wall the entire time.

Won't have to do this much longer.

The constant whirring of his brain stopped. He froze. What next? Really? Not just in theory, on a Net screen, but here in reality. What would happen after interfering in just one visit? What changes might confront him when he stepped back out of the pod? This was the part he hadn't planned out. He'd had a distant notion that everything here would be erased. Copil would never have died and his teaching career would never have ended. He would somehow suddenly be back at New London University, still lecturing. He wouldn't know what DOHR was.

But even that had been a series of cloudy dream images. A vague future he hadn't ever expected to come true. Facing a new reality, he had no idea what would happen to himself after this was all done, *if* it could be done.

"You can head on in now, Samson. It's all yours."

The electronic lock of the chamber door clunked behind him, making him jump. His heart felt like it had doubled in speed and intensity. Staring up, he was sure he was levitating again. His body gravitated toward the pod, floating him up the few concrete stairs to its open oblong cut-out. Something that had become routine, a part of his job, a mechanical function, now felt foreign and terrifying, as if he had been asked to do it blindfolded. The smooth, milky orb welcomed him. He stepped inside and the sliding door behind him zoomed into place, sealing him in—the idea of backing out an impossibility now.

The air was warmer, and sound became muffled and closer, the world beyond dulling away as if submerged underwater. The seashell skin of the pod looked lilac and pink from the inside. After a few seconds of waiting and gazing up and around, Alex's calm voice echoed from a concealed speaker.

"Same as always, Dyrne. Camera and mics ready to record. Observation reference: E001633 ready to commence."

Dyrne felt the throng and shudder of the mammoth machinery that filled stories far above him. The buzzing headache of reality rang through his consciousness, whistling through Alex's words.

"So here goes. Observation of Sarai Tailor, 2223. Preparation for her first synth rights march. Good luck, Samson."

31
FEBRUARY 2225

'SYNTHPHOBIA = IGNORANCE'

Sarai painted the tall, bold letters onto another placard, lining it up with the others drying on the cramped floor of the small apartment. She couldn't afford holographic boards. The brave statements lay in rows, looking up at her in their fresh defiance. She pulled a strand of her burgundy, curly hair to inspect it, scraping off paint with her nails, then rose from her crouched position, hands on hips. Looking around the small flat, she sighed, trying to figure out what task was next amongst the stacks of open folders and leaflets and books and scattered stationery.

The walls had been painted white over a dark grey that still showed through in streaks underneath; she hadn't found time to do anything about it, and it still didn't seem important enough to bother with now. Dotted around the edges of the room, where there was free space amongst the piles of papers, were a few ornaments and keepsakes: a childhood drawing, a chunky, glinting amethyst formation, an old-fashioned photograph frame and a black-silk wrapped set of "seeing" cards she didn't know how to use—a silly relic that she enjoyed toying with. Maybe she should tidy it all away. Or bin it altogether? The other university girls had scoffed at it all. Living with them in the dorms hadn't worked well for anyone. Amongst other differences, Sarai couldn't understand their apathy toward the synth cause, and on her own, she could devote more time to what really mattered without interference. At least that's what she told herself.

She traversed the piles of papers to the corner-desk and sat down on the small stool. A cool glow shone down from the skylight above, and she wrapped her feet around the stool legs. As well as the rally, Sarai knew she ought to focus on her upcoming assignment for Post-War Studies, so lifted her new Mobile and opened her half-completed essay: 'Introduction of the Synthetic Repopulation Programme'. A vague first draft of '23rd Century Decline of Creative Industry', which her tutor had guided her toward, lay abandoned. She had resorted to forging ahead with what she knew best and ignored the fact that not only the professor but the other students would be sick of hearing about the topic at this point. Apparently one of them had even threatened to leave the class if it was going to 'turn into a synth agenda course'. Sarai didn't care.

As she reviewed her last few paragraphs, a loud buzz interrupted. A still image of an elderly gentleman appeared on the glass. Sarai recognised him instantly and sprang upright in the chair. She waved her fingers over the screen.

"Hello?" she answered, stopping herself from pre-emptively using his name.

"Hello. Is this Sarai Tailor?" The voice was slow and croaking. The image feed followed: a thin face, weary and creased with time. Behind him Sarai saw the outline of a navy armchair, framing him like a throne.

"It is. Is this Edom?" She blurted.

"This is Edom Morrigan, yes. I hope this is a convenient time. My daughter spoke to me about your work. She said you'd like me to get involved somehow…"

Sarai gripped the edges of the seat to stop herself from jumping up and prancing around the room. Her feet dragged back and forth against the floor. Her bold self-introduction in the library to Edom Morrigan's supposed daughter had paid off, and now she was talking to the man himself. And as if this validation wasn't enough, he had referred to Sarai's University campaigns and protests as 'her work'.

"That would be wonderful, yes, if you could, in any way. It's a bit of an old-fashioned way of doing these things, but I'm hoping that's why it might work—people aren't used to seeing marches like this." She forced herself not to ramble. "I didn't think we'd hear from you. This is incredible, though."

There was another pause before the white-haired man spoke again.

"I'm not sure how I can help."

"Well, we're having a march at the beginning of next month and were hoping to find some kind of guest to give a sort of speech outside the government offices." Her words gathered speed. "If it was you, I think people would respond."

"...You know, I haven't spoken out much in public. A lot of people know who I am, but I haven't been involved in much... activism." The voice trailed, his head dipping. "... Although I know I should be. It's difficult for me... but I would like to help."

She exhaled, realising she had been holding her breath. She continued, steadying herself, to further explain the rally and make tentative arrangements to meet with Edom, stopping after every few sentences to gush with gratitude. The fact that this could help with her paper hadn't even occurred to her yet.

The initial discussion didn't last long. All Edom had offered were brief suggestions and hesitant arrangements. But he was the first. Not only was she speaking to the first and longest-living synth, but he was going to help her. They agreed, thankfully, to meet in person in the coming weeks and talk more.

The assignment was forgotten, and the Mobile abandoned at the desk. Sarai bustled around the room, hopping between the few uncluttered areas of floor space, gathering various notes and deciding who to contact first about her new key speaker.

It was then that she glanced over to her row of placards and saw it.

How had that happened? She bent over, examining the half-wet and half-ruined poster. It lay beside the others, positioned as she had left it. But the thick, black "IGNORANCE" had been smeared across the white board. She squinted at the illegible sign, baffled. Then she glanced to the second sign: a half-footprint was stamped in its corner. Tutting at herself and rolling her eyes, she realised she must have stepped right across them whilst pacing the room, oblivious in the midst of her giddiness.

Standing upright and tutting at herself, she tiptoed through the paperwork to the kitchenette sink around the corner. Lifting her right foot, she yanked off her tatty shoe. No paint. Wrong foot. She put it back down and, shifting her balance, grabbed the left one. Pulling again, she dumped the shoe in the sink, ready to wash the sole. She squinted.

No paint.

Standing upright and turning at herself, she limped through the pathway to the bathroom, back around the corner, taking her right foot, she yanked off her dirty shoe. "Going back," she said, she down and shifting her balance, pushed the left one. Putting aside the damp cloth, she into the sink, ready to wash her sole. She squinted

No point.

32

NOVEMBER 2270

Blackness. The lights and screens of the chamber had vanished beyond the shell of the swallowing egg. The colossal telescopes groaned and vibrated. A tiny but piercing electronic whistle squealed, blocking out all peripheral sound before light and colours flashed everywhere. The curved canvas all around shone with whizzing blues, whites, purples, greens, and black in shooting straight edges before slowing down to oily swirls.

The room solidified around Dryne.

She was there.

Looking right through his skull, Sarai stared ahead, tucking purple-tinged curls back behind her ears. The images always appeared like this, jarringly present after the initial glares and blurs. She was a younger version of the woman he had met at the University induction. For years he'd pored over the news sites and published holographs and security records; they had imprinted themselves in his consciousness. But she was no longer a holograph or words on paper or pixels behind glass or a vague memory from one day. Now she was present and real, separated by nothing more than a thin, buzzing film of electric time.

The apartment was soundless. Freshly painted posters lay around the floor and walls, emblazoned with fearless phrases of protest. Dyrne remained still, calming his heart with nothing but willpower. The familiar sensation of dreaming grew in his mind, abated only by clenching his eyes shut and re-opening them, finding the same images circling around, unchanging. He thought of his training. Even when historians might be out of view of a subject, their movement should be conservative and controlled.

Within seconds, she was wandering around the small flat,

traversing the placards and piles of papers covering the place. He observed her stances and expressions, alternating between pensive thought and frantic movement. She clambered amongst the folders and posters and open boxes. It was a jungle of cardboard and paper. Looking down by his side at the three-dimensional projection rubbing against his grey pod suit, he spotted one particular box, filled with household utensils and useless, ornamental items. A purple, jagged gemstone stuck out of one crate while a black, silk-covered rectangle lay perched on top of other items. Peering in further, he saw the worn corner of a thick, ancient-looking book. The words "Spirit World" were visible on the blue cover. The paraphernalia reminded him of archaic objects from a much earlier era altogether. He had found nothing about Tailor's interest in this sort of thing during his research. He knew she was omni, but these were signs of something more: older superstitions.

Sarai moved to a corner of the room, resting at a small desk in front of a Mobile—like Dyrne's own. Hers looked newer, though. As she began scanning through documents, he knew he ought to advance. Raising each leg and prodding forward with care, he felt the smooth movement of the pod shift and rotate underneath his suited feet; a giant rat in a wheel. Glancing down, he found that none of the images he passed through reacted to his presence. No transference. He wondered if Alex was watching. Approaching Sarai's turned figure with less stealth, he crouched, trying to glimpse the document she was reading. At that moment, the Mobile screen lit up with the anticipated image of Edom Morrigan, accompanied by a loud, continuous tone. Answering the call with a startled "Hello", Sarai stared at the screen as Dyrne listened in to the unfolding conversation he had read about in various interviews and Netcall logs.

Dyrne had always been aware of Morrigan. Like knowing how to speak or count, he couldn't remember where or when he had first learned about the original metaganic. The name was simply there in his mind, one of his earliest pieces of ingrained knowledge. His parents must have told him about Edom from a young age. Rather open of them, he thought now. He'd never considered it before.

Listening to the girl's naïve ramblings about her protest rally and her eager requests for Morrigan's help, Dyrne felt both gratitude and resentment toward her: thankful for her commitment to synth rights, bitter about the ultimate sequence of cause and effect that would inexorably lead from moments like these to her adoption of a synth child. A child who would never have privacy; who would be known as metaganic wherever he went. Dyrne watched the chain begin to form in front of him, each awful link sinking into its place.

The chain he would now break.

Turning his body with great precision, giving the impression of manoeuvring to survey the rest of the small apartment, he raised his hand toward the power control for the Mobile. Knowing he had to move quickly, he nudged the main glass panel in the wall with his finger.

Nothing. The power remained. His motion didn't transfer. Knowing he could neither react nor try again, in case Alex noticed, he waited with patience, eavesdropping on the rest of the Mobile conversation before considering another move. Gazing around the projected image of the flat, his eyes rested on the most blatant and ubiquitous option available. Considering for a moment the unintended sabotage of Sarai's protest, he subtracted the thought from his mind. Retreat was not an option.

•   •   •

"Pretty smooth-going for first observation of the cycle," Alex commented as the now-blank pod door slid open, releasing Dyrne from its exhilarating cocoon back into the present.

"Yes," he replied, before speeding back to the corner of the room, desperate to unzip from the damp, choking hold of the hot pod suit. Removing the rubber gear was always less smooth a transition than putting it on. Pulling the fastener down to just below his chest, he diverted any unwanted attention by asking Alex how long the observation had been, forcing the physicist to turn back to his screens.

"You were in there for...twenty-three and a half minutes. Co-ordinates were right on target, so I didn't have to adjust too many settings. The recording will come out the same as usual—patchy here and there—but audio was good and you got in pretty close without much transference. Visual at least."

Alex had paid close attention. Not surprising, Dyrne assured himself. It was the first visit, after all. His focus might lapse the further they progressed into the cycle. Allowing him to continue talking about details of the observation and technical specifics whilst facing the screens, Dyrne took the opportunity to shift with haste from the grey, sodden pod suit to his usual clothes. Thrusting his arms into the sleeves of the shirt, he felt it press uncomfortably against the perspiration on his back. He laid the used, damp suit flat on the bench, wary of saying anything about it or drawing Alex's attention to it. The familiar act made him realise nothing had changed. Alex was still here. They were still in DOHR. Dyrne's neat pile of clothes lay as he had left it. At what point would his impacts on the past begin affecting the present? And how?

"So next visit is...?" Alex asked, leaning over the metal railing from his platform.

"Phoebe will be coming to observe a little more of Sarai at University and some of the others organising the rally," Dyrne replied, feeling even more guilt at how futile all of her decoy observations would be.

"OK. And you?"

"I'll be following up with Sarai's visit to Morrigan's residence. It happened 22 days after today's events."

Alex nodded, wide-eyed. "Pretty good, Samson. You know your stuff. Better than you did with Daley's visits, that's for sure."

"Mm."

Turning to leave, exhaling for what felt like the first time since entering the chamber, he began scouring the visit in his mind. The gemstone, the black silk box, the spirit book. They were too unusual to ignore. He locked the nugget of gold away for safekeeping.

As he stepped into the corridor, Alex called out again. "Bit of kinetic transference right at the end there. And what was she doing with her shoes? I couldn't see."

Dyrne slipped behind a mask with expert stealth.

"She was checking for paint I think."

"Oh."

"Yeah. She must've stepped on one of her signs by accident."

33
MARCH 2225

Sarai squeezed her chapped lips together. Looking at the pock-marked, green door in front of her, she tottered on the top step. She'd taken one of the new Line tracks out here, where there were no more scrapers and fewer people. She rubbed a turquoise ring on her finger for luck, and after a few moments, a key clunked in a lock. Bolts unclicked on the other side of the door and the small house opened.

A short woman in her forties smiled, beckoning Sarai inside. She wore a uniform—a dark grey tabard over a plain white shirt and trousers. She also had an ID badge pinned to the tunic although there was no chance for Sarai to read it. The woman ushered her in from the small hallway into the main room of the house right away. Her first impressions were of old-fashioned décor—off-white wallpaper, geometric patterned floors and various matching pieces of blue furniture. The only sign of the 23rd Century was a holograph on a table at one end of the room. Then she saw the high-backed navy armchair and recognised it from the Mobile call.

The streaming sunlight from the window behind it made it difficult to see him at first, but after the initial silhouette faded, the recognisable figure became clear. He was thin but tall and sat upright. Round blue eyes looked up from heavy, creased lids at Sarai. He didn't speak.

"Mr. Morrigan, I'm Sarai Tailor."

Morrigan nodded while she spoke—of course he knew who she was. An outstretched arm gestured to a small couch at his side, and she sat, removing her frontpack and setting it on the floor at her feet.

"Thank you for letting me visit you. I didn't think you'd give me your home address."

The nurse excused herself and scarpered off into an adjoining room, closing the door behind her. Edom still hadn't spoken.

"As you know, Mr. Morrigan, I am organising a rally in New London to promote, um, synth rights." It was in saying it aloud that she was forced to consider what term she should use in front of Morrigan. Would he be referring to himself as 'metaganic' now?

"I'm not sure how far I can walk for you." His voice was thin, but Sarai thought she could see a smile.

"Oh, you don't need to walk anywhere, sir—"

"Sir, ha. Not everybody calls me that."

Despite studying the treatment of people like Morrigan for years, hearing him talk this way first-hand made her shudder. An uncontrollable swell took over and she deviated from her practised lines.

"I've written about the programme—and you—in essays and presentations for university. About your treatment. And your rights. I think you're incredibly important to a lot of people, not just me."

He shook his head. "Who would've thought? A synth."

Sarai wanted to reach over and hold his hand. He didn't seem to realise his own importance.

"It's not me you ought to study," he continued, looking down, "but those who berate me."

The heaviness in her stomach grew. "Well, I think you're extraordinary, Mr. Morrigan. The first of the post-War synthetic programme. I can't imagine how some of the backlash against people like you must feel. But you've survived it all. You're living proof of—"

"—There's a difference between surviving and living, Miss Tailor. And believe it or not, I don't hate those people who hate *me*."

Sarai sat back a little. "I think you could help others like you, sir."

Edom continued as if she hadn't spoken at all. "You know that I was given a code before I was given a name? A series of numbers." He looked right at her, almost whispering. "We all were; the first batch."

Sarai winced at his choice of phrase.

"I wasn't given a name until after I was fully grown and ready to be... delivered." He looked away again, gazing off to the far side of the room. She spotted sweat glistening down his forehead. "We've lived like codes, though.

Like products, a series of extra digits to make up numbers. Nothing more. That's all they wanted. A population injection."

Sarai felt a tightening in her throat, before licking her lips and forcing herself to speak.

"And I don't want anyone to have to feel like a code anymore. Do you? You are the first, but you can also be the last. The last to have to live as a second-class citizen." She was surprised at her own assuredness, but looking at him, couldn't tell if she'd caught his attention. Eventually, he answered, still slowly, grit in his throat.

"And how can I help? The problem is... people don't want to be reminded of me—the one who started it all. I worry I'd only cement this country's prejudices, Miss Tailor, not change them."

She clenched her teeth at the irony—this great symbol of a new era, the spark of one of the greatest post-War biological revolutions sitting in front of her, feeling powerless.

"But you can help the others like you," she urged. "There were thousands after you. Synths are still being born, for different reasons now, admittedly. But being born into a world that still doesn't always accept them. They need some hope. And you can help people like me, too. I'm different in my own way. Some of us are fighting for you." She tried smiling, but he still wasn't looking at her. The bright burst of hope that had brought her here was fading. She desperately needed to reignite it. Following his stare down to the coloured, jagged patterns in the floor, she inched forward, the couch creak awkwardly beneath her.

"Tell me about your adoptive parents. No one knows much about them." She hadn't planned on saying any of this, but knew she had to do what she could to make this rally, and all her efforts, a success. She noticed a shift in his gaze. "They must have been kind people. What would they think now? That you spoke out for yourself and other synths like you? Or that you shied away, alone, separate from your children, being looked after for the rest of your life by a stranger?" She pursed her lips and inhaled deeply.

Silence between the two filled the air. Distant clanking of cutlery tinkled from the room next door distracting Sarai for a moment. She turned toward the noise. It was then that the holograph she had caught sight of earlier crystalised into a sharp image. Squinting, she saw a younger Edom with his wife and three grinning children gathered around them. They stood in front of one of the first New London government buildings to be constructed.

As she looked back to Edom, she found him staring somewhere else.

"Did you see that?" he gasped.

She turned to look behind her, then up and down.

"No. See what?"

Was he avoiding answering her again? Had she pushed too far and ruined everything? Or was he even frailer than he looked? He didn't answer her, instead scanning the wall, looking for something. She sighed.

"Mr. Morrigan? Can you try to help at our march? You don't even need to speak if you can't. Your presence alone—your visibility—would prove so much..."

Finally, he looked back at her.

"I... I'm not sure, Miss Tailor. I... I need to think this over. I do want to help..."

The light flickered on Sarai's left as she felt someone brush past her hair. She turned, ready to smile for the nurse, perhaps now catching a glimpse of her name tag.

But no one was there. Edom was the only other person in the room. And as she listened now, she could still hear the distant sounds of movement from the next room. She turned back to face the withering man, finding him, again, staring wide-eyed and sweating at the empty space beside her. Goosebumps prickled on her skin.

"You saw that, too," the old man whispered, still looking off at some invisible point.

A fizzle. The holograph flickered and faded. The metal frame flipped over.

Seconds later, the kitchen door opened. The nurse reappeared, drying her hands on a towel.

"Mr. Morrigan... Oh dear, you don't look very well again." She scuttled to him and pressed a hand against his cheek. "I knew he wasn't up to this," she muttered, crouching down.

Sarai pressed herself back in the chair, trying to understand what had just happened. Edom continued to stare at the far end of the room. The woman turned back to Sarai.

"I'm sorry, but I think you'd better leave now. He's having another bad day."

Nodding, Sarai stood and fumbled her way around the chair.

"Please think about it, sir," she blurted. "You can contact me on my Net."

But he didn't even register her presence, mumbling whispers between dry lips with wide eyes fixed on nothing.

Without looking back, she left, the image of the old man's terrified stare haunting her.

34

NOVEMBER 2270

"Is your brother coming to meet us here?"

"Oh, no. We'll meet him nearer the scraper he's working in."

Dyrne wasn't sure how he'd tangled himself into this lunch meeting and now he couldn't manoeuvre his way out of it. He didn't want to disappoint Phoebe any further. At least it might take attention away from his visits.

Mann had only spent one night at Dyrne's. Since then he'd stayed in a rented travel room instead; he suggested to Dyrne after the first day that this had been his intention all along and that it would be much easier for work. This made things easier. Dyrne could worry less about what Mann might see or ask. Yet, he'd been surprised at the soft blow he felt hearing Mann say it, even though he knew it was his own fault.

"So remind me what he does," said Phoebe, throwing a few items into her frontpack then beaming at Dyrne.

"It's, um, something to do with power..." he half-guessed, shrugging.

"Political power? He's in government?" She sounded impressed.

"No, no. I mean energy-power. Nuclear. I think they want to begin implementing more of our systems farther north."

"Aah."

Leaving the compact enclosure of DOHR and stepping into the relentless openness of the street, Dyrne directed Phoebe to the east side of the city. A handful of other suited men and women crossed their paths in silence, faces either staring at Nets or immune to interaction.

"It's good to be out. It gets so claustrophobic in there." Phoebe yawned and rubbed her gloved hands in the cold air.

"Yes, feels better," Dyrne lied. With each footstep away from the place, his temperature rose. He wondered what Mann might tell Phoebe. And what if someone back at DOHR was reviewing his recordings right now, noticing things? Realising? An autochemist they passed pulled Dyrne's eyes to it, making his guts gurgle in pain.

As if reading his mind, Phoebe began discussing her most recent visit—an observation of Tailor's first pre-rally meeting in the New London University buildings. Dyrne had purposefully given her this one. He preferred to avoid the place, still, even from the safety of a pod. Phoebe's interest in the cycle had been growing, though: sightwriting her reports ahead of schedule, asking to review Dyrne's visits, discussing the cycle with other historians. She had even suggested doing some of her own research into Sarai. He cauterised this desire, though, telling her it was unnecessary; that his own research was exhaustive should she want to find anything. The danger of what he was doing presented itself in new ways every day.

They stopped at a small corner-park, just a block short of where Dyrne had told Mann they should meet. He figured that his brother could spot them from there; any further distance for them to travel away from DOHR, even one more block, was excessive. Perching on the edge of a stone bench, Phoebe lay back, wrapping her arms around herself, letting her head fall back a little with closed eyes, puffing out icy, rhythmic breath through her red-tipped nose. Dyrne leaned forward, resting his elbows on his knees and rubbing his face.

He looked across to the grey, granite building opposite them, examining the film of frost beginning to form on some of the windows. His focus shifted to the tall, shadowed entrance, through which a thin, dark-haired woman had just marched. Within seconds, a long, black car appeared on the street from the direction Dyrne and Phoebe had come. It was the first car he had seen today—sleek and elusive. He turned to glance at Phoebe who was still resting with her head facing skyward, breathing softly, oblivious. Looking back, he caught sight of the car for another few seconds before it grumbled off down the street, evading his gaze. As it turned the next corner, though, vanishing from view, he saw someone else.

Thinking it might be Mann, Dyrne shifted, ready to stand or at least raise a hand for attention. But squinting over at the man, Dyrne could see he wasn't quite broad or tall enough to be his brother, and his posture exuded far less brawn and confidence. He was ambling in their direction on the opposite side of the street. Habit drew Dyrne in; watching without being seen, absorbing the sight invisibly. But as the man grew larger and closer, step by step, recognition clicked like a key in a lock. First the hair: dark brown and curly, not long but longer than Dyrne's. Then the prominent forehead, pale and wide. With a sudden direct glance across the road, making eye contact, the stranger slotted into place, the lock dropping open.

Sapphire eyes.

Even from this distance, now directly opposite him, the piercing, blue spotlights shone at Dyrne, knocking him back against the bench with a thud. Phoebe was roused from her daydream, eyeing him sideways.

It was him. The prisoner. The ragdoll man he had seen restrained in pod chamber 6, out here in the open streets of the city. But now he was dressed in a neat office-suit with shining shoes.

How? Not possible.

"You alright?" Phoebe asked from far away.

"... Mmm," he answered, frozen, still tracking the impossible man walking off. It *was* him. The same person.

Dyrne opened his mouth, ready to explain what had just happened or to ask her to look across at the stranger. But he withdrew the thought like a hand pulling away from flame. She wouldn't know what the prisoner looked like and he couldn't tell her how he'd sneaked his glimpse of him at the pod chamber.

"Dyrne!" His brother's call penetrated his daze. As Mann glided confidently toward them, dressed in his expensive grey suit, Dyrne stood, wiping his fingertips on his trousers.

"You must be Phoebe." Mann reached out with a strong hand to greet her, smiling from his square jaw, showing neat, perfect teeth. Dyrne turned to look back down the street, searching for the ominous stranger, hoping for a final glimpse, but found only empty pavements.

"Good to meet you," Phoebe responded, blushing, or so Dyrne thought, looking back to her.

"Hey, Dee," Mann said, turning to his brother, pulling him into a hug. Looking over Mann's shoulder while pressed to him like a small child, Dyrne saw Phoebe, clasping her hands together and smiling.

Walking back westward, Dyrne watched Phoebe and Mann chatting with ease. Thinking about it now, they were a perfect match, Dyrne realised; both self-assured, buoyant extroverts who needed no help talking to strangers. Mann should go to one of her omni nights. The pair made it easy for Dyrne to assume his usual background role, straggling along beside others, remaining safe and unnoticed. He wondered if he had subconsciously arranged the whole thing this way.

As their voices melded into background chatter, his mind's eye returned to the inexplicable blue-eyed doppelganger and wandered with it. Perhaps the prisoner had a twin, or at least an older or younger brother who looked incredibly similar to him. He glanced at his own older adoptive brother, feeling a flash of envy.

They had arrived at an eatery without any input from Dyrne. They sat at a table in a back corner—Dyrne and Phoebe on one side with Mann on the other—and placed their orders via the table Net, collecting their drinks from the wall-dispenser. Still, Dyrne remained on the outskirts of the conversation, listening to the easy words flowing between his brother and his best friend. He switched between watching their bobbing reflections in the shining, black table top and staring out of the far full-length windows onto the street, surveying the face of every man in a suit who walked by, allowing his thoughts to whirl.

Perhaps he was dreaming again. They had been growing more vivid and more powerful. He had yet to experience another lucid dream, like the night after the omni gathering, but maybe it was happening now— the dreaming mind placing different random elements of his life together in one illogical scenario: Phoebe, Mann, the prisoner, a lunch cafeteria. He tried to make himself float up from the table and out through the window. But no success. This was reality.

He arrived at the most obvious explanation: the tired and confused walls of his mind were collapsing in on one another; an illusionist playing tricks on himself. In his exhaustion, he'd implanted the vision of the captive on a distant stranger across a road in a part of the city he rarely visited. He had experienced headaches before during busy visit cycles and had heard other historians complaining of the same affliction. Was madness finally claiming him?

"Didn't we, Dyrne?"

"Sorry?" He snapped back to Phoebe, who waited for his response.

"I was just saying," said Phoebe, "we heard someone talking about a ghost recently, didn't we?" Dyrne's memory jumped to Sarai and the 'Spirit World' book he'd seen. "Francis's friend, Luna, at my apartment?"

Dyrne sank further back against the chair, studying her with caution. "... I think we did, yes. What made you bring that up?"

Why is she talking about this?

"The building is haunted, apparently," said Mann, leaning on the table.

"What building?" Dyrne asked in a high pitch. "Ours?"

"No, mine. The building I've been working in this week. The one I've been talking to you about."

Phoebe looked at Dyrne, eyebrows raised.

"Oh. Yes, sorry. Of course."

"So where does this rumour come from, then?" Phoebe asked. On one hand, Dyrne was glad for her intervention which removed attention from him. On the other, the idea that they would be talking about the subject at all made him clench. He kept listening, sidling his way around the cliff-edge of the conversation.

"Who knows?" shrugged Mann, taking a gulp of his nutrient water. "But some of the folks there claim to have seen mysterious figures, heard strange noises late at night, the usual crap." Phoebe laughed, cueing Dyrne to follow along. "But it's so weird how they all buy into it. It was one of the first things one of the women who works there mentioned to me."

A young girl appeared with three plates of food, slipping them onto the table.

"Bizarre, isn't it?" Phoebe smiled, pulling her dish over. Ignoring his meal, Mann leaned forward again as if to broach some serious topic or offer wise counsel.

"I often wonder where people get these ideas. I mean, I know the concept of ghosts and spirits, and the supernatural has been around for a long time—how long have people been believing this stuff, Dyrne?" He turned to Phoebe. "Dyrne's the history expert in our family."

"Oh. Yes, I think he's mentioned an interest once or twice."

Both looked to Dyrne, waiting for an answer.

"Um, well, really for millenia, in some form or another. From what evidence there is left, there's been some belief in the afterlife or reincarnation or spirits walking among us, in every civilisation in every place."

"Well, there you go," Mann continued. "I thought omni had taken the place of it all—at least it's based on some research about the mind. But here I am, coming down from up north to New London where you'd think people would be a little more... forward-thinking." Dyrne was sure he saw Mann's eyes flickering in his direction. "And I've got people at the nuclear programme, of all places, telling me about ghosts. Ha!" He gripped his fork and began chopping at his vegetables.

"Well, people must be seeing something," Phoebe blurted, as if defensive.

Dyrne leaned his head on his palm, resting one elbow on the table, biting at his fingernails.

Mann shrugged again, chewing.

"Well, I've never seen anything, have you?"

Phoebe licked the back of her top teeth with her tongue, pausing. "... No."

"But even if I did see, let's say, a shadowy figure, or a holograph fall from a shelf—I don't think that 'ghost' would be my automatic assumption."

"And neither would mine," Phoebe smiled devilishly, dangling her foot over the plunging precipice of the conversation.

"So why do people still do that?" Mann continued. "Why do people assume that visions they can't explain are ghosts—visions from the past? Why not something else?"

"Because we're obsessed with the past." Dyrne's quiet voice somehow rose above them. Phoebe and Mann turned to look, as if they had forgotten he was even sitting with them. "No one cares about the future. It's the past we can't get, well, past." The words slipped like sand through Dyrne's hourglass mouth. He even laughed, his staring eyes unchanging.

Phoebe uncrossed her legs and sat upright.

"I'm not obsessed with the past," Mann protested with an arched eyebrow, his fork held mid-air. Phoebe remained silent, staring.

"Maybe not obsessed." Dyrne blinked and looked across the table at his brother. "But it's all that drives us underneath. It's how we function."

Phoebe eased her way back in. "But... then shouldn't society learn from its mistakes? Why does history notoriously repeat itself? Isn't—"

"—I'm not talking about society. I mean us, individuals. We don't change. Like we discussed before..." He was drifting off into a dream again.

"Yeah well, Dyrne's perception of his past is somewhat revisionist," Mann said to Phoebe, chewing on food again.

Fast breaths and rushing, painful blood pulsed through Dyrne, grabbing him by the shoulders and shaking him from his musing. He pictured a bullet flying toward his chest in slow motion, with no way to avoid it, as if paralysed in one of his nightmares. The urge to make some noise, anything to stop Mann from continuing, burst to his extremities, but he remained powerless. What was about to hurtle from his brother's lips? Dyrne'd never told Mann about the real reason he'd left his University job—never even mentioned Copil. But what if he'd found out on his own?

Please don't say it.

"Dyrne, what happened in stage two school at the swimming proficiency assessments?"

Veering off course like a Line carriage switching track, Dyrne's racing pulse released him. Realising that Mann wasn't going to mention the University at all, he exhaled, feeling himself settle back against the chair, the throbbing in his head subsiding. He had underestimated Mann's sensitivity. To an extent.

"Why?" he asked, knowing the answer.

"Just tell Phoebe."

Turning to face his friend, still eyeing Mann with suspicion yet innately following the order of an older brother, he began.

"Well, I... Mann and I were at the same assessments; it was a small school, all age groups came to the pool together. And... the older boys in Mann's section, they, well, they hadn't seen me in swimming shorts before—"

"And what did they do after that?" Mann shoved the story along, as if helping Dyrne to avoid the mention of his scars.

"They all started sniggering at me. Whispering at first, then pointing. Then laughing hysterically." Mann shook his head ever so slightly while listening, which Phoebe seemed to notice. "Then they threw me in." Dyrne didn't feel his face redden like he used to. Memories like these were plentiful. "The teacher just turned away, ignored me."

"Oh, Dyrne," Phoebe pouted, rubbing his knee, making his leg jerk.

"What *actually* happened," Mann interrupted, "was that one or two boys poked fun at him, as boys do, and Dyrne slipped and fell in the pool. That was it. Mr. Milner didn't even notice."

"No, Mann."

"Yes, Dyrne."

"And you didn't even help me. Didn't… protect me. From those bullies."

Mann looked to Phoebe. "This is what I mean—revisionist. He exaggerated the story every time someone asked him about it after that."

Dyrne watched Phoebe look from him to Mann: like two entirely different species. Mann's handsome smile was bordering on smug. Dyrne remained stoic, hands clasped underneath the table, his thin frame hunched. He wondered which version of the anecdote she believed.

.   .   .

Ambling back to DOHR after leaving Mann at his haunted scraper, Dyrne and Phoebe walked without speaking, side by side. The remainder of their short lunch had rolled on uneventfully with Phoebe and Mann returning to small talk and discussion about the nuclear plans for Edenborough. Dyrne had regressed into his observational role again, saying nothing.

Now, as before, the frosty streets were quiet, and a grey, cotton quilt of clouds blotted out the ivory sunlight. Phoebe thought it might snow soon. Turning a final corner, two blocks away from scraper 84, the looming, elevated news screen glowed down from the flat, otherwise featureless front of one of the buildings ahead.

"Louis Apol set to win Central New London election."

The message vibrated below a large video image of the young, waving candidate, repeating on a loop.

"That's good news, isn't it?" Phoebe commented out of the quiet. Dyrne smiled but said nothing. "So was your brother's version of that story as accurate as he'd like to think?"

"It's accurate for him, but not for me," he said, nuzzling his hands into his pockets. "I don't think he means any harm, but he never knew what I went through at school; teasing, taunting. The isolation. He saw things pretty differently."

She probably hadn't expected such a sudden, open response, he realised. Truths like these usually had to be worked out with a needle. But he'd already turned himself inside out in front of her during his confrontation with Dr. Moth.

"I don't know if you've noticed, but my brother and I don't share quite the same physical traits," said Dyrne. Phoebe smiled bashfully. "While I was too busy hiding my umbilicus scars to worry about swimming, he was winning certificates and top grades, gliding through everything he tried, not just the water. So, of course, he doesn't remember these things like I do." Silence returned for a few brief seconds. "Maybe why our parents didn't see how life really was for me, having Mann telling them everything at school was fine."

"Hmm." Phoebe nodded. It was the most Dyrne had ever spoken to her about his parents, let alone his scars.

He noticed she wasn't saying much. After all her prodding at Dyrne and subtle provocations over time, he was finally exposing his truth to her. Maybe she didn't know how to react.

"Does Mann know about DOHR?" she asked.

He paused for a second before taking another step. "No, of course not. What made you think that?"

"I didn't. Not really. You just looked a bit worried at one point when he started talking about your 'version of the past', like he was about to say too much."

"Oh. It wasn't that. He just... he makes me nervous sometimes—talking about our parents."

"I see."

Dyrne gave her a sideways glance.

Approaching the plain, grey building that housed DOHR beneath its façade, they crossed the street together.

"Are you ready for the next visit then?" Dyrne asked, forcing more life into his voice.

"Yes, just need to check what's up first this afternoon. I think it's—"

"—Observation of work on the Eli Dujohn campaign. Autumn 2225."

"Yes, yes that's right." She grinned as he stepped up to the entry scanner. "I can see why Charlotte changed her mind about the cycle. You know every single detail of this by heart."

"I suppose I do, yes."

Alex had noticed the same thing.

Don't sound so certain next time someone asks. Idiot.

As they face scanned and entered the lobby, Dyrne's focus returned to the inexplicable man trapped hundreds of feet beneath them. Then the compass needle of his brain swiveled around to the same man out walking in the city. And he felt the answer rising toward him like a slow elevator.

35
MAY 2225

A tiny wail echoed along the corridor, followed by the brisk march of three green-robed men and women past the open office door.

"Thought they were birthing a little later today?" Dr. Hawthorne asked the woman beside her, whose name Sarai had forgotten already.

"We're at the beginning of a new schedule, moving to earlier starts this month," the woman reminded her.

"Ah." Hawthorne smiled, looking back at Sarai, who grinned with enthusiasm in return.

Her heartbeat hadn't calmed to a normal rate since entering the facility. A run of bad luck had almost prevented the meeting from taking place at all. Sitting in the small, laboratory office now, she gripped her folder of paperwork in her lap.

"So your Mobile campaign, Miss Tailor—tell us how we can help," the doctor said, clasping her hands over her blue and purple patterned suit skirt, leaning closer to Sarai.

It was a welcome change for Sarai to face so little resistance. Perhaps they were surprised at her young age—something she hadn't disclosed on the Mobile call. Deliberately.

"Well, I was hoping to record some images here, to show people the truth of what goes on." She shuffled in the seat, rethinking the informality of her baggy trousers, recycled sweater and casual shoes. "I think that's what people are scared of most—the mystery, the unknown."

"Mmm." Both women continued looking at her, unmoving, but smiling, awaiting more. Sarai pushed back her paranoia with a loose curl of dishevelled, hair:

"I thought I could also interview you—or some of the other doctors—

to ask about your work, and the infants…" Still, the women watched her expectantly. "And the idea is to piece together short announcement recordings and spread them on the Mobile network, dispersing the message throughout pages and news sites." Her voice had gathered speed as she spoke. "Of course, we'd have to find new sites and groups willing to share our message. As you obviously know, not everyone is sympathetic to the cause."

The uniformed woman spoke next. She was a doctor, too, clearly of some importance, but her grass green tunic and trousers signified she was at least one step lower in the lab hierarchy than Hawthorne. She looked younger than Hawthorne too, whose short, curled, light brown hair reminded Sarai of one of her old school teachers.

"So what is it you'd like us to say? Do you want us to talk through the gestation process, or the adoption procedures? Or do you want some of the staff's personal opinions on metaganic life?"

"Well, yes, all of it, I think," Sarai responded, with a manic nod.

The two doctors smiled at her, as if in mutual understanding of her inexperience.

"Would you like to see the labs?" The green doctor asked.

Sarai hadn't anticipated this level of access. Her worry was replaced by a thrill of excitement at the invitation, clenching her papers again. "Please, yes." Perhaps she wasn't making such a bad impression after all.

•   •   •

The sleek, glossy corridors smelled of bleach. Sarai gazed around, limping behind the quick footsteps of Doctors Hawthorne and Smith— she'd made the conscious effort to remember the second doctor's name after hearing a colleague calling out to her. Trying to keep up with the sharp pace of the two women, skipping every few steps to compensate for the nipping in her ankle, Sarai remembered a museum visit she'd had with her mother as a child.

The short-term exhibit had been an assorted collection of salvaged pre-War pieces of art and random cultural paraphernalia: grainy strokes of colour in wooden frames; bizarelly-shaped abstract formations of glass and metal tubing; crumbling stone imitations of human heads and faces. She couldn't tell if some objects were supposed to look the way they did and had always been like that, or if they were merely the molten debris and rubble of war. Her mother had strode through the exhibition halls, sighing and complaining while Sarai fell back at her heels, trying to absorb the extraordinary items that pulled her in. Despite her mother's disinterest, the memory had remained vivid as one last recollection of childhood magic. They didn't speak anymore.

"Hurt yourself?"

Sarai was jolted out of her memory by Dr. Smith, who'd turned back to face her and nodded down to her leg.

"Oh, yes, it's nothing. Just more bad luck—managed to trip at the top of my stairwell this morning. Not sure how. Near disaster! Caught the banister at the last minute but not without going over on my ankle first."

"*More* bad luck? Are you a jinx Miss Tailor? Should we be worried?" Smith raised an eyebrow, smiling.

"No, no, I hope not!" She laughed, too loudly. "Just seemed to have a series of things go wrong recently! My Mobile calls kept disconnecting every time I tried to organise my visit. Then someone broke into my flat the last time I was supposed to be here... and once before, actually. Although they didn't take anything. Still don't understand that..."

Smith had turned away again as Sarai realised she was probably talking too much.

Turning sharply, the three women channeled down a narrower hallway, reaching a smooth, black door at the opposite end. Hawthorne face-scanned for entry as a beep and the whooshing, disappearing door granted them entry. They stepped across the boundary line before the door shot back into its rigid place, antibacterial mist jetting out from overhead spouts. Sarai held her folder to her chest with tight arms, although realised as she glanced down that the spray had already dried.

She scoped around the stretching laboratory they stood in. Long blocks of black, shining worktops stretched ahead of them, peppered with coloured glass dishes, shiny metallic instruments, test tubes, machinery and glowing screens of text. Two scientists in long, blue tabards leaned over a complicated set of apparatus.

"Fertilisation begins in here," Smith explained. "You know where the DNA comes from. So let's—"

"—Actually, I was wondering if you could help clarify a few things there." Sarai realised she'd raised her hand as if she was back in school.

Both doctors resumed their habit of watching her, waiting for her to say more. Although this time, Hawthorne pursed her lips and leaned back a little.

"Well..." Sarai lowered her hand and fidgeted with a ragged thumbnail. "There just seem to be so many theories amongst the public."

"Conspiracy theories," Hawthorne made a dismissive laughing sound, without smiling.

"Yes, well, I know the eggs and sperm were all provided right before the War, by anonymous donors—people who the government told about the programme, I suppose. But it is confusing, or, I mean, impressive, how many there must have been, for the thousands of synths there are now. I suppose you could be matching up the sperm and eggs in numerous pairings, but... There's just no official release of numbers that I've ever found.

"And, well, there are theories, or *conspiracy* theories, if you like, about how there may be other sources you take the DNA from. Like... other donors who are alive now but won't come out publicly for some reason, or... from, maybe, the... remains of—"

"—Miss Tailor, we don't release specific numbers of the programme's donors in the same way we don't release information about who donated." Hawthorne cut Sarai off with the swift skill of a lawyer in court. "The donation system was designed to be anonymous. Those who created the programme decided it best that the genetic backgrounds of *metaganics*," she enunciated the word slowly, as if correcting Sarai, "shouldn't be known by the rest of the public. Metaganics deserve some level of privacy. Of course, they don't often seem to get it no matter what we do. And these other theories—don't waste your time with them, dear."

Smith had said nothing throughout the exchange, looking at the floor with her hands clasped behind her back.

Hawthorne continued to explain the finer details of the fertilisation process, describing how it had developed over the past 80 years. Her voice had returned to its pleasant tone, like a robot back on track after a temporary malfunction. Sarai listened, enthralled, taking hurried hand-written notes.

"Shall we take a look at the wombs?"

Without having to answer, Sarai was led to the far end of the long laboratory. As they approached, she realised the end-wall was an entire panel of opaque glass that became transparent only at a close distance.

"We like to keep the gestation tanks secluded and protected from bright lights and loud noises," said Hawthorne.

"Although it's perhaps more for psychological reasons, on our part, than anything medically beneficial for the babies," Smith added.

It was the first time either woman had used the word "babies" until now. Something tickled in Sarai's stomach.

Peering through the glass, she surveyed the hidden room. Dim lights that glowed from the edges of the floors and the corners of the room lit up rows of around twenty singular, thick chrome tubes reaching up from the shining floors. Resting atop each were faint blue, silky sacks, shaped like large kidney beans. It was difficult to see what they were made of—glass, plastic, rubber? She could have asked but her open jaw was stuck in place. She knew what the sacks were for, though. Held in each was life. Fragile and real. Another emerald-clad woman paced between the rows, stopping at each womb for a moment, checking small electronic screens attached to each of the tubes. To the far right, Sarai saw movement from one of the orbs. A small dark shape pressed against the shell, before moving off again, back inside. From the top of each tank, a thinner tube jutted out and led down into the base of the chrome stand. Looking around, though, Sarai noticed that although the wombs were roughly the same sizes, the thickness of the tubes varied—some several centimetres wide and some as thin as a finger.

"Why are those tubes different for each womb?" she asked. "Is it because the babies are at different stages?"

"Yes, exactly," answered Hawthorne. "Umbilical tubes. As the embryos grow, we have to detach and replace them with bigger sizes. One of the key things we've never been able to find much of a way around, I'm afraid. At least we've minimised the navel scarring though—used to be much more severe."

"Of course," Sarai mumbled, realising that what she had at some point dismissed as hearsay was fact.

"Well, that and temperature control," Smith continued, folding her arms, also gazing in at the gestation lab.

Sarai stepped back from the glass, turning to listen. "Temperature control?" She realised that Hawthorne hadn't spoken for several minutes, but was listening with a detectable furrow in her brow.

"Yes," Smith sighed. "Even into adult life, we've found that most metaganic people tend to have difficulty regulating their body heat. That's our biologists' main concern. We're not sure whether it's inherent in our fertilisation process or caused by the nutrient composition we feed the embryos, or the wombs themselves—"

"—Ladies. Shall we move on to the nursery?" Hawthorne turned and traversed back through the lab to the entrance. Dr. Smith stopped what she was saying, and followed.

After leaving the lab, Sarai was marched back down the thin hallway and into the main corridor, where they turned left, joining two or three other doctors moving in the same direction. Conversation had ceased, until they passed a glass window looking into a vacant lab room, smaller than the one they had just been in. Hawthorne continued to march ahead, but Smith stopped at the window, looking back at Sarai.

"This was the first lab, used for almost everything in the beginning. From fertilisation right up to birthing, the first metaganics began life here. The rest of the facility grew and was built out from this point after the government realised how necessary it might all become."

"So this is where Edom Morrigan was born?" Sarai asked.

"Yes—Edom. Have you been researching him?"

"More than that—I met with him six months ago!"

Smith looked at Sarai, wide-eyed.

"It was through his daughter—she's at University with me. Well, not with me, but at the same place at least. I was trying to encourage him to get involved in a syn—um, metaganics rights rally I was organising." She could feel Smith's sceptical squint and sped into a race again. "I thought he could speak out about what he'd experienced. And also show how he'd built a full life for himself—even though he seems to have distanced himself from his children a bit…"

"Mmm." She nodded. "And is he going to get involved?"

Sarai's eyes lowered, figuring out how best to be creative with the truth. "I was at his house explaining what I wanted and asking about his parents, and he got sort of spooked about something. I ended up leaving. Never heard from him again and he won't return my calls."

"Hmm. Not surprised I'm afraid. He's a bit of a recluse, isn't he?" She gazed ahead. "No wonder."

Smith turned, picking up her pace to catch Hawthorne, who now stood several metres along, waiting for the pair to follow. Sarai studied the dim, empty laboratory before shaking her head and limping into a jog.

After walking through several other corridors filled with the noises of quick chatter from other doctors and scientists and entrances zipping open and closed, the women scanned through a final set of double doors. Emerging on the other side, the light changed. Instead of shining black, grey and white surfaces and fluorescent lighting in narrow labs, they were now in a wider, open room, glowing with warm, soft light oozing in from a tall window. The constant layer of busy noise outside had faded away, and the smell of menthol and vanilla wrapped itself around Sarai like a quilt. The walls were mint green. Milling around the room, another doctor wandered between six frosted white glass cots in the centre. A twinkling sound chimed from somewhere.

An involuntary "oh" floated from Sarai's mouth.

"We have six newborns right now, another five due by the end of the month," Hawthorne explained, professor-like, with a lowered voice. "Well, seven newborns now. You heard one of the births whilst we were speaking earlier."

Sarai had long since stopped note-taking and gawped around the mellow nursery.

"In the penultimate year of The War," Hawthorne continued, "the Repopulation Programme began with nearly two thousand births. Numbers fell for the most part to around five hundred a year right into the 23rd Century. Right now it's about two hundred each year. Makes it less difficult to home them all at least. We're still offering financial incentives, though. By the way, this is off the record."

"...Yes," Sarai replied, still dazed. She'd studied the metaganic programme since just before beginning University at seventeen. But seeing it here in person felt like she'd been researching in a dark room and now someone had torn the walls down, illuminating everything with sunlight.

"Of course, our purposes are slightly different today. The programme really carries on as a failsafe in case of... well, just in case. A repopulation programme needs to be ready at any time."

Sarai squinted and began working through what Hawthorne was saying. How could the synth programme continue forever in case there was another War? Where was all the DNA coming from? Surely they'd run out of those pre-War donations eventually. Unless they began 'repeating' the same synths at some point. She inhaled, ready to interrupt, before stopping herself, remembering how irked Hawthorne seemed to be at her last set of questions.

"Of course, most people don't realise the extent of our research into genetics and natal medicine."

Sarai gazed around again.

"I feel so strange. Like I've been waiting to come to this room for years. Like I have some sort of... connection to it... all this."

"Sounding very omni there, Miss Tailor." Smith smiled. Hawthorne shook her head a little before turning away.

"No children of your own?" Smith then asked.

Sarai was jolted out of the stupor she had fallen into. Something had pushed past her shoulder, and a breeze ran its fingers through her hair.

"... No." She blinked, turning to Smith, then looked around, confused. "Not yet, I'm only twenty-one."

"Oh," Hawthorne twisted back to Sarai, inspecting her face. "You seemed... more mature, when you contacted us."

"Any younger siblings? Nephews, nieces?" Smith asked.

"No. No, I'm an only child, small family. Why?"

"Just curious. And would you like children one day?"

BLEEEEEEEEEEEE!

All three women winced. The piercing wail swallowed the room and cut through Sarai's head.

"Chemical alarm!" shouted Hawthorne. "Everyone out, follow me!"

The two doctors about-turned, rushing back to the door they had come through. The others in the room hadn't even waited for Hawthorne's command and were already gone, the automatic door clicking shut behind him.

"What about the children?" Sarai yelled above the din, gesturing to the tiny, static cribs that lay forlorn in the middle of the room—unwanted eggs abandoned in a nest.

"We leave them!" Smith shouted. Hawthorne had reached the door now.

"Why? Why can't we take them? We can't just leave them alone in here!"

"Protocol! In an emergency we leave everything! Come on, Miss Tailor!" Beckoning her over, as if about to take her by the arm, Dr. Smith urged Sarai toward the door and out of the room, the blaring alarm still shrieking out above everything. "They'll be fine—they're being monitored by the machines!"

Pulled by the elbow, Sarai stopped resisting and allowed herself to be hurried out. Unable to refrain from giving a final look, though, she glanced back at the six vulnerable white boxes.

A translucent grey shimmer hovered by one of the cots, choking her breath.

"There's—there's smoke in there! There's smoke beside the babies!" She called to the two doctors.

"There's no smoke, Miss Tailor. It's not a fire alarm."

"I saw something though!" She insisted.

"Will you move, Miss Tailor?" Hawthorne snapped. "There is no time for this! Out!"

Gripped by tight fingers, Sarai was forced out of the building, leaving the children behind, the thin blur of eerie light still wavering in her head.

36
JANUARY 2226

Yawning, Sarai squeezed through the heavy door, pressing it open with one awkward elbow, hands full with folders. It banged behind her as she slumped back against it. She eased off both shoes before depositing the bulging bag and papers she carried into a new pile beside the couch. Lightposts outside shed a dull light through the small window covering everything in a faint glow, and she had to wave both hands in the direction of the sensor before the overhead tubes flashed on, one of them flickering every now and then. Home repairs had been low on her list of priorities for some time now. In the months leading up to graduation, life between her voluntary work and studying had been squeezed in a vice. She knew she ought to get the place fixed up before leaving next month, though.

Removing her over-sized, maroon coat, she threw it across a table strewn with worn, fading placards and dropped into a chair in front of the Mobile, setting off the automatic face scan, zipping it to life. "Smith," she called to the machine. The picture of the doctor in her green uniform appeared on the screen.

As the tone buzzed and she waited for an answer from the other end, Sarai leaned her head on one hand, glancing around the messy kitchenette. Her stomach growled.

"Hi. So how was it?" Heather asked through the speaker.

Sarai looked back to the friendly, freckled face waiting behind the glass. Heather was at home, out of her uniform and draped in casual beige, laying on a long couch.

"It was... OK. Not quite as good as I'd hoped," she replied, rubbing the sides of her mouth.

"as good?"

"Yes, well, I mean, not 'as good', but... as easy."

Heather laughed, leaning back. "If you thought a job in government would be easy then you'd better get out now while you can."

"It's not a job yet, they don't pay us for these internships. Graduation isn't until next month."

"Hmm, so councilor Dujohn promotes slave labour then," Heather added, raising an eyebrow. Sarai understood her scepticism. Working in the metaganic field for so many years, facing opposition from some cohort of politicians every day, it was no wonder she'd become cynical.

"It's not slave labour if I volunteered for it! And hopefully, the experience will result in a job offer at some point." She could hear her own naïveté.

"Mm, very omni of you—willing your future into existence with nothing but optimism!" Heather grinned.

"I've met a few government officials already and Eli has introduced me as 'an advisor'."

"Oh, Eli. On first-name terms, hm? Were you nervous being up there in front of everyone? Or is it second-nature now?"

"Not quite second nature but I've gotten used to my nerves. I mean, there are worse things, and this is so important." She was gazing downward in a dream, staring at nothing in particular, rubbing her face again.

"And how was the audience?"

"Not exactly receptive." She reached back, untying her mane of burgundy hair and rubbing it loose. "I thought most of the people who came to hear the new manifesto would be supporters, and a lot of them were. But so many just wanted to complain."

"Ha, sounds familiar. Bigotry is louder than acceptance. They're the ones who want to say their piece. It's easy to forget there are those who value equality—they just tend not to have a reason to mouth off."

"Eli's not even suggesting anything particularly radical. Just trying to break down the discrimination barrier—removing the mandatory declaration of birth status on job and housing applications. I thought I'd be used to it by now, but it's still so difficult hearing these people—the ridicule, the irrational ideas, the prejudice. The fear."

Heather sighed. "That's it, Sarai. Fear."

"People are obsessed with knowing which family lines the DNA comes from and who the donors were. They can't bear this element of the unknown."

"Hmph." Heather gave a quiet sort of laugh. "You've said that before."

"And don't you agree?" Sarai propped herself up on the couch, leaning on her elbows, frowning.

"I think that's part of it for a lot of people, yes. But I don't think everyone is as ignorant as that about the programme anymore. In fact, I think it's something different altogether. I don't think people are afraid of where synths come from. I think people are afraid of why synths exist in the first place."

Sarai squinted back.

"Those people you met today don't hate synths because their ancestors are a mystery. Almost the opposite—those people hate synths because of what they *do* know about them."

"What they know? What do you mean?" She leaned closer to the Mobile screen. Had Heather been holding back secrets about the programme this whole time?

"Think about the purpose of the programme, the facility, Sarai. Metaganics are still being born in our labs in case one day... it happens again. A second War."

"Yes—but—well, not just that; you gather other medical research..."

"We do, but let's be honest: that's all just by-product, no matter what Hawthorne says. Metaganics exist to serve one primary function. And if there was no chance of anything like another War happening, the programme would be rendered unnecessary. They would have shut it down long ago."

Sarai nodded, eyes fixed on some far away spot.

"Their existence implies the likelihood, the expectation, that there could be another War. No one wants that ever again. It was over a hundred years ago and we're still living with its repercussions."

Sarai squinted, trying to work her way through the theory.

"Even still, why would this make so many people hate them the way they do? I understand their fear of War, but the discrimination goes beyond that."

"Well that's another thing—it's more than fear alone. It's resentment. Metaganics represent those who will live on if we try to wipe ourselves out again. People see it as unfair. They hate the synths because they are advantaged. Superior."

Sarai scratched at her scalp, blowing out through puffed cheeks. She'd called Heather for a chat; a chance to relax and forget the day. Now the conversation was anchoring her down into a dark sea.

"Just my thoughts," said Heather. "So… did you just have to stand on the podium and look pretty or did Dujohn actually let you get involved?"

"He asked me for clarification on a few things about the programme. It really would've been better if you were there—you could have explained things better than I did. Eli even let me answer a couple of the questions—paranoid worries about metaganics being clones of dead enemy soldiers."

"Impressive."

"And then someone accused me of being a hypocrite."

"What? How?"

"Well after saying something about the adoption process and how important it is to encourage people to become parents—like you and Hawthorne spoke to me about—a man in the audience asked why I hadn't adopted yet. Said I should come back and lecture them when I'd adopted 'one of those things' myself."

"Did he realise you're twenty-one?" Heather laughed, raising her voice in disbelief.

"Obviously not—I don't think."

"And did he ask Dujohn the same question?"

"No."

"No, of course not. He's a 'he'."

"Anyway, some of the lights blew at that point. Sort of brought it all to a halt."

"Lights blew?"

"Yeah, they just sort of fizzled out. One of the tech guys was trying to figure out what had happened afterward—some wires had been pulled loose or something."

"Hmm." Heather frowned.

"The adoption thing, though... it's stayed in my head. Shouldn't it be something I'm thinking about? Eventually—"

"—Who was that?" Heather shouted. She sprang forward, her eyes searching through the glass beyond Sarai to the flickering background.

"Who? The man who asked the question?" Sarai responded, bemused.

"There! In your flat! Is someone with you?"

"What are you talking about?" Sarai turned to look over her shoulder around the four static corners of the cluttered living space, the light tube still blinking intermittently. "There's no one here."

"I'm telling you, Sarai, someone just walked past behind you. A man or something." The light flickered off.

A slow frost crept across Sarai's neck. Never dreaming of saying it aloud, especially not to someone like Heather who was grounded in science, Sarai leapt to the instant idea of something otherworldly. A spiritual form. Not the first time she had felt this. She had even read about it in the few existing pieces of literature she could track down on the subject, including one of her own books—an inheritance. Swallowing the notion, she shook her head and pretended to laugh.

"The only thing here is this absolute mess I need to finish packing." She gestured with an open hand, not turning her eyes to look at what might be behind her.

"There's something very odd going on, Sarai. It's weird."

Struggling to stay afloat in her sudden vulnerability, Sarai recoiled at Heather's words. Was it an accusation? Any use of words like 'weird' and 'odd' sent her spinning in circles back to school days and pointed fingers singling her out; images she had made sure to banish from her brain. Heather continued staring with a raised eyebrow.

"I'd better go now, anyway. My thesis still isn't done, and Dujohn gave me some paperwork to glance over for some thoughts."

Listening again, Heather leaned back from the screen. "You're still going to do that tonight? Get some sleep, girl. You've had a long, important day."

"Long yes, but important—not sure yet."

"Give yourself a bit more credit. Myra Hawthorne didn't let you visit the facility last year for no good reason. Even she saw how dedicated you were."

"Well, we'll see one day, hopefully. I just want someone to look back on all this and see that we made a difference."

"Mm. Hopefully, there'll be people left to be able to look back."

Sarai felt another shiver she couldn't explain.

After ending the Mobile call, she stretched her limbs, cat-like. Putting off both food and sleep, she delved into endless electronic pages of the dissertation. Although she knew it could be tackled in the morning, she had decided that continuing to work on past midnight was preferable to turning to sleep in the unknown dark just yet.

<h1 style="text-align:center">37
APRIL 2226</h1>

Sitting in silence, alone, Sarai stared ahead with the prototype Net resting in her lap. On the other side of the tall windows, the white city rolled out below, a two-dimensional, distant carpet from here; unreal and disconnected. The new family-sized apartment stretched behind her while her still-unpacked boxes lay dotted around with plenty of room to walk around them—unlike the old flat. The fuzz of silence thickened the air. Everything magnified her isolation.

The first thing she'd done was hang her degree certificate on the wall, where it now glinted back at her. In the end, she hadn't achieved the classification she had been aiming for—some of her research papers vanished before the final submission—but had been offered a government advisor position from Minister Dujohn's team nonetheless. She had accepted without much hesitation, knowing that opportunities for her to work elsewhere may have receded, with legislated synth discrimination and unchecked hate crimes rising more than ever. Now she sat, considering a new path.

The adoption application glowed from the Net screen resting on her knees. She looked down at the grey pinstripes that signaled her entrance into adult life. She'd be one of the youngest people requesting to adopt a metaganic baby, she thought. But she felt it would be her inevitable duty and was determined not to be labeled a hypocrite; another undesirable name she could do without. Talking about metaganic adoption hadn't been enough to make real change. She had to set an example through her actions.

Sarai pictured herself as a first-year student four years earlier, determined to take on the activist role and make a genuine difference to the metaganic cause. She'd been ignored at every other organisation she'd joined, even laughed at by a group of girls who didn't seem to think much of her dyed hair and odd accent. The synths she'd met, though, had laughed at her jokes, indulged her theories, let her join them.

Now here she was, suited up after a day in a government office, sitting alone in her oversized, lifeless apartment, preparing to become a mother. Shaking her head, she lifted the clunky square Net and wrote on the screen.

A grunt. Someone behind her. Turning in fright, knocking the Net to the floor, she peered over the back of the armchair around the near-empty room. Nothing.

It was happening again. This feeling. Something was with her, she knew, yet the barren apartment lied, telling her there was no one. Sarai eased herself to her feet and crept toward the hallway, craning along it for any sign of movement, knowing at the same time that there would, of course, be no explicable source. No person at least. Tick. Creak. Nothing. She squinted into the dark corridor, listening. Then the thud and spill. Leaping up, her nerves seizing her body in a tight grip, she almost tripped backward. She jerked her head around to look into the kitchen. Chips of amethyst scattered around the floor like stars on an astronomy chart and the seeing cards flowed like surf from the black silk wrapping. The box had tipped itself from the table, emptying its archaic contents, mocking their uselessness.

Next was the smash. The frame of the degree splayed out in bits. The thick piece of paper flopped face-down on the floor. Sarai stared at it through a film of catatonia before exhaling, shuddering.

She abandoned the apartment. It lay desolate for a week. Home to the ghost.

38
DECEMBER 2270

Murmurs spread through the carriage around Dyrne. Pairs of commuters began chatting, the fervour increasing, while others annunciated more clearly on Netcalls instead of mumbling in their usual morning drones. Even those sitting alone became more animated, shuffling in their seats and looking around to others with excited glances. The sun, showing itself now, glowed through the windows. Dyrne shifted his weight to one side, glancing over the shoulder of the man in front. His own Mobile had become more unreliable than ever and he had stopped reading from it on the Line every morning. All the research he would ever need was complete anyway. After the man in front had calmed his frenetic bobbing, he held his Net with a steady hand. The news site headline became clear: "Election Result: Dr. Scholtz wins Central New London."

The building energy spilled from the carriage into Central New London station and beyond. It flowed from person to person down each narrow street out to the city's extremities. They drank it in. The large humming news site screen close to scraper 84 projected bold images of the capital's newest election winner for all to admire, waving a stiff arm to a waiting crowd. A clear margin of votes, apparently. No mention of Louis Apol. Dyrne bowed his head and carried along his route.

Even entering DOHR, the lab floor was busier and more alert with historians gathering in packs and shooting across paths between workstations to chatter. He could just make out their words—discussing the election results—and sensed the friction of responses. Most people smiled, but others folded arms and shook heads. Diverting straight to his cubicle, he removed his frontpack and scanned into his Net. At the same time, a cackling laugh pierced his eardrum. Wincing, he glanced through the uncovered glass and watched Geraldine with her head back and mouth open, a spiderweb streak of saliva stretching between her lower and upper teeth. As she leaned in, Dyrne was sure he saw her squint his way with disparaging, beetle-black eyes. He turned back to the Net and tried to convince himself that it was paranoia, clawing its way back to him. He shunted the thought for now, as he spotted the familiar blinking, white icon in the corner of the screen. Opening the Alert, his heart pummelled into overdrive with dreaded familiarity.

Sender: C. Hould.

'*Mr. Samson, please meet me in my office as soon as you receive this.*'

The blunt message punctured him like a blade through a parachute. Geraldine looked away again as soon as he eyed her.

He grazed the glass with his knuckles at first. Gulping, Dyrne knocked again, too hard the second time. He pictured one of the older government officials pulling the door open, studying him with a sneer and beckoning him inside with a subtle jerk of the head. How would they question the historians? Would there be a panel? A Netcall to some other, even more secret government facility somewhere? Or a machine? Some kind of beeping, metal monster to be strapped and hooked into to detect his lies?

"Come in, please!"

Or had Hould told them about his birth status? Discovered his connection to Copil?

Over-compensating and pushing on the door with too much force, Dyrne fell over his feet into the small office, his face already flushing.

No officials. No panel. No machine. His shoulders deflated.

"Mr. Samson, thank you for coming so soon."

"Mmuhhm," he garbled back.

Hould, jacketless, leafed through pages in a red folder, standing half-way down the long meeting table as if she had been waiting for Dyrne to appear. He guessed what she was reading.

"I just wanted to clarify a few things, Dyrne." Her use of his first name frightened him again. "Routine procedure for something like this, but one of your most recent observations—your visit to Tailor after her government promotion..." She glanced up from the folder at him, as if to check his acknowledgment.

"Mhm. Yes," he answered, a petrified little boy, desperate to please with the answers she'd be looking for.

"There was a lot of transference. Mostly kinetic."

Fuck.

Had Alex raised this? Brought it to her attention? Of course, it was too obvious. How did he think he could get away with this?

"Observations with high sighting counts come straight to me above anything else. I have to check up on them."

He forced his body to relax again, straightening his back. Her tone didn't seem accusative just yet, only inquisitive.

"Oh, yes. Of course." He clasped his hands behind him, rubbing moist fingers together.

"Seems like you made quite an impact here. Boxes falling, noises, something smashing. What do you think led to this?"

She still seemed to be asking innocuous questions, assuming Dyrne wasn't deliberately doing anything, merely asking what he 'thought'.

"Well, it—it tends to be the pattern that as a cycle goes on, transference goes up. I—I think we begin getting used to the surroundings in the visits and can become too... comfortable."

Stop stuttering.

"I was exploring some items and thought I was out of sight of the subject," he went on. "I needed to be more careful, more gentle, really."

"Mm." Hould made a noise somewhere between a purr and a growl. Then she nodded, looking back to the pages again. Was this enough? Or was she as good an actor as he, assessing his performance, measuring the degree of his deception?

Taking the initiative, he leapt forward, adding, "Of course, there's also only so much control we have over these things—the physicists and us. Sometimes transference is an inevitable part of the process."

It was obvious she'd already know this, but she nodded, before tilting her head to one side, as if weighing up probabilities in her mind. He couldn't resist his body any longer and swallowed sticky dryness loudly. Hould spoke again, her voice changing, lowering just a fraction.

"You remember the meeting I called a few months ago? Before the regulation changes?"

"Mm."

"There are scenarios we wish to avoid." She looked up again. "Remember what I discussed with you—everyone? About our work affecting events? Important events."

His fingernails pinched the flesh of his palms, and he was aware of his vibrating heat. For those few moments while she spoke, he was convinced. She knew. It was over. He balanced on the outside edges of his shoes, desperate to speed up time and vanish from the room that felt as if it was shrinking around him, Hould growing larger and larger. But cowering from her, she only looked back at him, waiting for the simplest of responses.

"Yes. I do," he heard himself say, just loud enough.

"Now, I know you know this, Dyrne. I just need you to remember it. This incident could have been harmful, affected whatever Tailor was doing at the time."

'*Whatever Tailor was doing at the time.*' *She doesn't even know.*

He exhaled again. Hould hadn't read Dyrne's entire report—probably hadn't even watched the recordings. Nothing about the adoption application. He felt the tense wires stretched across his skin release a notch.

"Oh, of course. And I wouldn't allow the cycle to continue if I thought such impacts were taking place. I couldn't do that." The most blatant lie he had spoken aloud yet. And with each word he knew the end was coming, presenting itself: a swallowing, inevitable blackness. The shame would assume its place deep in his chest as soon as the meeting was through.

"OK," she replied. With a shiver, he edged himself back to his flat soles: a stranger inside his shoes. "As I say, just a routine check, Mr. Samson." And as she smiled and turned away, giving silent permission for Dyrne to leave, he closed his eyes and felt himself sink deep into his hollow body, leaving his old self behind in the room; another relic to be added to a glass case on Hould's shelves.

• •

"What the fuck have you been doing?" The seething words hit him as his left arm was gripped from somewhere and pulled into his glass cubicle, his other elbow whacking off the hard edge of the entrance. Phoebe's furious face appeared and burst through his daze, her green-eyed glower like some chemical fire. Now on high alert, he saw his glowing Net screen behind her. The end of his last visit paused on the glass. Printed copies of his reports lay scattered on the desk.

"Well?"

"God, Phoebe, what the hell is it?" He pulled his arms from her grip, fearing the worst but refusing to relent. He'd surrendered to complete deceit now anyway.

"Your visits, Dyrne! All this shit with Sarai Tailor—the transference. What are you trying to do?" Each word became less shrill and more desperate, her eyes glistening.

He opened his sticky mouth to find the words he wanted. "... Why are you even looking at my visits? Why are you at my desk?"

"Geraldine saw you going into Hould's office—again. She said you'd been called in about your last visit. I was worried. So I watched it."

Dyrne squinted, inhaling to speak before she cut him off.

"I am on your team for God's sake—would've thought I could watch the recordings. I see now why you've avoided showing me."

"Why is Geraldine even reporting to you on where I am? How did she even notice? She must have read my fucking screen. Or been watching me or something." Geraldine, he noticed through the wall, had conveniently disappeared from her desk.

"You're avoiding the issue, Dyrne." She stared at him, boring through his skull. Dyrne was cornered; trapped like the rat, he'd always been called. But she *could not* know. Desperate to fabricate an explanation, he fought to ignore the pounding heartbeat and squealing blood slicing through his thoughts. But Phoebe spoke before he could.

"Are you... trying to sabotage the metaganic programme even further? ... Stop yourself from being born? ... Kill yourself?"

He watched tears dribbling down her face, burning him like acid. He felt his own throat swell and heat build in his chest. Everything he had wanted to avoid was happening.

"No." He crumpled into the chair, burying his face in hands. "No, Phoebe."

"You *are*, Dyrne." More tears running now as she wiped them away with frustrated hands. "You're trying to stop Sarai Tailor from getting anywhere, from saving the adoption programme, from promoting the few synth rights she did. Why are you doing that to yourself?"

He thought that holding more guilt was impossible, but now here it was, piling on him again and again, pouring into edges and crevices inside that he didn't know existed. It saturated him.

"Phoebe, no. Please stop crying." His voice was congealed, knotted. He tried to take her hand, but it drooped by her side as she gazed down at him with bleary, reddening eyes. "I promise you, I'm not trying to—to do that. I know *you* might want to kill me sometimes, but I don't, sorry to disappoint." She managed a sad smile, but no laughter. He carried on, trying to convince her. And himself. "I've had a lot of transference on the visits—I'm guessing you've seen. That's what Charlotte was talking to me about. Just a routine check because I'd had a lot. It's fine, sorted now. I've to continue as normal. She's checked everything over."

Lies.

"I didn't mention it because it's, well, a bit embarrassing," he carried on. "Even Alex has been laughing at how clumsy I've been."

More lies.

She kept staring at Dyrne, and he couldn't tell if she was listening or judging.

"Look, the cycle's nearly over isn't it? All your visits for me have been great, incredibly insightful. And I only have one last visit. Still here, aren't I? If I wanted to kill myself there are a hell of a lot of easier ways, I'm sure. Chuck myself on the Line in front of the morning carriage. Overdose at an autochemist. Come live with you and your mood swings for 24 hours, or so Francis tells me." Finally, a laugh, and more rubbing of bleary eyes. "Come here." He stood again, hugging her, not caring who might see and wonder why. No point now. She breathed hot sighs into his bony shoulder, and he turned her, glimpsing the Net screen, still frozen on the image of Sarai's haunted apartment.

"God, I'm sorry," Phoebe soon managed, sniffing and pulling herself back, pushing hair away from her face. "I just worry about you, Dyrne."

"You shouldn't. I know you do, but you shouldn't," he replied through a smiling veneer. "I'm fine. It's all going to be fine."

He watched her rub her pink cheeks, knowing that he had caused this and that he was now responsible for her unwarranted apology. He also realised that he was catching sight of, not the past for once, but the future. A potential future. This would be her reaction if he *had* tried to kill himself. Or if he vanished from DOHR after manipulating Sarai's life enough. Or whatever would happen to him. He still didn't know.

He forced the conversation away in a new direction. "Well, seems like there are bigger problems to worry about." She looked back at him, furrowing her brow. "The election results. This Dr. Scholtz. Thought he was some kind of ultra-conservative."

"Mhm?" Phoebe responded, still confused.

"I thought Louis Apol was certain to win."

"Who?"

• • •

Lurking like an assassin, Dyrne perched on the edge of the seat, one hand clutching a thin, black folder. He was ready to pounce when the time was right. Some of the lights in the other half of the labs had turned off, and the omnipresent electric buzzing filled the air, interrupted by his stomach groaning. Behind him, the government officer who patrolled the elevator door to the pods had begun pacing. Dyrne had even caught him yawning a few minutes ago.

Since Phoebe's breakdown, he had spent the rest of the day presenting a façade of laughter and nonchalance, visiting her every hour or so, making sure she was kept amused and preoccupied. Underneath, the insidious paranoia that she would mention her suicide theory to anyone else in the building, even by accident, gnawed at him. At one point, when Hould had emerged from her office to speak to one of the physicists at the Hub, Dyrne had told Phoene an embellished childhood story about Mann, just to keep her attention fixed on him without distraction.

Almost every grain of sand in his hourglass aligned. Phoebe was conciliated. Hould was appeased. Alex hadn't reported or even noticed Dyrne's deliberate transference. And he knew how to manipulate Sarai Tailor through a veil of fifty years; how to stop her adoption of a son; how to prevent Copil's death. The stored pieces of amethyst, the turquoise ring, the silk-wrapped seeing cards, the spirit book. She believed in mysticism, ghosts, the supernatural. If anything was going to influence her decisions, it would be a sign from 'beyond': an illusion Dyrne had the power to harness.

And it was already working. Phoebe hadn't even heard of Louis Apol— the liberal, metaganic rights-promoting man she'd asked about just days ago. Her blank face when Dyrne had mentioned his name had shaken him with thrill and sickness. On one hand, he was achieving what he wanted: affecting Sarai Tailor's actions, creating a ripple of consequences, editing life. On the other, he was inadvertently wrecking what Sarai had worked for: synth equality.

The single sand-grain that still stuck was the intruder. Somehow Dyrne knew he was important; connected to all of this.

After Phoebe and the others had gone, he waited, staring at Hould's office door with the new plan whirring in cycles through his mind, practising every detail. All the while, behind the din of everything else, the captive man constantly signaled out to him—a distress flare from pod chamber 6. He'd kept track of how often the agents switched position— seldom—and had concocted the beginnings of schemes and possibilities. But for now, this had to be kept in a bottom drawer of his brain.

Seeing the glowing light turn off in Hould's office, he sprang to his feet as she exited and closed the door behind her, locking it twice with a beeping sound. He would have to do this without the bold encouragement of relaxant fizzing through him. He thought back to that lucid dream and closed his eyes, remembering the feelings it had given him. Control. Freedom. Snaking his way to the main elevator so that they would arrive at just the same moment, Dyrne appeared at her side, surfacing from the empty glass maze. Hould twitched in fright.

"Doctor, I was just leaving too. I stayed late to work on something extra." He didn't even give her time to respond as he held the folder out, guiding it to her one empty hand.

"Oh. Thank you, Mr. Samson." She had no option but to take it. "It's late, even for me."

"After our meeting earlier, I just felt this was important."

She looked down at the thin, unmarked plastic cover, showing no immediate interest in opening it. The elevator clunked into place behind the silver door.

"It's one final visit alteration, for my current cycle, in light of what I've uncovered while observing Tailor." He chose his words carefully as they both stepped into the lift, Dyrne squeezing through the door right by Hould's side. She glanced at him with a raised eyebrow.

"It's a little late in the cycle to be amending your approved plan, Mr. Samson." Her stubbornness made him wish she *was* using his first name now. At least that would be a sign he had penetrated formality.

"Yes, yes, I understand, Doctor, but again, considering what the observations have revealed, I feel this could be essential to understanding Tailor's motivations... like we initially talked about."

She paused, looking ahead, before sighing. "I'll read through it tomorrow, Mr. Samson. This kind of document shouldn't be leaving the facility." She transferred the folder to her other hand, holding her briefcase down by her side.

"I was hoping you could take a quick look right now, just to give me your thoughts. It would be helpful..."

She blinked, pressing her eyes closed for a second longer than felt normal then turned to look at him. He could feel her scrutiny, unraveling his pretence and peering right into him.

"It's just that I've been working on this all day and..." He faded off once more. After more silent seconds she blinked again and with a half-frown lifted the folder and flipped it open, scanning the few pages. Dyrne took the chance to wipe his forehead on his sleeve, as he chewed the inside of his lips, awaiting her verdict.

"And this isn't already documented?" she asked, after glancing over the pages.

"Well no. It was only on the last visit I overheard her making a Netcall arranging this. And the paraphernalia I spotted in the visit we discussed earlier seems to suggest it might be an important influence. One that hasn't been investigated or catalogued anywhere."

Another pause.

"We usually shy away from the paranormal here, Dyrne. For obvious reasons."

This time it was he who stared back without words, hoping that he could use her habit against her, encouraging her to fill the space.

"But if it's the last visit in the cycle..." She sighed.

Dyrne suppressed a smile.

"And if this can tell us something we genuinely don't know about her..." she said. "Brief Alex on it in the morning."

"Thank you... thank you," he uttered, stepping back a little and pressing a hand against the elevator wall.

As the lift slowed to a halt, the door shot open revealing the pretend world of the foyer, the huge security agent standing guard as a permanent fixture.

"Oh, and Mr. Samson," Hould added, stepping out onto the marble floor, "try not to be seen on this one."

39

He stayed awake.

Whenever the nightmares made him too afraid to sleep, he would sit with light tubes on in the living area, re-reading books and distracting himself with thoughts of Phoebe, Yusuf, Alex, Hould, Mann, his father. Anyone except Copil.

But tonight he stayed awake with a new compulsion: he was a sponge, soaking up every second left. The need to sense and experience everything—something he hadn't done in five years—was inescapable. He was now, ironically, living; his reward for what was coming, although he couldn't allow himself to think of it as that.

In the silent, dark flat, he was a blind man regaining his sight. Leaning on the living room windowsill, he watched the soundless street outside and everything in it bathing in glossy moonlight. Leftover rain made pavements and gutters shine. The chemical clouds had parted, and some stars could even be seen. A rarity. In the opposite building, a narrow window flicked from yellow to black. Were other eyes looking back at him from their silent rooms?

Gazing down at the empty vehicle space by the pavement, Dyrne pictured his brother's expensive and unexpected car that had appeared there a week ago. Mann was leaving tomorrow morning, returning home to Edenborough and his wife and children. Dyrne wondered again what he had really come here for, and whether he'd found it. Probably not. Dyrne could have invited him to stay for the week, or at least the final night. Could have met him every day. Could have agreed to call or visit their father. Could have allowed his brother's arrival to become the beginning of a change for him. A happy ending. But that wasn't the ending he had chosen for himself. He had known since taking the job at DOHR two years ago that he would never do any of these things for Mann.

They had met in the Central Gardens after work where Dyrne gave him a warmer goodbye than he had a welcome. He offered Mann the extra key to his apartment.

"Next time, you can just stay with me for as long as you need."

In practical terms it was pointless. There wouldn't be a next time, Dyrne had figured that out now. But it somehow didn't matter. The gesture was enough. Mann hugged him, predictably, although this time Dyrne embraced it, even hugging back before watching his older brother go, disappearing down a long street and off around a corner, oblivious that this would be their last encounter. In this timeline, anyway. This universe. This dimension. This thread. This life. Dyrne didn't know the scientific term and didn't think asking Yusuf or Alex would be a smart idea.

Exhaling the thought away, his breath clouded the glass. As the misty patch dissipated, two dark, moving figures emerged on the other side below. A man and woman crossed the little street toward his building, skipping over a puddle, looking like they were giggling together. Although observing was usual practice for Dyrne, he wasn't analysing or even trying to memorise what he was seeing anymore. He was just letting it happen, a distant witness to the images flowing beneath him. The couple stopped on the pavement, the man holding the woman closer to him as they kissed. Everything Dyrne hadn't allowed for himself presented itself, like those dramatic pre-War performances on television screens and theatre stages. Love. Excitement. Intimacy. Even his friendships were tempered with the invisible barrier he had created.

The man and woman had disappeared, possibly into the same building as Dyrne. They might have passed him by on the stairs or held the entrance door open for him countless times and he wouldn't have realised. He had only ever watched people when it served a purpose.

For another hour he stayed awake, ignoring the shelves and piles of books and folders he'd become addicted to. Instead, he surveyed the blocks of buildings and lines of rooftops stretching along the horizon and was soon able to hear the faint noises echoing from places he'd stopped exploring, remembering the great breadth of the city he had become deaf to. Nostalgia wafted over him; vague memories of watching the world from his window at night just like this when he was a child while Mann slept in the top bunk. Back then he'd look out and think of the things he would experience one day. Now he thought about the things he'd never experience.

He wondered how different things might have been if Copil had lived. And what would happen if his plan for Sarai worked. Synth rights were changing for the worse because of his interventions. But maybe it could still change. Without a child, she'd continue campaigning, and moving past the setbacks and hauntings. A dingy, crumpled flyer for a synth support group wouldn't be necessary. He smiled.

Knowing he'd need at least some rest, Dyrne slipped back to bed, keeping the small window untinted, watching the inky indigo sky one last time. Allowing the whirring temperature control box to lull him into haziness, he curled onto his side, pulling the thin sheet over his back. He watched the yellow flyer until he couldn't resist his lead eyelids anymore.

A final picture of the intruder floated in the darkness. Wearing a pod suit. Stepping out from a pod. And his doppelganger, walking the streets elsewhere in the city, oblivious. Dyrne's instinctive, psychic feeling of finality blanketed him again with familiarity. Everything that had been consuming his head blended like watercolours mixing, flowing and arranging themselves with sleepy ease.

Dyrne dreamt of his hourglass. Full.

40

After sightwriting the last sentence of her final report on Sarai Tailor, Phoebe leaned back in her chair, sighing. It was after 1700 and the other historians and physicists were either drifting to the elevator or tidying their desks. She'd usually be doing the same but wanted to spend just a little extra time teasing out an idea for her next bid. Pulling her chair closer to the Net screen again, she delved into her Netfiles—morsels of stories and possibilities she'd nibbled at with intrigue but had never bitten into. She might have been further into this process by now had it not been for her preoccupation with Dyrne's recent behaviour. So many oddities about the recordings she'd seen and his unwillingness to run his reports by her. She'd already embarrassed herself in front of him with mad accusations, her paranoia pushing past its boundaries and spilling into Dyrne's workstation. But even though he had reassured her, she still felt a seasick-worry slopping inside.

Thinking about it now, Phoebe wasn't even sure how he'd been allowed to visit Sarai Tailor at all. She was interesting enough, and obviously meant a great deal to Dyrne, but had never, in the end, amounted to much, apart from her synth adoption later in life. She'd been a bit radical as a student and seemed to be a helpful figure in the formative years of one or two of the other well-known activists. But her own career had fizzled out by her mid-twenties. She'd never made much of a political impact.

Phoebe's curiosity about the two older government officers, who had arrived minutes ago and entered Hould's office, had also kept her in the office late. She hadn't seen Dyrne all day so couldn't speculate with him about their presence.

As the noise around her dwindled, urging her to follow suit and shut down for the night, she gave a final glance to a file she'd created over a year ago. It listed references from a myriad of writings and artworks from different eras and countries—lost and existing—all connected to a female figure known as Jeanne d'Arc. Tomorrow she'd investigate the DOHR catalogue further. Ready to disconnect from the Net, a shadow across the screen made her aware of someone lingering behind her.

"I'm going now, Phoebe."

Recognising Dyrne's voice, she turned to find him standing, hands motionless by his side, unblinking.

"Heading home already? Not like you to leave so early."

"No, not home," he replied robotically. "I'm going down to the pods for the final visit of the cycle."

"Bit late isn't it? Everyone's leaving."

"There was something wrong with my pod suit. Then I forgot location notes. Had to come back up. And I got delayed again... But Alex promised to stay. We'll get it all done tonight." He looked right into her eyes the whole time, emoting nothing but some sort of daze. Or something else, like longing. Phoebe nodded.

"... Everything OK, Dyrne?"

He didn't answer at first. Only looked at her as if he was trapped in a vacuum and hadn't heard her say a thing.

"... Yes. Do you think... Maybe I should..."

She stood and threw her coat around her shoulders. "Should what, Dyrne?"

"Never mind. Everything done now. Going to be OK."

He must be tired. Or even at a loss—finishing the cycle he'd waited for and worked on for so long. Maybe he was feeling an anti-climax to it all.

"Great. Well," she chirped, turning to power down the Net, "I expect I'll hear all about it tomorrow. I'm off now. The last of my reports is done. Going to start work on my new bid tomorrow. You know, it's pretty impressive how you gathered all your research on Tailor so quickly. She only died a couple of months ago."

Dyrne was still staring, but took a step back, touching the glass wall behind him. "Well... she'd had the stroke quite a while before that. Was in hospital for a long time so... I sort of... started getting ready then. It seemed inevitable." Phoebe raised an eyebrow and Dyrne looked away.

"I know—it's morbid. And I know I could have just asked her relatives, but she didn't have any—"

"—Stroke?" Phoebe interrupted. "What do you mean? That's not how she died." Dyrne stared again, his mouth miming vowels as if he had lost his voice. "She was addicted to relaxant, Dyrne. That's what killed her. Come on, you've researched everything about this woman. I knew that just from reading news sites."

"...Yes. Yes, I just... I'm getting mixed up." His head fell, shaking side to side.

She rubbed him on the arm. "Long day, eh? Come on, walk me to the lift."

As he followed, she continued chatting, half to Dyrne, half to herself, and weaved through the glass pathway in the direction of the elevator. Fixing her frontpack in place, she noticed Dyrne had fallen a few paces behind, trailing numbly after her. When she stepped into the elevator, turning to give one final wave, his wide eyes hit her.

"Phoebe... Thank you."

"For what?" she giggled.

He looked as if he was searching her face, scouring for the answer in her skin, suddenly unable to speak her language. And as he took one more small step and raised a hand, opening his lips to speak, the silver door snapped closed, deleting him.

41

The silence buzzed as Mann sealed the front door closed behind him. He eyed the corners of the vestibule ceiling, wondering if there was an alarm system, but he hadn't seen Dyrne pressing anything when he'd arrived last week. He waited on the spot for a few seconds, listening, just in case Dyrne had somehow come home already. But he knew there was no real chance of this. Dyrne was addicted to work.

Mann opened the inner door to the apartment before slipping the new key back into his coat pocket. Again, he surveyed the place, observing his brother's habitat. Piles and shelves overflowing with books were at odds with the rest of the untouched, cold room. An un-living room. He knew when he'd arrived a week ago that he'd probably been the first visitor Dyrne had had in months, maybe even years. The fumble to find an extra cup, the obsessive arrangement of every object in its unmoved place, Dyrne's discomfort at sitting in what must have been a 'different' chair. Even when they'd both entered, he had stood in one spot, staring at Mann like he was an intruder; a zoo animal who'd wandered into the wrong pen.

Now Mann took his brother's place, standing on the same floor tile. He glanced over to the kitchen counter, clocking the holograph that reflected his younger self back at him. At least he could tell their father this—that Dyrne hadn't forgotten them.

Dropping his luggage, he sauntered to the couch, flopping down into it, rubbing his face and yawning. His focus rested on the square table in front of him. Dyrne's Mobile. Scratched and outdated. It was odd that he had left it here. Surely he'd use it on the Line to prepare for work? Or maybe the Census department didn't allow them to since they were working with data and information about the public. Mann reached forward and brushed the screen. It was still turned on. No face scan required. It was so old that that part of the software must be defective.

A news site zoomed to the fore.

'*Protests over Scholtz election win.*'

Mann shook his head.

'*Extra police presence required. Damage to news screens in Central New London. Disruption to Line services.*'

"Ah." That explained his cancellation. Next Line to Edenborough wasn't until later that night.

He skimmed through parts of the report and a few other articles. But as he rested the device on his lap, the pages shuffled and a new box floated toward him. In the middle of lines of words, one name stung him, a needle in his eyes.

'Copil Tailor.'

Tailor?

The couch fabric burned his lower back as he shot upright, gripping the Mobile. He scrolled further down the screen. Sarai Tailor's son.

He fucking lied. Of course, he knew, she'd died.

He scrolled further again. And further. And further. Screeds of information, dates, names, alerts, holographs, University documents, adoption paperwork. Endless. Mann's heart pounded with each new page, his stomach lurching every time he read the name.

And this wasn't just notes or idle interest. This was something else. The detail, the minutiae of these two people's lives. Mann's heartbeat choked him. He had peeled back Dyrne like the cover of a book and found something terrifying. Something unknown. A sick obsession. Morbid fanaticism. What was he doing with this level of information? What was he hiding? Lying about?

But Mann had lied too. Had lied for five years. Of course, he knew why Dyrne had left the University job. It was Isabella who'd found the first article at the time. 'Synth equality campaigner's family tragedy'. Same university. Same month. Dyrne never admitted knowing anything about the boy, but they knew he must be lying. Too much of a coincidence. And now the mother was dead. Mann had asked to spend time in the New London office the day after he'd read about it. He didn't know what he'd expected. Dyrne feeling depressed, isolating himself even further, quitting another job even. But not this. Mann couldn't even tell what *this* was.

Dropping the Mobile with a clunk, he leapt up, sickness swaying him. He didn't notice the hourglass tipping onto the floor at first. It was the crunch underfoot as he wobbled that drew his eyes. Tiny pieces of broken glass and scattered sand. Leaving it behind, he stormed to the apartment door. He glanced a final time at his own holograph before lurching through the entrance, a missile aiming for his brother.

42

Dyrne stared at the silver elevator door as it slammed shut. She was gone.

He holographed the image in his mind—her hands, her hair, her green eyes—locking her away. Surely his memories would survive with him.

Turning to survey the empty glass maze of workstations, the only movement was that of soundless shadows passing across the frosted window of Hould's office door every few seconds. The government officials' late arrival had sent electric shivers along his nerves. Glancing to the pod elevators, he realised the usual officer was absent—possibly on a changeover with the two others below, although he'd noticed on some recent nights that no one had stood guard here at all after most of the historians had gone home. As weeks had passed, security was easing up. After all, what harm could a bunch of historians do?

Treading silent footsteps, he traversed the glass-lined pathways to his own desk, picking up the thin mock file he'd have to take down to Alex; he must maintain the act to the last minute. Before leaving, he scanned the cubicle and its contents one last time, wondering what they'd soon be replaced with. His obsolete frontpack and jacket hung by a hook and he touched the scattered files on Sarai Tailor with fleeting fingers. Simple printed words on paper to anyone else; a suicide pill to him.

Gliding to the pod elevator cage, lungs heaving, Dyrne soaked in his surroundings to salvage as many extra seconds as possible. He leaned in to the wall panel to face-scan a final time.

Clunk. Clunk. Clunk.

Machinery behind the opaque door signaled its movement, and with a loud beep, the white entrance slid open. Stepping back abruptly, expecting to be met with the intimidating glare of one of the towering government agents, Dyrne saw, for the first time in days, Yusuf. He couldn't even remember the last time they had a conversation. Their eyes skimmed each other for a moment.

"Evening, Mr. Samson," Yusuf nodded, smiling coolly.

"Hello, Yusuf."

He stepped out and passed Dyrne then stopped.

"I just spoke to Alex. He tells me you're running a little behind schedule tonight."

Accusation in his voice?

"Yes. Long story. Just going down now to... to finish." He forced a smile.

"You may have to wait just a little longer."

Shit.

Dyrne stared at Yusuf.

He's set me up. They're coming for me.

"Not too long, I hope," said Yusuf. "It's just that they're... well, I'm not sure I'm supposed to mention it but, they're moving him out tonight, soon... the man down there."

Dyrne felt the tension in his shoulders melt, his concrete stare dissipating. The prisoner was being moved. It would explain the government officials' sudden arrival.

"I didn't want to stay to see him again," Yusuf muttered, looking down. "You may have to stop as soon as you get down there. I think they're getting ready to open chamber 6."

Yusuf's words melded and swirled in Dyrne's head. The intricate clockwork of images, thoughts and ideas fixed into place, as he gazed back to the open elevator shaft.

"Thank you, Yusuf," Dyrne mumbled back. He abandoned his old friend like an outdated tool and lunged into the waiting, dark elevator. At the same moment, the elevators at the opposite end of the lab all opened in unison. A troupe of guards stepped out, ready to march in Dyrne's direction. The cage doors swallowed him whole, and he descended.

•　　•　　•

Walking along the uniform, darkening winter streets, Phoebe watched the heels of those trotting in front, guiding her toward the Line station. The streetlights had already buzzed to life, and their dim, fuzzy glow magnified her daze. More commotion than usual echoed around her. The dying glimpse of orange sunlight gleamed off one of the shining memorial planks in the Gardens and into her eye, making her stop and switch to a new daydream. 'Saab, Sachs, Sadler, Salisbury...'. The lost family names gilded in bronze made her wonder how different the UE would be now had they lived on and what the world was missing without them. Some she'd even visited.

"Phoebe!"

Instinctively, she assumed Dyrne had called her. Maybe he had left the labs after all. But turning her head, it was someone taller and broader who jogged toward her under the lamplights.

"Mann?"

Dyrne's brother lunged toward her. His face beamed pink and he panted as he spoke.

"Shit, Phoebe. Do you know where Dyrne is? Still at work?"

She paused, knowing that revealing DOHR's location could be tricky.

"I think he's still at the office, yeah. Why?"

"I don't know where that is. He never showed me. I thought waiting by the station would be the best bet for finding him. Can you take me there?"

She sifted through the five or six basic stories she'd been given to memorise in case of questions like these, but still chewed her lip for a second before answering, staring at Mann. He wasn't a stranger. Did being Dyrne's brother make things different?

"Well, I have to get the Line home. I'm in a bit of a hurry to meet my husband. Can't you just wait for Dyrne here? Or meet him at his apartment?"

"The Line's all fucked up because of the Scholtz protests. Delays and cancellations. You won't get home anytime soon. I really need to see him now. Can't you take me?"

She dug her nails into the straps of her frontpack, thinking of the next best alibi.

"Sorry. I should start walking if I can't get the Line. I definitely won't have time to go back to the office. Whatever it is, I'm sure it can wait. Dyrne's fine. I just saw him five minutes ago."

Shit.

She shouldn't have said the last part. Now Mann would know the office was only five minutes from here.

"He'll be leaving soon, too," she blurted.

This lie wouldn't matter. She wouldn't stick around for him to discover it. Mann half-turned away, hands on his hips, as if looking around to figure out which way Phoebe had walked from. She needed to move now.

"Sorry, Mann. Just wait at the station entrance for him. I need to go." She swivelled to move off, but Mann called again, shocking her frozen.

"Do you know anything about Dyrne and Sarai Tailor?"

Her chest spasmed and she tottered, still facing away. Too many seconds passed and she felt Mann's eyes boring into her back.

"Mm?" was all she could manage, edging around to face him again, people skimming past them both.

"Sarai Tailor. The synth rights activist who died. I don't know what or why but something weird's going on with Dyrne. Something to do with her. He's been... stalking her or something. I found an insane amount of information on her in his apartment. Everything about her life you can imagine."

Every sentence drilled into Phoebe's guts. Seven years she'd worked at DOHR without leaking a thing. Not even to Francis. How had Dyrne been so stupid, leaving research lying around in his apartment?

"Well... I guess she must have meant a lot to him. A sort of role model. We don't know what it's like for him being metagan—"

"—This is more than just admiration, Phoebe. It's fucked up. And it wasn't just the woman. There was all sorts of stuff on his Mobile about her son. Copil."

The pummelling in Phoebe's stomach changed. It became deeper, its vibrations changing frequency.

"Her son?"

"Yeah. The one who killed himself. Listen..." Mann reached out to take Phoebe by the forearm, pulling her to the edge of planted gardens, out of the growing river of commuters. She allowed herself to be yanked along by him. "I don't know if you know this about Dyrne, but... he used to work at New London University."

This she knew, but Mann's bulging stare and tight grip let her know there was more. She sensed its enormity like an oncoming Line carriage zooming right to her.

"He taught that boy. Right before he died. Dyrne quit the next week. We always knew there was a connection, that it had messed him up or something, but he won't talk about it…"

Mann said more, but all Phoebe heard was ringing; a supersonic whistling shrieking through her. Pins and needles pricked at her skin all over. She gazed at nothing and saw Dyrne in the labs. Remembered his goodbye. His empty face.

She heard her shoes clipping over the pavements before she realised she was running. Back to DOHR. Back to Dyrne.

Arriving at the deep core of the place, feeling a punch of cold air, Dyrne noticed, again, the absence of the usual waiting agent. Hearing murmurs from the other end of the corridor, he gulped back any remaining fear and stepped forward, working his feet, legs and swinging arms into a stride.

He pictured Mann and tried to emulate his stature.

Reaching the T-junction at the end of the echoing path, he snapped right, marching blithely past pod chamber 5 toward the two black suit-clad imposing agents who stood in front of the closed door of chamber 6. They abruptly stopped talking upon seeing Dyrne. One of them held up a halting palm.

"Where are you going? Your work should be done by now."

Your work.

Did they even know what was going on in these concrete chambers?

"Pod chamber 8. My *session*," Dyrne chose the word carefully, "got delayed. Working late on it."

Blinking, the first guard regarded Dyrne for a moment before easing up and budging a half-step backwards. "Fine. Move on."

Dyrne stumbled ahead, head bowed, scarpering to chamber 8, where the door lay ajar, as predicted. He paused, before pushing it open a little further, and stepping inside.

"Finally!" Alex called out from his raised console platform.

Dyrne didn't answer, though. Didn't even look to Alex yet. He remained where he was, his hands still holding the door edges.

"Well, come on, let's do this," Alex drawled again. This time Dyrne held up a 'one minute' finger in the physicist's direction.

Prizing the door toward him, he snuck a glimpse back out into the corridor. One of the guards stood with his back to Dyrne, blocking the view of the other. He became conscious of his thumping heart. The officers mumbled to one another for a few seconds without moving much. Then it came. Some signal. Some command via a hidden earpiece, or so Dyrne assumed. The guard nearest him stopped speaking and dipped his head, bringing his fingers to the side of his head, focusing on invisible words from some hidden device. Next, he gave a nod. At once, both men stepped back, one gripping and yanking back the heavy black lock across pod chamber 6, the other pushing down on the chunky handle with meaty hands and shoving the door open. They both vanished inside.

Dyrne stepped back into the corridor.

Muffled words. Clanking of metal. The heaving sound of physical effort. Then they piled out. The disheveled, handcuffed prisoner flanked by the two officers like silent executioners. His worn pod suit was stained, emanating sweat. Yusuf had been right. They were moving him. He supposed it was like some omni karmic exchange. It was his time to take the prisoner's place. Pumping blood inflated his throat. The guards moved fast, already jostling the prisoner down the corridor. The heavy heart-thud pulsed in Dyrne's head, banging his eardrums. It had to be now.

"I know who you are." He tried to shout but couldn't tell how loud he'd been over the pounding in his ears.

It was enough, though. All three stopped and turned.

The brilliant blue eyes were bloodshot, straining through falling, greasy, brown curls. They met Dyrne's gaze with an entire gravity of their own. The background buzz of machinery was all that filled the air.

"Thought you might be the first to figure it out, Dyrne." His voice was cracked but gentle.

Dyrne hadn't even paid attention to one of the guards stomping toward him. "Shut up and get in there!"

He had to make his last seconds worthwhile. But what else could he say? Each of the guard's booming steps were ticks on a clock.

"You're a historian." His words spilled out as the heavy hand thudded against his chest, shoving him backward.

"*Was* a historian," the man called back.

"Stop fucking talking to him!"

Gulping hard and craning over the guard's gladiator frame, more words poured from Dyrne, unable to stop yet. "What did you change? In your visits?"

"My mother was killed when I was four. Car crash. Decided the sight of a figure in the middle of the road would be enough to make her swerve the other way."

The second officer grabbed the intruder by the collar, dragging him away. At the same time Dyrne was pinned against the wall beside the pod chamber door with two battering ram arms, his shoulder blades banging into the concrete. Twisting his head to the side, bleary-eyed and useless, he watched his anonymous colleague being hauled off, disappearing around the corner forever. After a few seconds, the guard released Dyrne. He hunched over, panting, avoiding the bulky man's stare.

"Get in there and don't come out! We'll be reporting this to your superiors!"

Dyrne ignored him; the words meant nothing now.

The guard stepped back and turned, striding down the corridor. "Almost managed two months without letting this guy speak to anyone," he muttered, shaking his head.

Pushing the chamber door open again and stepping straight to the corner-bench, Dyrne pulled the waiting pod suit from the shelf with limp hands.

"What the hell was going on out there? Come on, get in the pod and let's get this over with."

"...Yes. Let's. Sorry, Alex. I just had to... figure one last thing out."

"Yeah, yeah, just get a move on."

After mindlessly shrouding himself in the suit, he turned to Alex, holding down vomit, clenching damp fists. He stared at his friend, taking another mental holograph to store in his mind.

Finally, he looked at the huge sphere again. It had magnified itself now. Zipping up the suit, vision darkening, Dyrne's body carried him up the steps into the embracing, open womb of the pod.

43

"I just think you ought to have given me more warning, Michael." Dr. Hould sighed and rubbed her palms together in her lap.

"Look, Charlotte, we can't keep him down there any longer. The guards are saying he's an utter mess. Could barely stand yesterday." Michael Windsor stood with one fist clenched, knuckles resting on the conference table.

"I've been adamant from the start we shouldn't have kept him down there," Charlotte responded.

Rowan Etheridge, hunched over at the opposite side of the conference spoke up. "You should be happy we're getting him out then."

"But I thought you couldn't risk him being outside these walls, talking to anyone? Another prison inmate, a nurse, a police officer—this is what you told me."

"Look, there's no one left in the labs to see him now." Back to Windsor. The two men alternated speaking duties as if they had prepared the routine. Hould noticed he'd ignored her question. "And if we're going to get him in a vehicle we need to do it now, while everyone's preoccupied with these election protests. We've given our guards the order anyway, so there's no point in debating this."

"You're moving him right now?" Hould jutted forward in the seat, pressing her hands on the table edge.

"Yes." Etheridge again. "We checked the visit schedule in advance. All observations are finished today. No more historians or physicists left working."

Hould teetered on the edge of telling them the inevitable truth. There was still one historian and one physicist left. But she swallowed it down. Another few minutes could pass before it would have to bubble up. Besides,

Dyrne and Alex would be in their chamber at this point, the visit underway. They probably wouldn't even witness the prisoner's removal.

"What else was it you wanted to tell me about?" Hould pressed on. "Something to do with your personnel investigations."

"Yes," Rowan spoke, eyeing Etheridge at the same time as if to ask silent permission to continue. "One of your historians. We have a problem."

"If this is about Geraldine Schue, I already know. She was in here this afternoon. Gave me a pretty accurate theory about our intruder. She's figuring it out." Hould exhaled and eased into the desk chair, gripping the underside of the armrests.

"Schue?" Etheridge squinted at her. "No, no."

"Which historian, then?"

"How much do you know about Dyrne Samson's past?"

She pulled on one of her lapels, clearing her throat.

"What I need to: Samson is a former history lecturer, published writer—an expert basically." Her steady voice betrayed the worry gripping her insides. "I don't need to know about his personal background, if that's what you mean."

"You do this time, Charlotte." Etheridge leant a wrinkled hand on the table as if reaching out to grab Hould.

"... So what is it?" she asked.

Both of the elderly men glanced at each other again.

"Do you know who Copil Tailor was?" Etheridge placed his withered hand back in his black suit pocket. Hould watched each of his movements.

"Some connection to Sarai Tailor, I assume. Her son I suppose?"

"Yes—her son," Windsor responded.

"Her adopted son," Etheridge clarified.

"... Oh, yes. She adopted a metaganic. That's right, I read all about this in Mr. Samson's bid application. Died young. Killed or something terrible. Huge impact on the rest of her career."

"A synth, yes." Etheridge spat the words as if they were curses. Hould narrowed her eyes, sinking further back into her chair.

"Let me guess. This all has something to do with Samson being metaganic himself. I do know this. I didn't think your investigations would be so concerned with birth sta—"

"—That's not the problem," Etheridge interrupted. At the same time, muffled voices swam around the labs outside. While Hould wondered what was happening on the other side of the door, neither of the men seemed to hear.

"The problem is," Etheridge continued, beginning to show strain, "that Copil Tailor attended New London University."

Like a holograph emerging from a Net screen, a clearer image of her superiors' message began to unfurl before Hould. The muttered sounds outside continued.

"But," she sputtered, still trying to make sense of it and refute it at the same time, "Why is the fact that Samson taught at the same University—"

"—No, Charlotte." It was Windsor who interrupted this time, sighing and clasping his hands in front of him. A clock ticking sounded amplified, echoing around the room. "Not just the same University. Copil Tailor had been studying Pre-War History. Dyrne Samson was his professor."

The distant conversation beyond the office walls grew closer.

"What is that?" Etheridge turned now. Windsor, the more limber of the two, turned away from Hould to walk to the door. Shock settled in as she saw her rules and meetings and order and control begin to crumble like sandcastles. Opening the door, Windsor stepped out.

"Sir, we've extricated the subject from the lower levels," a gruff voice boomed from just outside.

"Yes, so why are you talking to me? Get him out of here!" Windsor croaked back.

"Sir, we need to inform you—there's been a problem. The captive's identity may have been compromised."

"Compromised? What?"

Hould and Etheridge listened, staring at the open doorway.

"Sir, one of the facility employees spoke to the subject. I tried to stop him, but he continued conversing. The employee seemed to... *know* the subject, sir."

Hould rose from her seat onto melted feet. Her insides sank into hollow legs.

"Dyrne," she uttered, staring off at the shelves.

"Eh?"

"Dyr—Mr. Samson... He's here now. He's down there."

"What?" Etheridge seethed through stretched lips. "In the pod chambers? While we've been moving the prisoner? Why? How? No one was scheduled to be down there!"

Clink. From outside, the familiar sound of the main elevator doors slid open. And now someone was shouting. A woman. Hould's focus shifted for half a second, recognising the voice as Phoebe Rush's. She knew Rush was close to Dyrne. Hould looked back to Etheridge.

"I approved one final visit. Just yesterday..." She swallowed like there was glass wedged in her throat and wiped her sweating hands on her blouse. "But it's too late to stop it now. The visit's begun."

44
APRIL 2228

Stepping into the narrow, purple hallway, Sarai felt like she had traveled back in time. The building was one of the older residential structures on the city outskirts, with its dark stairwell and broken banisters. The flat was dingy, cramped and stuffed full of antique furniture—two cupboards, chairs, small tables, little cabinets—none of which matched. She was already peering back over her shoulder to the paint-flecked door, setting herself a mental time limit for staying—a time limit that kept flickering in her mind. The idea to come here was ridiculous.

"I know what you're thinking—silly amount of things I've gathered over time." The elderly lady in a loose-fitting patterned skirt and ivory cardigan smiled as she showed Sarai the way in.

"Not at all," Sarai lied. "They're lovely." She looked away from the woman as she spoke, worrying about her relaxant-breath as she squeezed by.

"I'm in the process of getting rid of some. Smoothing the flow of the place." Sarai wasn't sure what this meant. "It's difficult, though. They're fascinating; all with their own little histories." The woman stroked the curved back of a worn, mahogany chair as she passed it. "We'll go in here."

She pushed open a door into a much wider room. Sarai felt like they were now in a different apartment. The space was bare, with a small cloth-covered table and two chairs on either side, facing one another. An even smaller, circular table stood beside the farther of the two seats, with a wooden box and some other unusual ornaments on it. The walls were painted a more reassuring bright white and a broad window gave a view of the upper reaches of a leafy garden area below. Some of the trees were beginning to brown. As Sarai glanced across, she caught her faint reflection.

Her hair was tangled, her skin blemished. Her eyes bloodshot. Again.

"Sit down, sit down, dear. Now is there anything I can get you before we begin? Water? Tea?" the woman asked, touching Sarai on the elbow.

"No, thank you," she replied, trying to smile, her voice fluttering. As she slipped onto the chair nearest, it wobbled on one leg underneath her weight. Looking at the small table opposite, she could see that the ornaments were similar to some of her own that she'd inherited from her estranged mother: jagged gemstones, a spherical purple crystal, and a small silver candle melted to a few inches.

The woman sat in the chair opposite Sarai after closing the door. It had taken several months to find her, looking at Net advertisements and obscure pages, asking session leaders at meditation classes, even enquiring at the two remaining churches in the city, much to their disapproval. Sarai had almost given up on the idea of finding one of these fabled voyants until overhearing a conversation about ghosts between two omni women at an equality activist meeting—one she hadn't organised herself. Her focus on the movement had wavered, having other worries occupying her mind, like finding a new job—her employment under councilor Dujohn had been terminated after his recent re-election loss. She'd been staying inside more, too.

"So what brought you to me today, dear? You must have been looking hard. Not that easy to find people like me anymore." The woman sat forward, smiling, joining her mottled hands on the table. A milky stone glowed from one of her freckled fingers.

Sarai let out the sob of a lost child as unexpected tears poured down cheeks that bloomed ruby. She surprised herself, more than the voyant probably. She shook her curled hair before wiping her face.

"I'm so sorry."

"That's quite alright, dear." The woman reached over to pat her forearm, asking for no explanation.

"This is silly, sorry," Sarai apologised again, rubbing at her eyes. "I don't know what I'm doing here."

"Yes, you do." The woman still smiled.

"I know this whole idea isn't popular practise now—I don't mean to offend you. I do think of myself as omni. The others, though... they've said I'm mad for coming here—said this isn't what omni means anymore."

The voyant nodded, blinking. "But why are you *really* here, dear? What is it you've come for guidance about? Are you looking for contact from the other plane?"

"No. No... I don't think I am."

The two women looked at each other across the cloth-covered table for several seconds before Sarai felt the voyant's silent encouragement urging her on.

"I want to ask about... adopting a child."

"Oh."

"Well... a metaganic child. I do a lot of work to promote anti-discrimination and they still need volunteer parents. God, this is why they think I'm crazy—leaving a decision like this up to... Anyway, the metaganics are—"

"—You don't need to explain yourself to me, dear. A child is a child."

Sarai allowed herself to breathe more evenly, wiping a final tear and exhaling. "It's just that every time I've tried to take the process forward, or even just discuss it, things have always happened. Bad things—an injury, things going missing... apparitions." The white-haired voyant looked back at her with a knowing smile. "I've started to think they're signs—that I shouldn't be going ahead with it." She sighed again, closing her eyes and waving her hands palm-up as if knowing every word was nonsense.

Turning to the small wooden box beside her, the woman opened the lid, lifting out a black silk-covered block. Sarai recognised the shape, similar to her own seeing cards; the same cards that had been knocked inexplicably from the box in her kitchen, as if calling to be looked at. She didn't mention this, though.

"I like to use the cards to help advise me, dear. They're a tool for guidance to come through."

"Come through?"

The woman nodded, unwrapping the black fabric and shuffling the long cards in her adept hands. "There's a presence here already. I saw him come in with you."

Sarai closed her eyes, shuddering. She fought the urge to turn around to check each corner of the room. Was it really here again?

"Him?" Sarai asked, trying to steady her voice.

"Mm, I feel a masculine energy, and from the silhouette I glimpsed I'd say it was a male spirit, yes."

Sarai's stomach folded in half and she felt icy water slither across her shoulders. After shuffling the blue-backed, frayed cards herself, as instructed, she handed them back to the woman, who had become quieter now, taking deep breaths.

"Adopting a child... adopting a child." The voyant repeated the soft mantra as she lay twelve cards in a circle on the table, like hours on a clock. "Is this a wise option for Sarai?"

Sarai was impressed the woman had remembered her name, having probably only mentioned it once when she originally sent her a Net message—something the others at the omni group had told her not to do. She realised, too, that she hadn't even remembered the voyant's name.

A shadow passed over the window; a brief cloud probably. But Sarai saw that the voyant's hands had stopped moving and as she looked up to her face, found that she was gazing at the window.

"Let's begin."

One by one she turned the first six cards in the circle, revealing an array of assorted pictures and shapes—all simple, black scrawlings in white card: waves at sea, a black cat, a spider, three coins, a crescent moon, a tiny shoe.

The nameless voyant passed her open palms over each of the cards, 'feeling' the pictures one by one as if blind, reading Netbraille. She then rested both hands on either side of the circle.

"Some interesting cards have come up, dear," she began. "Did you have your own problems in childhood?" she asked, still looking down at the mystic images spanning the tabletop.

"... Problems? It depends on what you—"

"—With your mother?" the voyant cut in. Sarai couldn't tell whether this was a question, a guess at the truth, or an affirmative statement.

"Well, I don't speak to her anymore. So yes, we did have..." As Sarai looked away from the cards to the woman's face her words stopped forming.

The voyant stared above Sarai's head, her eyes a shock of white all the way around hazel irises. Instinctively, Sarai swung to look behind, wincing already. A white glimmer in the air shot out of sight. She jerked back toward the voyant, hunching as if something was about to hit her.

"What is it?" she squealed.

"... The presence, dear. The visitor," she replied, her voice now higher and thinner.

"You look scared! Why are you scared? Aren't you used to this?"

And what was 'this'? 'This' had happened before. More than once. A paranormal explanation was the one she always returned to, no matter what the other omnis told her about the 'old ways' and 'superstitions'. She gripped the edge of the rickety, creaking chair.

"I'm not scared, love. It's just... incredibly clear today. More than usual, that's all. A strong spirit." Sarai sensed that the voyant was embellishing now; making these thoughts up as she went. The woman looked back to the obscure pictures and flipped the next card.

"What is that?" Sarai asked, her voice hollow. "It looks like a grave. A tombstone." The grey rectangle with scratched writing couldn't be mistaken. "What does that mean? Something bad." She wasn't even asking now.

"It... it has different interpretations. It isn't always negative."

"But it is *usually*?"

"The card can represent closure, the end of a cycle, yes, but the beginning of another, too." She sounded desperate, even more than Sarai, clinging to an explanation that neither of them believed.

As if to cement the thought, the voyant yelped. Looking down, the card shifted on the table, tilting from side to side, taunting the two petrified spectators. Sarai pushed backward in her chair. The tiny grey picture of the tombstone flew from the table, cutting straight at her. She screamed, jumping up and batting it away to the floor like a poisonous insect attacking her. Falling back over her own stumbling feet toward the wall, she watched the rest of the cards pounce from the edges of the table in a blur of edges and pictures, as if being thrown by an invisible child in a tantrum.

"I'm sorry Miss Tailor, you're going to have to leave now!" the voyant yelled. She leapt from her chair, tripping on her billowing skirt as she rushed to the door. The colour in her face had faded, freckles standing out like ink spatters against ghostly white skin. She pulled the handle.

A primal, guttural howl.

The old woman grabbed her gaping mouth with one hand and her chest with the other, falling to the side against the edge of the doorframe. Sarai took shaking steps to her, trying to steady the voyant who looked ready to topple backward into the room. Sarai peered out into the corridor, throwing her own hand up, echoing the old woman's gesture of horror.

Every piece of cluttered, worn furniture down the length of the hallway was toppled over, piled on top of one another, upside down and impossible.

45
DECEMBER 2270

A flash.

Black.

Nausea pummelled him. He felt himself topple and regained his balance. The sound of his breath was close, magnified, wavering. In. Out. In. Out. He reached forward in the darkness. The edges of his fingertips brushed the smooth, cool skin of the pod where the barest light dully traced the outlines of his hands; an electrical leftover. Feeling with his palms and turning on gentle feet, Dyrne felt for the thin edges of the sheath covering the entrance.

No physicist to open it.

Pressing his weight against it, he pushed on the rectangular section of the pod until it clicked and slid away from him. Still blind, he felt his way through the hole and edged the first foot out, searching for the concrete step below, like dipping toes into freezing cold water. Finding the stone floor, his eyes drank the tiny shred of light and he stepped out with the second foot, pressing his way down the few steps to the ground.

No real thoughts yet. No voice in his head. No speculations. Just physical immediacy and the innate need to escape.

A laser-thin rectangle of glowing light framed the pod chamber door. He teased his way to it, hands splayed out wavering in the darkness like a frightened animal.

Please Alex.

He approached the cold metal and grasped for the handle, yanking it toward him.

It had been left open.

The tiny, dim lights from the stone corridor bled through the open doorway, illuminating at least some of the chamber. Looking back, the corner bench was empty: no pile of clothes to be found. Only another folded pod suit like the one he was wearing, resting on the shelf. Hanging over the console railing, though, he could see a folded white lab coat. Darting back, he grabbed it, noticing as he lifted, the metal tinkling of something hitting off the railing—a security tag attached to the lapel.

'Alexander Myers'. One final oblivious favour.

Flinging the coat around himself, he snuck back to the corridor door, peeking his head out first. The silent strip was empty, of course. Passing under the tiny glowing lights should have been a familiar act, but now it was foreign. The door to pod chamber 6 lay open, empty. It was identical to every other chamber. No signs of anyone having been kept captive in it for two months. Because they hadn't. Not here. Not anymore.

He rushed on, lumbering the lift cage and rising to the office level. As the elevator trundled to a jolting stop, the white door above shot open. Confirmation. No officer guarding the entrance. No security troupe waiting to grab him. He looked around the empty floor with vague recognition. The glass workstations were set out as he knew. Hould's raised office rested on the left as it should. The silver exit elevator doors lay ahead on the far side of the office floor as expected. But this wasn't the same place. He was a stranger here. The tiny differences glinted at him, like little changes in a dream of a childhood home telling you it's not home at all. The intruder must have felt like this when he'd returned from his visit. Dyrne wondered if he'd known Yusuf and Charon or if they were abnormalities to him.

Dyrne passed through the crystal walkway, glancing in at the strangers' workstations, empty and abandoned for the night. Postponing the observation for as long as possible, keeping Alex waiting until long after 1700 had worked. Everyone in this place had gone home.

Peering at Hould's mezzanine office, he noticed the light behind the frosted window. She was still in there, despite the misleading silence. Unwilling to take any chance of discovery, he tiptoed through the remainder of the cubicles, rushing past what was his own, resisting even a fleeting glance at whatever new items and documents might fill it now. He stepped up to the silver door of the lift, hearing the quiet beep of the motion sensor registering his presence. As he waited on its arrival, one final magnet pulled his gaze over his shoulder.

Phoebe's station.

Her distant glass box glinted back at him under the dim fluorescent lights. He could have found his way there in the dark. It was memorised. He knew somehow that even here, in this version of the present, this was where she worked each day.

The whooshing sound of the metal door slid open, and he twisted his head back, stepping in, swallowing his thick heartbeat. Turning around for his final look at something he could never see again, his fingers twitched. His breath fluttered.

He had felt like this at his mother's grave.

After the years, forever planning and preparing and forcing himself toward leaving this place just as he was now doing, the accomplishment only made his chest ache.

Hearing the distant click of a door handle, he glanced in its direction to see Dr. Hould's office door open and a foot emerging. Timed perfectly, the elevator door zipped into place and shot him upward, like the sand in his hourglass reversing backward, erasing itself, leaving everything below, a buried secret abandoned in his past.

At the entrance lobby, the elevator ejected him. He recognised the young receptionist: the nameless boy who had existed here every day before the government guards had taken over. He glanced around at Dyrne, confused, opening a silent mouth at this stranger in a lab coat and grey rubber suit, but saying nothing. Marching ahead, Dyrne crossed the marble foyer, his plastic soles making sticking sounds on the cool, tiled floor. He stepped through the glass entrance doors that opened automatically, releasing him into the freezing, cloudless night. Wasting no time waiting for the receptionist to raise an alarm, he ran for the first time in years into the dark, unknown city.

46
MARCH 2271

The watcher sheltered himself behind a line of trees, his eyes peering over the dark, turned-up collar of a stolen coat. On the opposite side of the road, Mann Samson emerged from a shining, black car and slammed the door. A tall, blonde woman stepped out from the passenger side. Her hair bounced as she skipped to catch up with her husband. They walked arm in arm to the familiar entrance of the apartment building.

His observation was brief. The building door was opened, the brother and his wife disappearing inside, passing another couple who were leaving. He allowed himself the cheat of a glance up to the window of the blue-walled flat he knew they were headed for. Then he turned to leave. This was as close as he could get. They had their own Dyrne now.

• • •

Phoebe Rush was more difficult to watch. For other reasons. He could only spy her springing through the Central Gardens, away from the Line station. She rummaged through her frontpack as she weaved amidst the stream of other passengers. He knew she might glance this way at any moment. He wanted to feed his heart but knew that her inevitable blank stare would stab at it. His face would just be one more among the crowd. He followed the back of her wispy hair until the city absorbed her, swallowing the last of his abandoned life. He knew he should leave soon—he rarely entered the dangerous centre of New London anymore—but closed his eyes for a few more seconds, tracking the memorised steps that Phoebe would now be taking to a DOHR where Dyrne Samson had never worked.

• • •

He had seated himself in the dark row farthest from the altar, a lone parishioner in the church. The flimsy, weathered jacket just about covered his bony torso. Matted hair fell over one eye. Soft choral music played from a speaker somewhere, echoing under the curved ceiling. The windows were green, and the light shining through the watery glass made him feel he was under the capsized hull of a ship. But safe. He bowed his head.

Coming here had become a habit; a discreet place to avoid questioning looks, to be alone with his memories—the last part of his life he couldn't delete. None of this was the reason for today's visit, though.

He had found Copil.

With a different name now. But his birth number was identical, labelled and filed with all the others, including his own. This church was a place he liked to visit, apparently.

There were no more weekly masses or sermons here. No marriages or baptisms or even funerals. A gathering was sometimes organised by older members of the community, still grasping at old ways and comforting traditions. But the building was merely waiting now, either to be demolished or to evolve. In the meantime, it served as a safehouse for some, a meditation spot for a few, and a museum relic to be studied for others.

The doors behind the waiting man opened, and he lifted his head. A sudden shaft of sunlight beamed straight down the aisle, illuminating the once-white altar, its surrounding statues and the empty spots where gold boxes and huge candles might have been years ago. The light shut off with the dull thud of the doors. A pair of shoes clicked over the marble floor and strode ahead. The young man took a seat near the front. Dyrne's pounding heart overpowered the gentle, synthetic music. He rubbed a thumb into the opposite, moist palm and watched, fixated. The heat bubbling behind his skin dissipated, though. He realised, of course, that Copil could never recognise him. He was still making this mistake.

Now a smile teased his lips. Copil did nothing, said nothing. His existence was enough. No more Phoebe. No more Mann or their father. No more DOHR or Alex or Hould or Yusuf. But Copil alive instead. He wasn't a University student here. Wasn't taunted and teased with no one to protect him. Wasn't the adopted son of famous activist Sarai Tailor.

She never adopted anyone.

The momentary joy began its predictable fade soon enough. The smile dwindled like a dirty mark being wiped clean. A final splinter was still lodged somewhere in him. Watching Copil now, he could see what had changed. He saw an older version of the boy he knew. He saw the edges of a beard, upright posture, a suit jacket. He saw a man who had survived his nineteenth year and lived on.

But he remembered how easily this had been ruined.

Despite everything he had altered, Dyrne's own memories could never be 'visited'; no machine could delete what he had been capable of.

As silent seconds flowed, he closed his eyes, laying his head down again, leaning against the bench in front with both arms. Before coming here, he had cast his vote for the December election, fraudulently claiming to be the real Dyrne Samson—a lecturer at New London University. Louis Apol was running for re-election.

Pressing his forehead into the wooden pew, his thoughts rounded back to Phoebe. She would be proud. Even now, his imagination snaked back to the centre of New London, through the Central Gardens, four blocks ahead then right, across the street to scraper 84. Just to see, to observe. But reality kept him away. He stuck to the outskirts of the city, the traditional home for the synths and other outcasts. He'd even spent those first few nights in the forestry preserves.

Opening his eyes, he looked forward along the wooden rows to see that Copil had gone. Knowing it was time for him, too, to leave—his last observation complete—he leaned back and stood with hands on his knees feeling his back ache and his thighs twinge. The Metaganic Support Centre was nearby. He'd memorised the address from a giant news site screen that had displayed the proud message: "Metaganic Support: Coming Together." Today he'd make his first visit.

Exhaling, ready to leave the gentle cocoon of the church, he turned to step into the aisle. But behind him, a whisper grabbed at his ear. He hurtled around. Floating off along the pew away from him, a shimmering, white silhouette morphed and gleamed and vanished. A woman.

A ghost.

ACKNOWLEDGEMENTS

Thank you to all the readers and writers who helped me along the way with their advice and feedback on *Turning the Hourglass*, including: Michael Alperstein, Tegan Whalan, Eric Murray, Brian M. Start, Kellie Riek, Umber Bhatti, Alex Dook, Dan Levinson, Cullen W. Monk, Rachel Grant and Anna Hedley.

Thanks also to the Black Rose Writing team for all their help with the process of publishing my first novel.

Particularly special thanks to Melissa Wiggins and Alex Pantazis for the time and effort they've spent on this novel as well as their ongoing support and encouragement—it's been invaluable.

Finally, thank you to you, whoever you are, for reading *Turning the Hourglass*. I appreciate it whole-heartedly and hope you enjoyed it. If you have a moment, please write a review at the outlet you bought it from. Reviews help keep the novel alive and guide other readers to their new favorite books.

ABOUT THE AUTHOR

M.J. Keeley is a writer and teacher living in Glasgow with his partner and clan of cats. He studied English Literature at the University of Glasgow and has had short fiction published by Centum Press, Medusa's Laugh Press, Mother's Milk Books, and Havok magazine. In addition, he is a contributing writer for award-winning online magazine *The Wee Review* and the *Neon Books* blog. Matthew can usually be found reading, writing, or cat-worshiping.

Join Matthew's mailing list at: MatthewKeeley.co.uk
Like him on Facebook: Facebook.com/MatthewKeeleyAuthor
Follow him on Twitter: Twitter.com/MatthewJKeeley
Follow him on Instagram: Instagram.com/MatthewJKeeley

Thank you so much for reading one of our **Sci-Fi** novels.
If you enjoyed our book, please check out our recommended title for your
next great read!

Culture-Z by Karl Andrew Marszalowicz

In the year 2190, mankind has made great strides forward in the worlds of
technology, science, and greed. However, when all three get together one
last time, this oblivious generation may not exist much longer.

View other Black Rose Writing titles at www.blackrosewriting.com/books

and use promo code **PRINT** to receive a **20% discount** when purchasing.